Missions

Book 1: Cambodia

by Danny Tyran

July 2022

Copyright

Table of Contents

Introduction

I was sitting at a table in a bar talking and having a good time with my buddies when he walked in. I noticed because who wouldn't? Several of my friends had turned their heads too and I could see that no one was left indifferent. Even the less gay among them seemed to have felt if not desire, at least envy when they saw him.

He was tall: six feet four inches at least. His complexion was tanned, like that of someone who had just returned from a beach vacation. His blond hair was short on the sides, but long enough on top to have it gathered in a sort of ponytail or a rough bun. His shoulders were broad and his hips narrow. His jaw was shadowed by a sand-colored beard. He had a dimple on his chin. His lips were so perfect and sensual that they made me want to kiss them. His long, slender fingers wrapped completely around his bottle. You could see his muscles under his t-shirt, which was as black as his pants and shoes. But what struck me most was his frank, direct gaze, so clear that it reflected the light like two silver moons.

"Do you know who he is?" Alex asked me, noticing my interest.

"No. But he reminds me of someone."

"It's Zach Mendel. The sadistic dominator who's been banned from almost every BDSM establishment in and around the area, that's him."

Zach Mendel was my favorite freelance journalist. I had only ever seen him in pictures and never expected to run into him here. This man represented for me Freedom of expression with a capital F, the Right to Information with a capital R and the Courage with a capital C. I know; it's a lot of capital letters, but after all, he was my international star! I had studied to become one too, not so much a star than a good journalist. But I had only just finished my training and had very little experience in this field. And today I learned that my star was not only a Dominator with a capital D, but that he was a fallen angel.

"And why was he banned?" I asked when I caught my breath.

"His last submissive accused him of abandoning her in a situation so perilous that it could've cost her life."

"If he's straight, what is he doing here?"

"No. He's bi. And this bar doesn't turn away bis or even curious people of both sexes."

"We should've questioned this girl more to know the exact circumstances of this famous 'perilous situation'," said Thierry, who was sitting in front of me.

"What do you mean? That he is accused of endangering a life is not enough for you?" asked Alex to him.

"Since when do we condemn a man without having heard his version of the facts, and that the accuser's statements are automatically considered one hundred percent true?" Thierry retorted.

"Would you know more about what happened and about this dominator?"

Alex's scornful tone of voice made it clear that he doubted Thierry knew more about the situation than he did.

I turned my gaze in the same direction. A very pretty woman, who also reminded me of someone, went to sit next to Mendel and started talking to him. He had such a bright smile that it totally transformed him. He had appeared so stern to me before that I had mentally compared him to a priest with his black clothes and his water bottle. It seemed to me that all he was missing was the Roman collar to complete the picture. Except clergyman don't usually wear their hair so long, they aren't so supremely manly and handsome, and don't attend gay bars. At least I don't think so. I didn't date any priests, so maybe my opinion was skewed, based solely on biases.

"A dominator I know well and Mendel are old friends. They went to the same school for several years," says Thierry. "This dom said he was a virgin when he and Mendel had sex as teenagers."

"And how did that work out?" asked Alex.

"He ended up in the hospital. Not Mendel, but the other guy. Mendel is known in the BDSM community for his extreme sadism. It's said that he can't cum unless he subdues his partners or inflicts physical or psychological pain on them. Despite this, apart from this girl's accusation, no one has ever blamed him for anything."

"His old friend, is he a dominator or a submissive?" I asked in turn to try to understand how one dom could submit to another.

"In fact, he's a switch and he's much more maso than sado, but he doesn't want everyone to know about it. He thinks subs are reviled, as if they were less manly than other men. As far as I know, he considers Mendel his one and only master. Some people have a suspicion that they have a D/s relationship, but it's probably just Mendel, his friend and me who are in the know."

"Had he filed a complaint against Mendel after their first violent fuck?"

Thierry smiled before answering.

"No, he hadn't. On the contrary. He thanked Mendel and asked him when they'd do it again. I told you, he's very masochistic, as much as Mendel is sadistic."

"And did they do it again?" I asked, growing more curious as I glanced in Mendel's direction.

"Not immediately. Mendel was reportedly very disturbed by what he'd just experienced. After all, it was the first time, and he was afraid of going too far if they did it again. But the other nagged him and finally convinced him to try again. They still see each other from time to time. Actually, I think this switch is madly in love with his old friend Zach. But Mendel works as a freelance journalist. He travels a lot to write his articles and shoot his documentaries. He has been published in all the major periodicals around the world. Since he is fluent in… I don't know, eight or nine languages, he writes in all of them. But his frequent travels make long-term relationships difficult."

"But then, this girl…," I began.

"She had recently become his sex slave and professional assistant. She was the one holding the camera while he interviewed people or commented on the footage she filmed for him. And recently they were in Asia, I can't remember which country, when Mendel would've dropped her in a dangerous situation. At least that's what she claims."

"You think it's not true?" insisted Alex.

"Who knows? If she was in love with him and he broke up with her on that trip, she may have sought revenge by telling this story and saying only what was consistent with her version."

"What did he say?" I asked.

"He hasn't said anything yet."

"Nothing? Don't you think that's strange? If he was innocent, as you seem to think, wouldn't he have been quick to defend himself?"

"I don't know. But why don't you go and talk to Mendel about it?" asked Thierry, looking at Alex and me in turn.

Mendel was getting ready to leave with the woman who had approached him earlier. I remembered now where I had seen her: she was in the journalism and audiovisual graduates' group, while I was a freshman. If I was not mistaken, her name was Monya.

I thought that if I didn't talk to Mendel right away, I might never get the chance again. I was looking for a job, and if he had fired his previous assistant, he must be looking for a replacement. That's probably why Monya had met him. She probably had more journalistic experience than I did, with only a few articles in my college paper and a few months' interim position at the local newspaper. If she got the job, I could forget about Mendel and continue my job search.

I have to say that besides being my idol and finding him extremely attractive, he aroused my curiosity and desire and excited my senses, like the aroma of food makes starving people salivate. I had a strange feeling that if fate had put him across my path, it was perhaps not without reason, but I didn't know why yet. Even so, I didn't dare go talk to him. He frightened me a little. This fear was as much an attraction for me as a deterrent. It made me want him more, but it just sort of made everything harder, it made me hesitant.

Alex, bolder than me, got up and went to talk to him before he was out with Monya. Even though my full attention was on Alex and Mendel, the distance, the stupid country music, which bellowed, "Not every night, not every day," and the chatter around me prevented me from hearing anything they were saying. Alex came back soon after with a look of both pity and rage.

"So what did he say?" I asked him.

"He said that if I wanted to know more, I'd have to spend a few hours at his house and let him do whatever he wanted to me. I'm curious, but not that curious. I don't want to run the risk of ending up in the hospital. I still have all my pieces in perfect working order, and I want to keep them that way," he replied, looking at himself as if to verify that there was no damage.

"He must've known that you wouldn't accept his offer. It was an indirect way to get rid of a curious," I commented.

Was I masochistic enough to please someone like Mendel? I wasn't sure at all. I knew so little about him. Maybe, despite my attraction, it was better to find out more about him before venturing into his house and between his sheets and claws.

5

Over the next few days, I asked people I knew from the journalistic and the BDSM communities about Mendel. In the first instance, he was either praised or denigrated. But I got the impression that those who were badmouthing him were the ones who envied him the most. They wished they had his incredible looks and the same kind of adventurous life he had. But to lead such a life, you had to be able to afford top-notch audiovisual equipment and travel around the globe. Most couldn't afford it.

"Mendel is a daddy's boy, at least financially. His parents are dead and his father left him a fortune. I heard Zach gave a good portion of it to a friend and to charities around the world. But he still had enough left over to buy a house and state-of-the-art equipment."

Eva, the journalist who told me this, was almost drooling with jealousy.

"How did his parents die?" I asked her.

"She died in a car accident when he was twelve. It seems that she was so drunk that she had to see triple. And he committed suicide two years later."

"Poor children!"

"Ah, well, they were probably happy when they died. Living with an alcoholic religious nut and a sadistic pedophile and incestuous man, it must've been quite a life."

I looked at her, speechless. So he would have inherited his sadism from his old man.

"His father was arrested several times for violence against his wife and kids. But each time he was released. When you can afford the best lawyer in the country… Oh yeah, Zach has an older sister named Karin who became a nun and lives in a convent. She didn't want to get a cent from her dear daddy, who allegedly raped her multiple times. That's why Zach inherited everything. But that's probably also why he prefers to give as much of his money as he can to whoever needs it."

"Their mother let her husband abuse her children?"

"Yeah. But Karin had enough and filed more than one complaint, hence the arrests. She'd have told the police that when their sweet daddy was bullying them, their dear mom would tell them to ask God to help the old man change and to find the courage to forgive him. She may also have prayed for her wonderful husband to die, but if so, she wasn't answered until after her fatal accident because he committed suicide two years later. I can't even imagine what those two years Zach and Karin spent alone with this wacko were like for the brother and sister."

What a family! What a childhood! But could I believe any of it? What if it was just gossip peddled by a reporter who didn't care about verifying the veracity of her sources?

As for the people in the BDSM community, everyone told me that Mendel Jr. was both feared and respected, at least before his assistant accused him.

"I believe that the reason there wasn't much pressure for Mendel to give his version of what happened in Asia was precisely because they were afraid of him. Knowing his unusual sadism, they must've wanted to avoid that he goes too far again, as with his first lover, or that he loses his head, like his father. So, when his assistant denounced him, they were too happy to blacklist him," commented a friend named Martin.

Martin, an old submissive who knew everyone and all the ins and outs of the BDSM scene, both in our city and in every city in the country and even beyond, was an inexhaustible source of information, usually reliable.

"It's not fair!" I exclaimed.

"As Mom used to say, 'If you think life and the world are fair, you're in for a big disappointment, kid'," said Martin.

"So, his father really was a sadistic pervert?"

"Yes, he was! People in the community had access to little Zac's medical records. He spent almost more time in the hospital than he did at home. He was constantly trying to protect his sister and mother from his father's brutality. It wasn't easy for a boy to stand up to a man who was as big and strong as Zach is today. Mendel Sr. was quick to push his son out of the way when he wanted to pick on them. And if Zach insisted, he'd beat him, sometimes to the point of unconsciousness or otherwise torture him. It's a good thing that someone staged a suicide."

"What?!"

"Oh, I don't have any proof. Nobody does, but…"

"Did Zach kill him?"

"Actually, it seems that it was Karine who tried to prevent him from murdering her brother, who was trying to protect her as always. She'd have smashed their father's skull with a heavy cast-iron pan or something like that. But it was concluded that he fell from a cliff. A suicide. That's why people fear Zach too, besides the fact that he spends more time in the most dangerous countries in the world than he does at home and always comes back alive. Most people doubt that he owes his remarkable survival only to miracles caused by the prayers of his pious older sister."

"Is he a believer?"

"It seems so, but what does he have faith in? Only he could say. All I know is that he chooses his travel destinations not only to do shocking reports, but according to the help he can give. He thinks of himself as a kind of missionary. He doesn't seek to convert people to Catholicism or any other religion, but rather to altruism. But some believe that he wouldn't always be so peaceful and that his old man's corpse wouldn't be the only one on his path."

I highly doubted that Mendel ever bragged about making his father's or anyone's body disappear or accused his sister of murder. So how could he know all this?

One thing was certain, the more I learned about Mendel, the more my curiosity and a mixture of fear and respect grew.

"Did he find a new assistant?"

"Not that I know of. Why?"

"I saw him last weekend with a woman who studied journalism. I was just wondering if she was one of his friends or if he'd hired her."

"No lo sé."

I would probably have to stop procrastinating and call Mendel to get an appointment. Would he offer me the same thing he offered Alex?

"Do you know his phone number?"

"I think it's on the Internet. But wait, I'll give it to you."

He did it, and I added it to my contacts. My masochism made me consider the possibility of a meeting with Mendel with at least as much fear as excitement.

Chapter 2

I found Monya's phone number, and she revealed to me that she had not met Zach Mendel's rather unique selection criteria.

"He's a weirdo, this guy! I was at his house for a job interview for a journalism assistant position and he asked me to lick his shoes. No, thanks! Not for me," Monya said in a tone of revolt mixed with disgust.

"Just that?" I thought. If she wasn't ready for so little, how would she have reacted if he had really shown her what he was capable of? I wanted to laugh and I admit I felt relieved: the job was still available!

"Didn't you know what he was?

"He's a freelance journalist, right?

"Yes, but apart from that.

"If you want to talk about all the gossip about his past and everything else… I was told about it, but I didn't believe it. It was all too far-fetched. It's just too much for one man, don't you think?"

I must admit that I, too, felt that in his case, reality almost exceeded fiction. I could understand why she had doubts, since I had them too. So, I wished her the best of luck in finding her dream job and said hello. Then I dialed Mendel's number, which Martin had given me, only to get a voice mail. I tried so many times that when he answered for real, I thought it was his damn answering machine again and almost hung up on him.

"Hello, Mr. Mendel. My name is Gabriel Jacob. I'm calling because I know you're looking for an assistant."

"No, I'm not."

"No?"

"I'm not only looking for an assistant, but also a slave."

Ouch! But that voice! What can I say? It matched perfectly with the memory I had of the man. Deep, very masculine, beautiful! And that very direct way of expressing what he wanted… I was smiling like an idiot. Good thing he couldn't see me.

"Yes, eh, I know. I'd still like to meet you for this job."

Silence. I was afraid he would hang up. So I hurried to speak. I might as well throw myself into the clutches of the devil himself by opening my mouth as not to be admitted into his hell for closing it.

"I believe I can also meet this expectation."

"Do you know me?"

"By reputation only, Sir."

He grunted.

"But I don't care about rumors, I prefer to make up my own mind," I pointed out.

He laughed.

"What if the gossip is beneath the reality?"

"Excuse me for contradicting you, Sir, but I doubt it."

"What have you been told?"

"That you drove your first lover to the hospital and that you helped your sister get rid of your father's corpse."

I admit that I had taken a big risk there. But it was better for him to tell me right away to go fuck myself somewhere else if I was wrong and had offended him than to go to his house and get the same thing, either a dismissal, or suffer an angry reaction. As far as the fuck part was by him…

He was silent again, but for so long that I didn't know what to expect. I was getting ready to apologize to him for my stupid accusations when he started talking again.

"Tomorrow, nine o'clock in the morning. Bring your portfolio. And don't be late or don't come."

"I'll be there…"

He had already hung up. I looked up his email address on the web and immediately sent him my e-portfolio, specifying that I would still provide him with the paper version.

I almost didn't sleep all night. This was due to the overly hot and humid weather combined with my noisy and failing air-conditioning, but also to the doubts that plagued my nerves. I wondered a thousand times if I was making a big mistake, the worst one in my life. But when I finally closed my eyes and calmed down, I felt surrounded by light and peace. Why? Was it fate telling me not to be afraid, as I was on the right track? Something in me still refuses to believe in all this metaphysical nonsense, but this serenity was so unfamiliar to me that I couldn't deny that I was experiencing it. Mendel's desire to go out and bring help all over the planet must have inspired me.

I got up at six o'clock. I would have done so earlier, since I hadn't slept, but what would I have spent my time doing: pacing around in my apartment? So, I lay there and masturbated three times thinking about him. Maybe I shouldn't have, because if he tested me, despite my masochism, I might not get a hard-on, and then what he might do to me would probably seem more painful than exciting.

I washed, dressed and ate as if I was in the twilight zone. But can you go and meet a sadistic dominator in your normal state? I doubt it. I was sure that all the masochistic submissives in the world would have understood my nervousness, my anxiety and the frenzy of my desire.

When I started to climb the steps to his front door, my legs were shaking so much I thought I would never make it. I rang the bell. He opened the door a few seconds later. My goodness! What a magnificent man! How could I not be seduced despite his terrible reputation?

He led me to his living room and invited me to sit down. I hesitated. Should I do it on the floor, like any good slave? He told me with a smile that I was not yet his property, so I could use his couch. I did so while handing him my portfolio. He then offered me a drink.

"Coffee, please."

I wondered as he left the room if I shouldn't have made it for us. It's a slave's job to meet the needs of his master, right? Then I remembered that he wasn't yet, and I felt a little twinge of sadness that he might never be.

The proud tilt of his head, the straightness of his back, and his noble gait, all that convinced me that I had been wrong to remain seated while he stood up to serve me. This was upside down, because such a man was born to have the world at his feet, or at least to have me at his feet, not the other way around.

He offered me an espresso and placed sugar and cream on the table between his chair and the sofa where I was sitting.

"Promise to tell me the whole truth and nothing but the truth and to keep secret anything I might reveal to you, demand of you or do to you."

I felt my heart rate increase and my body temperature rise several degrees.

"I swear to you."

"Come on, tell me everything," he ordered.

I almost asked him, "Everything about what?"

Then I thought he probably wanted to know everything I had found out about him. So, after taking a sip of his excellent espresso, I told him what I had been taught.

"I did not take my first lover to the hospital. The friars at our boarding school took him there after he had crawled more than walked from the shack where I'd brutalized him. As for sharing my wealth with charities, I prefer to offer my help directly to people in need. The middlemen tend to take too much from what we give them," he said when I fell silent.

My goodness! At least he didn't seem to be proud of the state he had put his first lover in.

"I was told that you felt remorse for treating the boy that way."

His face tightened. I thought I saw shame in it at that moment.

"That part at least is true. We were still teenagers. But I regretted my actions and was afraid to be my father's worthy son."

The pain in his eyes made me want to know him better, to find out everything about him, not through people, but from his own mouth.

"Did he mistreat you?"

Evading my question, he asked me who had told me everything I thought I knew. I did not hesitate to give the names of Alex, Eva and Martin. After all, they were not shy about reporting all the gossip they heard and had not made me promise silence, so why should I hide their identities?

"I know Martin. I'll have to teach him to be more discreet."

"He admitted that it could all be fake and that, at least, it wasn't verifiable. And he had nothing but good things to say about you, Sir. He believes that the reason you were in the hospital so often as a child was that you were always trying to protect your mother and sister from your father's assaults," I said in defense of Martin.

Mendel grunted. He didn't seem to find that what I had added cleared Martin of everything. I thought it might have been better not to reveal my sources to him after all.

"I looked at your digital portfolio. It's a little light, but if the rest is okay, I'll be happy with it."

I assumed that "the rest" was my slave qualifications, for which I had no resume, only the names of a few dominators who could speak well of me.

He then ordered me to tell him everything about myself. I did. It took me almost two hours to describe my very ordinary early childhood, my discovery of my homosexuality, my slightly more eventful adolescence, my studies, my search for a job until I wanted to call him to become his assistant, without forgetting my few experiences of service with more or less qualified dominators.

"So you're not a novice sub?"

"No, Sir. But let's just say I wouldn't necessarily recommend every dom I've ever been with."

"And would they recommend you to me?"

I thought about it to make sure I was answering honestly.

"Yes, except for one."

"Why not him?"

"He was very inexperienced. He had only his charm and his enthusiasm as a beginner. Everything excited him. But his ignorance made him make mistakes and blunders that were sometimes dangerous. And when I offered to explain to him how to do well what he was clumsily trying to do, he considered that I wanted to dominate by the bottom."

"A real jerk," commented Mendel.

"I think he was mostly very proud and felt humiliated that a sub was able to show him a thing or two."

Mendel grunted. He seemed tempted to repeat that this guy was just a jerk.

"Is he one of those people you would advise against?"

"At that time, yes, he certainly was. But he's taken classes since then, attending workshops and working with more experienced doms. He hasn't trained enough to improve his techniques, in my opinion, but he's still much better than he was."

"Give me your hand," he commanded in a tone so soft he could have read me a love poem in that same warm and tender voice.

I shivered at the thought as I obeyed him. My right hand was on his side, so I offered it to him after placing my cup on the table between us. He put pressure on a particularly sensitive spot and didn't let go, staring me straight in the eyes. I closed mine, trying to breathe slowly and deeply and find the courage not to resist him.

"Look at me."

I opened my eyes and turned them to his. I had noticed they were silver-gray with a thin charcoal line around them. But now that his pupils were dilating, they were almost entirely black. He was excited about what he was doing to me! I liked that idea a lot. I smiled at him despite my pain.

"Come sit here and lean against me," he ordered, spreading his legs.

I settled into his chair between his thighs, so firm and warm! He continued to press where it was most sensitive, where it hurt so much. Then he bent his head and sniffed me, like a hungry animal ready to devour me raw. His breath on my neck made me shiver and my dick got harder.

"Get your cock out. I want to see the effect I have on you."

I unbuckled my belt, opened and lowered my pants and briefs, proud to display my already rigid and imposing manhood. He didn't comment. He just started biting my ear, my neck, my shoulder. And Lord! It wasn't just gentle nibbles. Without stopping to pinch my hand, he was sinking his teeth in everything he could reach like a hungry wolf or a seductive vampire. I moaned. This only made him more aroused and accentuated his desire to penetrate me with his fangs or something else, because I could now feel his cock gorging with blood against my back.

"On your knees!" he growled after several minutes.

Oh, gladly! Far from refusing to obey him, as Monya had done, I held my pants and my belt so I could turn around and kneel between his legs. I was so happy at the thought of maybe getting the chance to serve him sexually that my gaze immediately focused on the swelling against his belly in his cloth prison. He'd let go of my right hand when I turned around, but he took it back when I placed it on his thigh.

"Get it out," he grumbled.

I didn't ask what; my eyes were on it. I thought, "With pleasure!" And I reached out my left hand, the one that had held my pants in place, towards his. Mine slipped to the floor. I struggled to undo the button, then the zipper. When I finally managed to open it all the way, I pushed my fingers through the slit to release his hot wand. He wasn't wearing any underwear and his hard dick gushed out. His heady smell made me dizzy for a moment. I smiled. Yet the pressure of his thumb on my right hand had not abated and my pain was becoming throbbing. But this pain, tangled with his warmth and scent, only fanned my desire and awakened my pleasure.

I apprehended the moment when he would order me to suck him so much his cock, of average length, was wide. It would probably enter my mouth with difficulty, so how could I push it into my throat? But he was silent. I was drooling with anticipatory delight. I looked up into his eyes, which were closed. Beautiful! My desire at that moment was so eager for him that I moaned.

"What do you want?"

I glanced at his cock. He understood.

"If, in order to taste it and become my assistant and slave, you were to allow me to make you suffer for several hours and in such a way that you would end the day where the man I still love ended up when we were teens, would you stay with me?"

I looked at his strained, pained face. He was afraid. Of what? That I would answer "yes"? That I would say "no"?

"I'm willing to let you torture me any way you want for as long as you want, if that's what turns you on and makes you happy, but if you send me to the hospital, you'll feel guilty and miserable. And I don't want that."

"You're trying to avoid more pain," he said with anger that made his voice rocky.

"No, Sir! I swear I'm not. The idea that my relationship with you starts with remorse, not mine, but yours, it's not…"

The next part couldn't get out of my constricted throat. He zipped up his pants, stood up, walked around me and stood behind me. He pulled up my t-shirt and ripped off my belt, then pushed me down to force me to put my upper body on his chair permeated with his smell and warmth. Then he started whipping me with my belt. He kept beating me with brutal force. In spite of my pain, I could not help but notice with what astonishing precision he was hitting me. Was this his father's instrument of choice? Not one bit of flesh on my back, buttocks and thighs was spared. When the strap wound up to hit the tender areas of my flanks, stomach and nipples, I would yelp in pain. And each time I heard him laugh. He forced me to sit up on my knees and pull me back by my hair, he took off my t-shirt, then continued to hit my torso, without mercy. Ah, the sadist!

While moaning and screaming, I tried not to struggle too much until I realized that he liked to see me writhing in agony. He hadn't asked me if I had a safeword. But I was convinced that if I had said, "Zach, stop!" he would have done so immediately.

Then he dropped my belt and pulled me up by my ankles. I found myself on all fours, then flat on the floor. He ran his nails over my welts. I could hear moans, but were they of pleasure or pain? Were they mine, his or ours intertwined?

He pulled his cock out again and lay on top of me. My mind was so engrossed in everything I was feeling that I didn't realize he had put on a condom. He fucked me without paying attention to my grunts of discomfort. It was like being penetrated by two cocks at the same time as it was so large. He went in all at once, stopping only when his balls hit my ass. Then he started his in and out. With every move he made, his clothes and the rug rubbed my welts, and the pain this stirred up made me wince. He knew this very well and didn't mind scuffing me. Oh, how good it felt! I felt so used, possessed. I had stepped into his hell and his flame so bright and burning was heating up my flesh and senses.

"Thank you, Master!" I said, gratefully, as his very first lover had done.

He let out a sort of growling laughter and his penetration became more brutal. Then he slid his hands under me to pinch my nipples and squeeze my testicles. Ooooh, the bastard knew how to hurt me and make me come at the same time. With each stroke, he brushed my prostate while squeezing my balls, scratching my nipples and biting me, sending me into a delirium of pleasure and pain.

"Thank you, Master!"

He grumbled a little laugh. However, he came out of me without having cum. I didn't understand why he had stopped and I was disappointed. Did he consider me unworthy of being impregnated by him or was he not excited enough by me?

"Please!" I begged him.

I didn't know if my pleas were for the pleasure, he was depriving me of or for the pleasure he was forbidding me to give him.

"I'm just getting started," he said, his member pointing to the sky, and with a proud, conquering look on his face, sending a wave of reverential awe and excitement through me with his few words.

"What a beautiful animal!" I thought to myself. But that was long before I thought of begging for mercy; for several hours later, I couldn't stand any longer the pain and being kept on the verge of orgasm at the same time. But begging him to stop was the one pleasure I still wasn't ready to give him. If I had to end up in the hospital for him to finally cum inside me and allow me to come too, well, I was determined to endure whatever he wanted to inflict on me.

"What a proud man you are!" he said.

"You haven't come yet, Sir," I said, my voice hoarse from grunting, moaning and screaming.

I knew that what was making my breathing so difficult right now was not just my fatigue, my unrelenting pain and my frustration at not having cummed; it was more the disappointment of not being able to get his. Mendel, on the other hand, was a little short of breath, but he still seemed in control and ready to continue.

"Is that why you won't stop me from hitting you? You want me to cum?"

"What's the point of all this if you don't?" I replied, my throat dry and tight.

He smiled, then started to make love to me, like no one before him. He was as gentle, sensual and tender as much as he had been hard, even cruel, before this moment. He caressed me and licked me with his eyes, his hands and his tongue. I was floating somewhere between his hell and my heaven! Many times I had hoped to meet someone who would give me so much pleasure that I would lose my mind and not know where I was or who I was anymore. Zach Mendel was that man.

"Teach me, Master," I asked him after we had both come.

"Teach you what?"

"To give you as much pleasure as you just gave me."

"You did," he said with so much conviction in his voice that I was amazed and pleased.

His obvious jouissance was one more pleasure for me, the greatest of all.

"How?"

"You were in enough pain to want to tell me to stop, but you didn't. And while I was stroking you, you needed to cum without further delay, but you held it back. You wanted me to do it first. At one point, you were so distraught with ecstasy… If you had seen your face! No one has ever seemed as entranced by what I did to them as you seemed to be. Believe me, you gave me a lot of pleasure, my dear slave."

I opened my eyes wide and looked at him with a big smile. He had accepted me! I was his slave and his assistant.

"Thank you, Master!" I repeated so enthusiastically that it made him laugh again.

Then he got up and went to take a shower. I joined him there. He allowed me to enter the stall with him and soap him up. I noticed several old scars. Had they been caused by his father or by incidents in his line of work? I didn't know, and I didn't dare ask him about them right away. But I stroked and kissed them deferentially.

He washed me like I was his little boy and he was a loving dad. Except that I was enjoying the feel of his soapy hands all over me and I was still slowly getting hard. He brushed my balls so gently that I thought I was going to spray him with my cum. He flicked my cock and it twitched, but he did nothing to relieve my crying need.

"You know it's not going to be easy, don't you?" he asked as he finished wiping me with a delicacy that made me shudder and desire him again.

Now it was my turn to laugh. He did too, but his laughter, amused at first, took on an intonation that silenced me, so much it was threatening like an impossible love and a forever unfulfilled happiness.

Chapter 3

After we got dressed, my new master ordered lunch. The restaurant had to be close by, because the delivery was quick. While we ate and for part of the afternoon, he told me all about himself.

Everything I had heard about his relationship with his family was just a shadow of what he had experienced. His mother was not in her right mind most of the time. She was drunk on alcohol, painkillers, soporifics and prayers. In order not to have to serve her husband sexually, as soon as he was home, she would rush to take sleeping pills that would knock her out all night and most of the following day. But one day, when he had unexpectedly raped and brutalized her again, she had fled in a car after swallowing three quarters of a forty-ounce bottle of vodka. Her children were at school. One of the neighbors told them that he had tried to talk their mother out of driving in her condition (she could barely stand), but she had broken free of his restraining hand and sped off to her death a few kilometers later when she ran a red light, killing the driver and passenger of the other vehicle. She went through the windshield and crashed into the wall of a building near the intersection. She was so disfigured that they held a closed-casket funeral.

Zach and his sister Karin's childhood had been hell, until their father was knocked out by Karin to defend her brother from the madman who was trying to stab him with a kitchen knife. They then carried the body and threw it, headfirst, off a cliff, fearing at every moment that they would be caught in the act. They returned after having erased all traces of their passage. It rained heavily during the three days they waited before calling the police. They told them that they did not know where their father was, but they had not seen him for several days. During this wait, the two children had agreed on what they should say and had even worked out variations and "hesitations" to make sure they didn't sound like they were repeating everything like parrots. They questioned and tried to intimidate each other to make sure that their story would hold up and that they would withstand the stress of an interrogation. When the police asked them why they had not called earlier, they readily replied that their father was often away on business for several days, which was true.

The brother and sister were then entrusted to their maternal grandparents, who sent them to two Catholic boarding schools, one for boys and the other for girls. Karine, who remained deeply religious, became a Carmelite nun. As for Zach, he keeps a very personal notion of good and evil, of neighborly love and of this supposed "God of love" who allows millions of children to live and die in the greatest misery without intervening.

It was at his boarding school that he met Arthur, whom everyone nicknamed Arty because of his many artistic talents. His milky skin, dimples, thick curly hair and long hemmed eyelashes gave him a deceptive cherubic look. Deceptive, because Arty was not afraid of anything or anyone, not even Zach, whom all the students and some of the teachers already feared.

"Why were they afraid of you?" I asked my new master.

He shrugged.

"I wasn't very friendly, with the other students. Some of them made fun of me because of my gloomy look and everything they didn't understand about my asocial behavior. Dad, although violent, was far from stupid. He was an exceptional businessman, who had multiplied the substantial sum inherited from his father by millions. As for Mom, she was a genius. She learned languages and musical instruments with ease. She was already remarkably talented at the piano at the age of four and, until her death, she could perform complex pieces very well, even when drunk. Dad passed on to me his natural aptitude for numbers and speculation and his sense of observation. And Mom taught me everything she knew. Because of all my knowledge and skills, the brothers asked me to assist the other boarders with their work. I did so, but only to the extent that they wanted to learn, not to make friends with them."

"But your multilingualism, your musical talent and your willingness to help students in difficulty should've made you popular with them, right?"

"Yes, but most of those who could've benefited from my assistance weren't studious or eager to learn enough to ask for it, they saw no reason to study languages they thought they would never need, and I only played classical pieces while they were only interested in rock and roll. All my skills only increased the distance between them and me, because they made me different in their eyes. So, I got closer to the Jesuits, even to old Father John. They all had an astonishing degree of knowledge and experience, and I became a little more educated through them. The students began to call me Brother Mendel. To them, it was a way of insulting me, of ridiculing my friendly relationship with the monks, but I was proud of this nickname. It was as if they saw me as an educated adult and themselves as ignorant children."

"Were there any who influenced you more than others?"

"It's hard to say. They all brought something to me, each in their own way and on different levels. Brother Marcus, for example, taught geography and history. He'd been a missionary. He told me about his adventures in Africa, Asia and South America. He'd tell me about the great misery, the simplicity and the kindness of the people he had lived with and loved. I was fascinated, not by his tenacious will to convert them to his religion, but especially because this man, now very old, had more than once risked his life to help them. I'd seen myself for years traveling to the ends of the earth to help when necessary and possible."

He thought for such a long time, smiling, that I asked him what amused him.

"I thought of Brother Andrew, who was the physical education teacher for all the classes at the boarding school. He was a sixth-degree black belt and had excellent knowledge of many other martial arts. He'd even developed a personal self-defense technique that he called the peaceful method, because it consisted mainly of subduing his opponents and putting them out of action quickly without harming them, at least not seriously. He once told me, 'Always do everything you can to avoid a fight. But if you're really forced to fight, try to make such an impression in the first few minutes that no one will ever want to come after you again. And take advantage of the surprise effect to run away. There is no shame in running away from your attackers, especially if they are numerous and dangerous.' I was happy with what he was teaching me, even though I was aware that this kind of method could only work if my opponents weren't armed and ready to kill."

Like his mother, Zach was a fast learner. But even though he tried not to flaunt his knowledge, he was increasingly mocked. Brother Andrew had told him that he'd probably make friends if he joined the soccer team and helped them win. So, Zach practiced regularly at his school's gym to improve his ball skills. But one day while he was practicing dribbling and juggling alone, his classmates' attitudes took a violent turn. George, a big guy who liked to play rough, showed up with his whole gang. He intercepted the ball and threw it viciously at Mendel's head, who promptly threw it back in his face with a frontal blow. George, angry and with a bloody nose, then wanted to impress with his great strength and started to jostle his opponent, who did not let himself be manhandled. After only a few seconds, George was on the ground, yelping in pain as Zach stomped away.

Father John, whose only job outside of celebrating mass and confessions, was to collect firewood for the fireplaces at the old boarding school, sometimes suffered from back pain. He asked the students if one of them could fill in for him for a few days and Zach readily agreed. A few days later, while he was out cutting and stacking logs, George tried to make him pay for the humiliation he had suffered. Zach faced a concerted attack from the bully and his cronies, but he fought back so hard that George and some of his friends ended up in the school infirmary. Probably for fear of being expelled by their school's administration, the whole gang then kept a respectful distance from Zach and even stopped insulting him. But they spread the rumor that Zach was a wild beast who should not be approached.

"That evening, Brother Andrew asked me what had happened. I told him with all the calmness that my anger allowed me. I assured him that if I could've done otherwise, I would've avoided fighting and that I'd done a minimum of damage since there were five of them against me alone."

Zach explained to me that George was well known for his brutality and tendency to harass those younger and weaker than himself. He had harmed so many school children before that, according to Zach, the physical education teacher seemed satisfied because, for once, George had had his lesson; but he feared that the bully would take it out on someone smaller than him. Zach asked Brother Andrew why the troublemaker wasn't being sent away. The teacher replied that without his wealthy family's fortune, the school would probably have ceased to exist years ago. "Throw him out. I'll make sure you get enough to keep you going at least until I finish my training or longer if I can," Zach assured him.

He then asked his grandparents if they could take enough from his inheritance to donate to the school to keep it open. They told him no. Even though the money belonged to him in its entirety, until he came of age, no one could take more than the small amounts needed to support him. He promised them that if they provided the brothers with what they needed, he would pay them back a hundredfold when he came of age. But his guardians were not as wealthy as

Zach thought they were and as his father had been. However, they had many friends and acquaintances who were. They raised money and the boarding school was able to remain open for several more years. When Zach came of age, he gave his grandparents so much money that they could live very comfortably for the rest of their lives, and he put a small fortune into his school account.

"Maybe when you heard about my charities, it was my old boarding school they were speaking of. But then, I only gave to Arthur and to people in need, not to charity."

"What about George?" I asked.

"He had to stay at home for several weeks. Then the school management talked to him and his parents. George promised to behave from now on. Father John said that if there were any incidents, he'd be expelled permanently."

"And did he behave better?"

"He seemed so afraid of me that I felt sorry for him. But he couldn't completely avoid me since we were on the same soccer team. He was our striker. I played forward. I was considered the 'false nine' because I often scored, which enraged Georges who thought he was being cheated of his goals."

"Did he try to make you pay for his frustration?"

"You don't take it out on your teammates. So, he'd just grumble when he thought he'd lost a chance to give us the lead because of me. But one day, when we were in the locker room, he wasn't looking where he was going and he bumped into me. What ensued was an avoidance waltz, each trying to get around the other. I laughed, put a hand on his shoulder and pretended I was dancing with him. Those who saw us laughed too. But George pushed me away roughly and said, 'Don't you dare touch me, you, faggot!' It was the first time I'd been called that name. Many around us went, 'Hooo!' Clearly, they were all expecting me to lash out at George to force him to swallow his words. He was big, but short. I was almost a head taller than him. And my build was already quite pronounced, at least as imposing as his. I said, 'Sorry, George, but you're not my type at all.' George wanted to hit me, but he had to remember what he was risking if he did, especially in front of witnesses. He just turned and walked away."

Mendel recalls the incident with a smile.

"And nothing else happened?"

"He complained when I was appointed to lead the team a year and a half later. I knew how to motivate the members. I gave them all a chance to show what they could do. I was always ignored in the classroom, but on the field, I was well liked. So, when our previous captain left us to study elsewhere and we voted on who would replace him, I got a strong majority. George claimed that it was his rightful place as he was the longest-serving player and the best scorer. In fact, according to the latest stats, I'd scored as much as he had, even though his position gave him an advantage, but I didn't comment. Everyone started saying that seniority and the number of goals scored per season were not relevant or sufficient criteria for selection and that I was the one they had chosen. Georges then decided to leave the team. But soon after, Arthur came along, and he was damn good at the game. He was much better than me. He was given George's position and we won even more games than before."

I considered that what was remarkable about Mendel's story was that he never complained about anything or anyone, not even about his dear father or the fact that his classmates ignored him. He found something good in everything he lived. He believed that having had such a childhood had taught him to appreciate all the happy things that happened to him afterwards. Father John's kindness had taught him to be more empathetic and generous. Brother Andrew's suggestion that he join the soccer team had helped him develop his muscles, his skills and his leadership abilities. Brother Marcus's stories had inspired him to travel and to step in to help whenever he could. And the company of all the other friars had led him to take an interest in many important subjects not found in textbooks.

Chapter 4

Sitting in his favorite chair, Zach Mendel, my new master, told me about the beginning of his relationship with his first lover (part 1).

Arthur, a.k.a. Arty, was a newcomer to boarding school following the accidental death of his parents. Like me, he had been entrusted to his grandparents, whom he hated because they were too conventional, strict and religious. In the hope of converting him to a more fundamentalist Catholicism and instilling in him a sense of discipline, they had enrolled him in our boarding school. Poor Grandma and Grandpa, they didn't know who they were dealing with.

As soon as he arrived in his new class on the first day, Arthur attracted attention by sitting at the very back of the room, next to me. I'd pretended to ignore him, but actually, I'd been won over at first sight. Yet I made it a point not to attach too much importance to people's looks, but rather to their value as a person. So why was I already so attracted to this one? I didn't quite understand it yet, but I'd soon find out.

Brother Jeremiah, the arts and humanities teacher, had asked Arthur to introduce himself, which he did more than briefly, giving only his first name.

"And to what do we owe your coming to this school?"

"The torturers who are my new tutors wanted to get rid of me. So, they thought that putting me here would be a good idea. Anyway, if they think that I'll become as religious as they are because of your religious drivel, they are wrong."

His body was tense, his teeth and fists clenched, and his tone was angry. I turned my head away to hide my smile from him.

"You're not in your parents' custody?" the brother had questioned, not paying attention to Arthur's challenging comment.

"No."

"Why not?"

"They died in a car accident," Arthur answered, swallowing his saliva and lowering his eyelids to hide the tears that had sprung up.

So, this little rebel wasn't as tough as he wanted us to believe. I looked at him with more interest as the teacher asked me to share my books and be so kind as to give Arthur a pencil and paper until he had his own school materials. I obeyed without question, although I'd have preferred to wait until I knew this new student better before getting any closer.

Arthur immediately began scribbling a demonized image of himself whipping up a bloody caricature of Brother Jeremiah on the cross, head down and half naked. But obviously, under the loincloth of the crucified pointed a rigid cock. This made me smile. Arthur seemed more interesting every moment.

The teacher then asked the whole class to draw a representation of hell. Arthur just finished what he'd started, so that in the end it was a real work of art, albeit a very irreverent one.

"Bring me your work," the teacher demanded when his class was over.

The astonishment on his face when Arty handed him his paper would've deserved to be photographed for the boarding school's annals.

Brother Jeremiah had once told us all that he'd always grade us based on the artist's talent and quality of his work, not on what was represented. And he valued freedom of expression much more than most of the other brothers. So, Arthur was surprised the next day to find that he was given an A for his drawing. He tried not to look too amazed, but it was obvious that he was expecting and perhaps even hoping for some negative comments and an E for this first work.

But Arthur couldn't help but clown around and poke fun at the quirks of teachers and students. He was a really talented mime, and his imitation of George's clumsy walk was worth seeing. But one day I got tired of Arthur's antics and disrespect for the brothers; especially since he kept sitting next to me. So, at lunchtime, I followed him to the bathroom and stood behind him, waiting for him to finish urinating.

"What do you want from me?" he asked as he zipped up his pants.

"It's 'What do you want from me, Sir?' for you, newbie."

I was so close to him that Arthur turned around with difficulty, but he still smiled at me with his usual bravado. I pushed him off and he fell sitting in the urinal.

"You're going to show respect to the brothers and father from now on, because they deserve it, all of them. Do you understand?" I ordered him harshly, my hands clamped on his shoulders to slow his efforts to get up.

Arthur froze with a grotesque grimace on his handsome face.

"Understood, Sir."

He put the emphasis on "Sir". Even so, I didn't have much faith in his submission, but I helped him to his feet anyway and walked out, figuring I'd soon see if he was sincere. And I almost hoped he wouldn't be too tame. I could already picture him crushed under my weight, groaning. If I could hold back my smile, I couldn't stop the burning swirl in my groin and cock.

His pants were wet, but Arthur didn't even bother to get them changed. Maybe he had no other. George, of course, noticed this and started ridiculing him, saying he had pooped his pants. Arthur turned around and gave him the finger. When George tried to slap him, I held his arm back with a firm hand.

"Don't do that, George! Remember what will happen if you bully another student, especially a new one like Arthur?"

"Let me go, Mendel!"

"Only if you swear not to bully him."

"What's the matter with you? Is he your boyfriend?"

"No, he's my valet, my servant, my factotum."

Hearing these words, Arthur froze on the spot.

"Your facto what? You can't talk like everyone else!" said George.

"Promise or I'll drag you to the director's office so he can fire you."

"I didn't do anything to your bootlicker," replied George.

"It's not for lack of trying. And anyway, that's YOUR story, not mine."

George looked at us in turn, then gave in.

"Okay. I won't touch him. I wouldn't want to get dirty anyway."

"Swear to me."

"Don't fuck with me, Mendel."

I hooked his leg while grabbing his wrist, and I began to drag him around quickly while he tried unsuccessfully to get up, screaming to let him go. I repeated to him, "Swear to me."

He replied in a panicked voice.

"Okay, okay, okay. I swear."

I released him so roughly that his face hit the floor. Meanwhile, Arthur, still in the same place, was watching the scene and was clearly amazed.

I then went to the cafeteria. Arthur followed me like my shadow and sat down opposite meat at my table. I didn't comment and started eating without saying a word. But something was bothering me and after a few minutes I asked him about it.

"You said your parents died in a car accident. How did they die?"

"A drunkard ran into them. It's a good thing she died too, otherwise I don't know if I'd have let her live much longer."

I felt a chill run through me. Was this driver my mom? Arthur seemed to have shut himself up in his memories. As for me, I didn't want to know more than that. We finished eating in silence.

That night, too, he followed me and sat across from me for dinner. I felt trapped. Could I escape him? Since we were in the same group, he'd probably be assigned to my dorm room. After dinner, I told him to do his homework alone. I had my own obligations elsewhere. But when I went to chop wood for Father John, he asked me if I'd be so kind as to help Arthur adjust to his new surroundings.

"Show him around the school and the neighborhood, so he can feel at home," he suggested.

I was caught like a rat in a trap. Father John was my favorite of all the people who lived here. He was very old, but still very lucid and energetic. He was always understanding and compassionate towards us, despite our youthful folly. He also knew how to see the best in each of us. So, I didn't have the heart to say No.

I told him not to touch the firewood; Arthur and I would take care of it. And I left to find Arthur. He'd returned to the cafeteria with his bag full of books and school supplies, presumably to study. He didn't know yet that we had a library where we could go to do our homework or that the dormitories had not only one bed per student, but also a small desk, where he could work if he wanted to.

"Father John asked me to show you around. But first I have to cut firewood for him. We'll pack up your things and then we can explore the area."

"Father John is the decrepit old man who looks like a tramp in his oversized clothes?"

I stopped walking, paralyzed. I'd just had a vision of the old man floating in his pants. Suddenly, an invisible fist crushed my heart, my breath was too short and I felt like crying.

"I thought I told you to show respect to the brothers and the father!"

I was in such a rage! He must have understood this, because I saw his frightened expression. Immobilized under a lamp, with his long eyelashes drawing a shadow across his cheeks with each blink, he looked like a fawn captivated by the headlights of a car or a child who fears the wrath of his father.

"But he's not even here. He surely didn't hear anything."

"Ah, you think that's respect? Saying the right thing when people can hear you, but insulting them behind their back?"

He swallowed his saliva and shook his head from side to side.

"Is that a 'no'?"

"Yes. Huh, no. Heh…"

His confusion almost made me feel sorry for him. Almost. Except that everything about him excited me: his undeniable beauty, his boldness mixed with vulnerability, his pain at the memory of his parents, his apparent desire to please me…

I ordered him, "Remind me to punish you for this breach of the rule."

He held his breath. He didn't dare look me in the eye. When he started breathing again, he was so tense that I thought he'd rebel. I hoped he would. But he answered respectfully, "Yes, Sir."

Then a shock went off from my solar plexus and electrified my whole body, especially my cock. It was as if thunder had struck me. And at that moment, it was me holding my breath. I'd never felt anything like this, for anyone! I didn't even understand the full extent of these emotions and sensations that were coming over me. And it scared me.

I ordered him to follow me, and we went to the dormitory, where I had him put his things on the bed next to mine. That bunk was free, because no one had wanted it: too close to me and to the window through which the cold air came in during most of the school year.

Then I dragged him to the door where I had to go out to cut wood. He was the one who split it while I laughed at his clumsiness. After explaining to him how to use the saw and ax better, I had him chop and stack more than was needed.

"Put your arms forward, that way," I said, demonstrating.

He obeyed me without question. And I put logs on his forearms up to under his chin. Then I ordered him to follow me, and we went inside. I walked briskly, deliberately making it difficult for him to carry the wood. I imagined him accidentally dropping his entire stack. I smiled as I heard him gasp as he struggled not to drop anything. But he held on.

Once near one of the large fireplaces, I showed him where to put his load. I sat in a chair, put my feet up on the footrest and let Arthur figure it out on his own. When he had everything placed properly, I said, "Half goes to another place."

I stood up, as if to leave. He tried to pile up as fast as he could in his arms what needed to be carried elsewhere. But logs were falling as he picked them up. The task was almost impossible for a single person; I knew something about it because I'd taken on too heavy a load the first day and it had almost all slipped away. So, I walked over and helped him with my most crooked smile. I'd have understood if he'd thrown everything in my face and told me to take care of it myself. But he responded to my mocking look by shaking his head and smiling back. I definitely liked Arthur a lot.

We went to the other big fireplace to put the rest of the wood there, and then I showed him around the place, including the kitchen, where Brother Francis was still preparing the necessities for the next day's meals.

"Can we help you, Brother Francis?"

He looked at us, one at a time, before answering.

"I told you, Zachary, that the job of the students is to study, to fill their brains with everything they'll need later on."

I replied, "Knowing how to cook is very useful, vital, even."

"Have you finished your homework? And your friend there, his name is...?"

Arthur held out his hand and introduced himself.

"We haven't done them yet, but Father John asked me to show him around the boarding school and the surrounding area," I replied.

"Will you be visiting your families this weekend?"

"No, not me, you know my grandparents live too far away for me to go there often."

"And your friend? Arthur?"

"I don't want to go back to those people. If he stays here, so do I," he said.

Obviously, "he" was me.

"Who are these people you prefer to avoid?"

"My maternal grandparents. But I'd never seen them before Mom and Dad died, except in pictures. My mother didn't get along with them. My other grandparents, I knew well, but they live in an old people's home and couldn't take care of me."

"These people are still your guardians."

"The first thing they did after they got custody of me was to blame me for everything I am and everything I do. They yelled at me like I've never been yelled at before, just because I like to draw and play the flute and the guitar, because I eat with an appetite, because I have insomnia and I go out at night to get some fresh air, because when I do get to sleep I have nightmares and my screaming wakes them up, because then I have a hard time getting up in the morning, because… because… Sometimes I need solitude, but if I stay in my room, they call me lazy, and if I go out walking alone in the forest, they say I'm just a bum. So, they decided that I was a hopeless case and decided to get rid of me by sending me to a boarding school. They are happier without me and I'm happier without them anyway. I want to stay here!"

At times, as he spoke his answer, he seemed to suffocate. He was in great pain, I could feel it, and I suffered for him.

"You loved your parents very much, didn't you?"

Arthur turned his head away. But I could see his Adam's apple bobbing up and down spasmodically. He was still trying to swallow his tears. I suddenly felt like hugging him tightly and assure him that everything would be okay.

Brother Francis put his hand on Arthur's shoulder and gave it a little squeeze, then said, "If you need to talk or… anything else, please feel free to come to me. I'll help you any way I can."

Arthur thanked him in a broken voice. Then the brother turned to me and added, "Take good care of your friend, Zachary. But you could wait until the weekend to show him around. Go do your homework tonight instead. I'll explain it all to Father John."

That's what we did. After retrieving our school bags from the dormitory, I led Arthur to the library while playing tour guide, telling him what was in each room we passed until we got there. Arthur sat at my table again, across from me.

Patting the seat to my right, I whispered, "No, come here. It'll be easier for me to help you if you need it."

He worked in silence for at least forty-five minutes until something he didn't understand made him grunt. Without stopping my reading, I asked him what was wrong.

He was having trouble with math. It was a trigonometry problem I'd done the day before. It seemed very simple to me.

"Start over and tell me, as you go along, what you're doing and why you're doing it. I'll tell you what's right and what's wrong."

"I can't do it. I don't understand any of this."

"Didn't you learn trig at your previous school?"

"Yes, but I skipped two grades, one in elementary and one in high school, because of my excellent grades. I think it was being taught at one of them. And now I'm here and I don't know anything about it."

So, I was dealing with a little genius.

"Okay. It's better if you forget about this assignment for today. Tomorrow we'll discuss it with Brother Philip, the math and science teacher. And if you're having trouble in other subjects, we'll talk to the principal. But, if you have skipped years, that means you're younger than the majority of the students in our class."

"Yes, but only by one year, since I did my first year of elementary school late because of the month I was born. I wasn't old enough to start at the same time as my friends."

"How old are you?"

"Fourteen."

I didn't understand why I felt such a need to protect him, as I'd have done for my little brother, if I had one. I figured it must have been his dimples, long hemmed eyelashes, and childishness that made him look so juvenile, but he really was younger than the rest of our class, all of whom must have been fifteen or even sixteen, for those who had started school late or repeated a grade.

"Have you finished your other homework and lessons?"

"Brother Frederic asked me to study a little bit of music history that I already know."

"Did you really?"

He gave a confident "yes" with his head. So, I opened my book to the relevant pages and asked him about it. In addition to the correct answers, he gave details that were not there. And his additions weren't only correct and relevant, but explained clearly, vividly and interestingly.

I nodded, pleased with my new factotum. I liked Arthur more and more. But I owed him a punishment and he hadn't yet asked me for it.

"Isn't there something you need to ask me?"

He looked at me with question marks in his eyes. He didn't immediately realize what it was, but when he did a few seconds later, he blinked. I leaned over and, after making sure no one would see us, gave him a tiny peck on the corner of his lips. He shivered. I was really enjoying this skin-deep sensitivity.

"I didn't want to offend him. I didn't understand the respect and affection you have for them. I won't do it again, I promise you."

"You told me you wouldn't make fun of them anymore when I first told you about them, right?"

He nodded with the same little boy's expression at the thought of punishment. I still had a fierce urge to kiss him. But this wasn't the right time; not when punishment was involved.

"I'm going to write this on your slate. We'll add all your mistakes if you make any more. And as soon as I can, I'll add them up and punish you for them. Is that okay?"

He nodded nervously, glancing at me with concern, then looking away. His cheeks were flushed. Ah, how beautiful he was! So touching.

"Say it. Do you agree?"

"Yes, Sir, I do."

His voice had become firmer. He was ready for anything. At least, that's what he thought. But he didn't know what was in store for him, and neither did I.

"Right."

We went to the dormitory. I asked the overseer, Brother Raphael that night, to give me the bedding I needed for Arthur, who chose the bed where he had put his things earlier and which was closest to mine, of course. The brother suggested him to move further away, where it was a little warmer, but Arthur turned down the suggestion with conviction, saying that he wasn't afraid of the cold. So, we prepared his bunk together.

We then went to wash ourselves in the showers. George was already there and ogled us as we got undressed, but he didn't say or do anything for once. Arthur scrubbed my back without my asking and I returned the favor, stopping only above his nice, round, firm little buttocks. I dropped the soap and as I stood up after picking it up, I found myself at the level of these two beautiful twin bubbles. I wanted to bury my nose between them, to sniff them, lick them, bite them and hit them. But I finished straightening up and turned off the hot water so that the icy spray would help me overcome the state in which this vision and the images it had provoked had put me.

Arthur had claimed to suffer from insomnia or nightmares since his parents died. Yet he was sound asleep within minutes of going to bed, despite the hubbub of the dormitory preparing for the night, discussing the day and complaining, as usual, about the great "cruelty" of the brothers who had overburdened them with homework and lessons. In his apparently dreamless sleep, Arthur looked like an angel. Poor little boy lost all alone in a world of which he knew nothing!

Chapter 5

Master Mendel's account of the beginning of his relationship with Arthur (part 2).

The next day it was time to get up for morning mass. I still hadn't shown Arthur the chapel and we had to go there for the service.

He had drooled on his pillow in his sleep. The image of the sleeping angel was a bit tarnished as a result. I shook him awake. He grunted. When he opened his eyes, he looked completely lost, probably not remembering where he was. But when he recognized me, he sat up and smiled at me in such a childish way that it moved me. I was amused to see his hair scattered around his head in such a mess that it looked like he'd been caught in the middle of a tornado while sleeping.

"Sleep well?"

He seemed to be searching for a memory of his usual waking hours in the middle of the night, and when he couldn't find any, he replied that it was the first time he hadn't had a nightmare since… He stopped there, but I understood.

He asked me what time it was.

"Five o'clock."

He went back to bed right away. As he started to cover himself, I grabbed his blankets, shaking my head no-no and smiling mockingly.

I yelped, "Get up. Now!"

He grunted again, but sat back down.

"Why do you have to get up so early?"

"Don't you hear the matins? They're calling us to mass."

"Mass?!"

He looked quite disgusted at the idea of going to listen to what he must have considered preachy and a complete waste of time, judging from the drawing he had done on the first day.

He was already sinking back under his sheets and into sleep, but I ordered him, "Add this to your slate. When I say, 'Stand up,' I want you on your feet right away. Got it?"

He straightened up and looked at me, his mouth open.

"But…"

"No 'but'. Get ready quickly or we'll be late. I don't like latecomers any more than the brothers like them."

He didn't look too enthusiastic, but he got up, dressed and followed me to the chapel. As always, I sat in the back of the nave; he sat next to me, as always. But after only a few minutes, he had leaned against me and gone back to sleep. I was tempted to jostle him to wake him up, but I was touched by the trust in me that his behavior showed. I couldn't bring myself to blame him. On the contrary, I wanted to pet him, like you pet a puppy that lies on your lap.

All the brothers and the not too sleepy schoolboys were singing hymns during the service. Normally, I would have stood, sat, and knelt, as the rite called for, but I stayed still so as not to disturb Arthur's nap. While I was singing with the others, he woke up, straightened up and looked at me. He seemed hypnotized. Then I saw his skin turn into goose bumps. What had caused this effect? Was I singing so out of tune?

At the end of the service, as we were leaving the chapel, he said to me, "You have a beautiful voice!"

So that was the cause of his shiver. What a strange kid he was! Sensitive and bold at the same time.

As we walked to the cafeteria, he added, "You should sing in a choir."

"Isn't that what I do?"

"Yes, but… I meant, in a more prestigious choir."

I laughed.

"I don't give a toss about prestige."

He stared at me so intensely that I, who could have stared the devil down, had to look away.

I then sat down in my usual spot in the cafeteria and asked him to go get me breakfast.

"What do you want to eat?"

I laughed.

"This is not a five-star hotel. Bring me whatever there is."

He left and came back with my tray in one hand and his in the other. So it was his skill, some physical strength and a lot of willpower that had saved him from dropping the logs the night before. He placed my meal in front of me.

I was still a little surprised that he didn't feel humiliated to serve me in this way in front of all the students and brothers. But I was soon to discover that I wasn't dealing with just anyone and that it took more, much more, to discourage or frighten him.

That night, unusually, we didn't have too much homework or lessons, so I went to the common room where there was a giraffe piano. I sat down on the bench, set up my score in front of me, and lifted the keyboard flap. Then I collected myself before starting to play. Arthur, who had initially remained in the hallway, came and stood beside me and watched me. I was too focused on my Satie piece to pay him any attention. But when the piece ended and I stopped, I noticed that he was crying. I closed the flap and turned on the bench. I motioned him to come closer and pointed to the floor. He knelt between my legs without the slightest hesitation.

"Why the tears?"

He replied in a vibrant voice as he swallowed and wiped his face, "This was Mom's favorite."

How likely was it that Satie's Gymnopédie was his mother's favorite piece of music? If I had played Beethoven's "Ode to Elyse" or "Moonlight Sonata", the best-known part of Bach's Piano Concerto No. 5, or Chopin's "Nocturne" Op. 9, I'd have thought it was just a matter of luck, but Satie certainly wasn't.

He was trembling in my arms. When he started to sob, I motioned for him to sit next to me on the bench and gave him a big hug.

"You're lucky."

This statement shook him a little.

"You can at least mourn the loss of your parents. I can't do the same for mine. My mother was an alcoholic who died by her own fault and my father was such a monster that I was glad when he passed away."

He looked up. His beautiful tear-streaked face was a study that not even Bach could have composed.

I asked him, "You play the flute, don't you?"

"Yes. And guitar. And other instruments, but not as well."

"What kind of flute?"

"A transverse flute."

"Did you bring it?"

"My… guardians took away my flute and guitar. They were gifts from Mom. I don't know if they threw them away or just hid them. But I don't have them anymore."

"What a cruelty to take away such memories of a child's mother! And what kind of morons would believe that being able to play a musical instrument is a flaw?"

He laughed through his tears.

"Morons like the ones who have been entrusted with my care."

I felt sorry for him, much more than for myself. I didn't even know how I felt about Mom and Dad's death. The other students had become my family, Father John was my counselor and protector, this boarding school was my new home. Arthur had lost the Love, the greatest of all, that a child feels for his parents. I realized that I felt as much affection for him as I do for a little brother when he is unhappy. My suffering and his, although very different, were linked.

I got up and went to look in a closet. I was happy to find a flute. I handed it to him. He took it and looked at me with so much emotion that I could hardly contain mine. Then I took a handwritten score out of my bag and offered it to him.

"Learn it. Saturday morning, after breakfast, we'll play it together."

He seemed both happy and nervous. Perhaps he was afraid that he wouldn't be able to play it as well as I hoped, as I had believed him capable of doing. This fervent desire to please troubled me, for I didn't yet understand it.

"Who composed it?"

"I did."

"Is it true?!" he asked, his eyes sparkling.

"Of course, it's true."

He smiled at me, apparently delighted to discover that I had the knowledge to write a score. He replied in a passionate voice.

"I'll learn it!"

My love for him hurt far more than the memory of my father's raging hatred, my mother's drunken recklessness, my sister's frequent absence from home as often as possible, or the indifference of the students at that boarding school. I said to myself, "Don't be afraid, bro. Don't be afraid of anything! I'll always take care of you." And I meant it! I really believed it. How could I've guessed that, a few days later, I would wonder if I should forget him altogether, keep him away from me? Poor little brother!

Chapter 6

Master Mendel's description of the beginning of his relationship with Arthur, his first lover (part 3).

The week went by without a hitch. Every day I offered to help Arthur with his schoolwork. But he didn't need much help, except in trigonometry and a little in languages. So, sometimes, after my homework, I'd let him finish by himself and I'd go and help the brothers with their daily chores of cleaning or cooking, studying history and languages with them or just listening to their stories. Occasionally, Arthur would accompany me and assist me. I'd give him instructions in ancient Latin or Greek, demanding answers in the same languages to help him improve his initially sketchy knowledge. At times he asked me,

"What's the point of learning this? These are dead languages. Dead! Nobody speaks them anymore."

I explained to him that they were much more alive than he thought, since they were the basis of many of today's European languages, such as French, English, Spanish, Italian, German… Opening an etymological dictionary, I gave him many eloquent proofs. He grumbled but tried to answer me in the language in which I had spoken to him at the time.

But when I'd correct him every third word, sometimes even in English, because he'd sometimes choose the wrong term, mix up idioms or construct lame sentences, he'd get impatient. I didn't care; all I cared about was that he improved his knowledge. And he was getting better.

Every night I heard Arthur practicing the score I'd given him. At first, when I noticed he wasn't in bed, I wondered where he could be. Had he gone to the bathroom or was he just gone walkabout? Then, when he didn't come back, I listened and heard a distant flute tune.

He had taken refuge in the attic and his music was coming faintly through the fireplace. The first few nights he kept making the same mistakes, always at the most difficult passages, but he kept repeating. Oh, my God! How I loved that kid! He wanted to please me so much. How could I not fall in love with that angel?

I lay there with my hands clasped behind my neck, smiling, satisfied with my factotum's efforts to please me and with the hold I had over him. It was normal if he had trouble waking up in the morning and keeping up during mass and in class. I let him sleep against me in the chapel. But that didn't stop me from scolding him if he didn't get out of bed fast enough when I ordered him to, nor did it stop me from adding his disobedience and grumbling to his slate. He then tried to stay awake and listen more carefully. Oh yes, he did try! But it was getting harder and harder with the accumulation of sleepless nights.

As planned, after breakfast on Saturday, we went to the community room and I sat down at the piano. Arthur had brought the flute. He set up a music stand next to me and shakily put his score on it. I could see how nervous he was. It was a sign of how important it was for him that we play together. He was almost pitiful. I thought to myself, "He'll never be able to do the play well in this state." I gave him my recommendations.

"Take three deep breaths, try to relax and think of something peaceful, then focus on the first few notes, only on them."

He nodded and obeyed literally while I carried out my own instructions. His obedience, so total, pleased me greatly.

When I began to play, he followed me, as well as he could, I'm sure, but he was still getting it wrong in the same places. I started the piece over to the beginning. He followed suit. It was a little better, but still imperfect.

I turned around on the bench, motioned him to come closer, and pointed to the floor, instructing him to kneel before me. Even though there were other students and Brother Frederic in the room, he did so without hesitation.

I put my hand on his head and stroked his tangled hair.

"You can do better. I've heard you practicing every night since I gave you this score. You can play it beautifully. I know it!"

He was staring at me so intensely. A few tears had formed in his eyes. He was in such need of understanding and comfort! Poor abandoned boy.

I placed a kiss on his forehead, then turned around on the bench and started playing again. He stayed on his knees behind me and followed me. We were now one instrument in the hands of Apollo, god of music, poetry, light, healing and the future. There was only "us" and the music.

Despite some applause, I kept my eyes closed for a moment after the last note and when I turned them to him, I saw that his face was flooded with tears. I didn't ask him what was wrong. I knew that his tears were due to the emotion caused by our harmony, our perfect symbiosis. I smiled at him, put my hand against his cheek and brushed it. He shuddered. Someone made a foolish comment about the "lovers" we were supposed to be, but I didn't care. Arthur tensed up a bit, but when I gently ran my thumb over his face, he closed his eyes and regained his composure.

The novelty and intensity of what I was feeling for him scared me. But when he looked at me and smiled, it seemed as if we were both in the same halo of light and warmth, isolated from the others and the tepid haze of the ordinary world.

It was almost too much, too perfect to be true. I know. It was unimaginable, unhoped for. But that's exactly how I felt about him in that moment. Since I was born, I'd been waiting for him, and there he was, at my feet, ready to give me his days and nights, ready to do anything for me!

I stood up and motioned for him to follow me. I explained, "We didn't finish the tour of the buildings and surroundings."

After putting his flute away in the desk drawer next to his bed, we finished the tour of the boarding school, including the attic where Arthur had played his instrument. I was tempted to give him his punishment then and there, but I was afraid we would be heard over the chimney. And I had to show him the huge land that had belonged to the brotherhood for over two centuries.

~.~.~

Before going out, we went to put on our coats. First, we went around the building. I showed him where Brother Raphael grew a vegetable garden during the summer and the fences on which his strawberry plants climbed. There were several fruit trees from which Brother Francis made jams, compotes, desserts and liqueurs.

I showed him the garage, which was more like a warehouse, where the lawnmower was stored, as well as various horticultural, DIY and repair tools and much more. It was also used to store any obsolete or surplus items that were not used at the school, but that could still be useful. Again, I could've used our relative isolation to amuse myself with Arthur, but so close to the main building, Brother Raphael, who was in charge of the maintenance of the grounds, could've popped up at any moment and surprised us. Even Father John could've gone to get wood for the fireplaces and we'd have been caught in the act. And sometimes other people would take a walk outside or delivery people or visitors would park near here. So, it wouldn't have been very safe to do it there.

We followed the path that started at the back of the school, went along a creek and into the forest. Further along the trail, a small house had once been used to welcome visitors, relatives and friends of the brothers and Father John. But due to lack of maintenance, it was quite dilapidated. However, I invited Arthur to enter. There was still a stove, which we could've lit if we'd had wood and more time, and if I hadn't been afraid that the smoke, which could be seen from the school, would alert the brothers. There was a kitchenette, a small bathroom, a room with a bed. The house must've been welcoming, but now it was dusty, damp and smelled of mold. However, Arthur and I weren't hard to please. This moment of solitude was too precious not to enjoy.

I had been so looking forward to the moment when I'd order Arthur, "Naked."

He stripped awkwardly, his hands shaking. He was shivering in the autumn chill of the room. I then ordered him to undress me. He did so almost religiously, without even touching me other than with my own clothes, as if I were the high priest of his cult and he felt too much reverence for me to dare touch me without express permission or to allow himself the slightest disrespectful gesture.

Once naked, I went around him to examine every inch of his flesh, not hesitating to trample his clothes, which he had left in a heap on the floor. His milky whiteness illuminated by the opaline light coming from the bedroom window gave him the appearance of a statue carved in the purest Carrara marble. He was magnificent! Even today, I don't think I've ever had a lover with such perfect beauty as his.

I ran my hands over his naked flesh, taking in every bit of him as he lay still and quivering. But this time, I had no intention of helping him ease his nervous tension. On the contrary, I was savoring it.

Spreading his buttocks and feeling his anus, I asked him, "Have you ever been penetrated there?"

He began to tremble, almost vibrating like a piano wire. I was playing the nerve strings of my new instrument, and I loved it.

He shook his head, no.

"Speak!"

"No, Sir."

His voice! He was having so much trouble breathing that he could hardly say those two small words. It was a delight to my ears. I slapped him so hard across the face that he lost his balance. But he came back to stand two steps in front of me. I slapped him several times, always as hard. And each time, he came back to his place, standing in the same spot, offering himself to me. Then I ordered him,

"Get down on the bed so that your ass is on the edge and your legs are dangling. And spread them apart."

He took the specified posture. I picked up my belt and started whipping him. The more I hit him, the more excited and confused I was by what I was doing to him, by his moans and cries. It was our first time. I'd only seen such acts committed by my father and they'd never been welcome. But Arthur kept his posture, letting me give him new blows, inflicting him intense pain. I turned the strap around my hand, so that I could hit him with the buckle. And I did it several times. He started screaming at the top of his lungs and squirming in pain, but he kept on doing pretty much the same thing, clinging to the blankets, twisting them frantically. And his contortions did nothing more than give me access to other parts of his body and electrify me further.

"Turn around."

My voice was now huskier than his had been before I started and my cock was pointing stiffly. When I saw that his was harder than mine, I think I lost my mind. I whipped him even harder, almost furiously for so long that he was bleeding all over by the end. But his blue eyes, now as black as my soul, were fixed on my face and he still had a raging boner.

I went looking for another instrument to torture him more cruelly. I found a walking stick near the outer door. And when I returned to the room, he hadn't moved an inch. He was waiting for me and watched me enter, his eyes locked on mine. I'd have thought that when he saw the cane, his mind would be filled with terror, but he was examining me from head to toe and seemed to revel in the sight. For some reason, it enraged me; I'd have liked to see fear in his eyes as there was in mine when my father used such an instrument on me. I growled through my teeth,

"Get face down on the bed. Make sure only your feet stick out."

He obeyed.

"Get your ass up."

I started hitting him with the cane on his buttocks, thighs and soles. I only dropped my instrument of torture when I heard him sobbing. Not once did he beg me to stop.

Then I pulled him to the ground by his feet. Then I grabbed his hair, forced him to get on all fours and fucked him without lubrication or mercy, thrusting into him impetuously, to the depths of his bowels. His moans, far from making me feel tender, intensified my pleasure and my ferocity. At a certain point, I believe that I was no longer totally inhabiting my body so much I was distraught, obsessed by my pleasure and by his suffering, as if my mind had merged with his. I have no idea how I'd have reacted if someone had tried to stop me at that moment, because I was possessed by an infernal force that demanded to be satiated.

After cumming, I lay on top of him for a few minutes, just long enough to catch my breath, without worrying about his orgasm or his injuries. Then I got up and left, leaving him alone, without trying to find out if, in the state I'd put him in, he'd be able to go back without help to the boarding school.

He came back; the next day, holding his ribs, limping and groaning. He'd been unable to get dressed completely and wore only his coat. His swollen and bluish feet had prevented him from putting on his shoes, and by walking along the path, he'd skinned them a little more. Someone found him lying in a corridor and took him to the infirmary of the boarding school. Brother Andrew, who had been a caregiver, was notified. After examining him, he thought it best to take him to the hospital.

They questioned Arthur to find out who had done this to him, of course. But he never told the truth. He claimed it was a stranger he had come across in the woods. In a way, he didn't lie, because I was a stranger to myself that day and we were well into the woods when it happened.

When he was able to come back to school and resume classes, he hobbled over to me and sat down at my table; just like always. The first thing he whispered to me was, "Thank you, Sir."

I shuddered. I didn't know if it was pleasure or terror. And he wanted to do it again as soon as he was healed of his injuries. I didn't.

Chapter 7

Master Mendel's account put me in a state of mind that must have been quite similar to his when Arthur asked him to try again: a mixture of unease and perverse excitement.

"Why didn't you want to try again with him?"

"I was afraid of myself, of not being able to control myself. His masochism was and still is such that he and I together is like opening a door to an extreme SM universe, almost without limits. But you must set limits."

"And did you recidivate?" I asked him.

"Not immediately. I told him that I'd gotten what I wanted from him and I wasn't interested in him anymore. And I ordered him to stay away from me."

Oh my God! I know only too well how I would have felt in Arthur's place.

"He must've felt rejected and hurt," I assumed.

"Yes. He looked at me blankly as he cried. But even that turned me on. His pain at the thought of losing me and of having been nothing but a plaything for me, a means to satisfy my baser instincts and sadistic pleasure made him even more beautiful, more desirable. Ah, Lord, yes, I wanted him!"

"Did he try to change your mind?"

"No. He kept away from me, as I'd demanded, but he didn't mingle with others any more than I did. Several went to talk to him to try to find out what happened to him, how it happened, and who did it to him, so much so that he finally got tired of their curiosity and yelled at them to leave him alone. He found himself even lonelier. He was increasingly perceived as a wild and potentially dangerous animal. But his loyalty to me, despite what I'd done and said to him, was probably the biggest factor in convincing me to get close to him again. For I believe it was during this period that I began to truly love him, and not just as the new kid being I had to help with his homework or the wounded little brother I should comfort and protect; he'd become my double, my reflection, my perfect match."

His voice vibrated as he said those last words. I could feel their truth. He still felt love for Arthur. It was obvious.

"And how did it go from there?"

"I had to get over the shock of being so much like my father. And I couldn't bring myself to hit Arthur again until he'd fully recovered. So, it took weeks since he had cracked ribs and was covered in various injuries, some of which healed quite slowly. In the meantime, I kept him in a kind of permanent Scottish shower, complimenting him whenever he did something really well, for all his successes at school, for his talent as a musician or even on the soccer field, where he insisted on playing despite all his bruises, but treating him like my servant, acting towards him with as much contempt as the nobles of the past had towards their valets. But the more arrogant and tyrannical I was, the humbler and more servile he behaved, as if he thought me worthy of being placed on the highest pedestal. All his actions were marked by respect and even love for me and his desire to get at least a little attention from me. My always so vivid memory of how I felt about my father's smugness and cruelty was charged with fear and hatred, certainly not respect and love. So how could he have such good feelings for the monster I had become? I didn't fully understand that until many years later."

"And did you still have sex during your boarding school years?"

"It was difficult, since we couldn't do anything inside and had to justify every outing. And we couldn't hang out outside for long without attracting the brothers' attention, who might come to check on us. But we enjoyed every moment alone. And, as I told you, I can't orgasm without causing pain or humiliation. But just the thought of what I was inflicting on him every moment of every day was enough to satisfy my sadism a little and mitigate it during our very rare fucks. But it didn't always satisfy his masochism; he wanted more. He'd have liked me to trample him, to break him. Once I said to him, 'If I let myself be taken where you dream of taking me, Arthur, your life will be in danger.' He replied, 'I don't care if I die at your hands.' But I'm not a murderer and I hate real violence, the kind that is inflicted on those who don't seek it or don't consent to it. I could even be considered a pacifist. So, I gave him everything I could without him having to go back to the hospital. But this watered-down version of what we both loved so much left us both unfulfilled. So, from time to time, we tried new games, more and more dangerous."

His pupils had dilated. Obviously, these memories still excited him. At the risk of awakening his desire and sadism and pushing him to start again with me, I asked him about these games.

"How dangerous?"

"Once, when we were both in the shed putting away the shovels used to clear the driveway and yard of snow that had accumulated during a storm, we were very out of breath. His gasps reminded me of his erotic, masochistic pleasure. I backed him roughly into the wall, forced him to turn around, then wrapped my arm around his throat and squeezed. I didn't release him until I felt him go limp. He hadn't even tried to push me away when he started to run out of air. Afterwards, I began to grip his neck in a vice during fuck. This allowed us to discover that his pleasure was multiplied tenfold if I strangled him and that he suffocated as he was cumming. My pleasure was also greatly multiplied by seeing his eyes bulging as he almost lost consciousness during orgasm."

I understood very well what he meant by "dangerous". I knew not to go too far with this type of play, not only because it could cause the death of the person being strangled, but because, even if they remained alive, it could cause irreversible brain damage if they went without air for too long.

His gaze had turned inward. He remained lost in his memory for quite a while before continuing to tell me.

"Another time, in the same shed after working for several hours outside, I crooked my leg at him as I pushed him to the ground, then sat on him. I then leaned in to kiss and bite him, feeling him all over. As I reached for his pants, I felt an unusually hard bulge in them and reached into his pockets. I found a pocketknife. We weren't supposed to have them at boarding school, but Arthur, the rebel, didn't always follow the rules. I opened the knife and examined it with fascination, imagining all the things I could do to him with it. Then when I looked down at Arthur's eyes, I saw that they were enlarged with terror. That turned me on. I smiled at him as I laid the edge of the blade against his throat. He tensed up at first and began to struggle. I pressed his shoulders to the floor and looked at him hard, ordering him to stop resisting me. He froze. When I put the tip of the blade back on his throat, I felt him give up the fight, surrender to my will. He was ready to let me do whatever I wanted to him; I saw it in the tenderness of his eyes and in the relaxation of all his muscles. He was offering me his life. I cut his skin lightly. A drop of blood beaded. I thought I was going to ejaculate at that moment, I was so excited! Under my buttocks, something hard, not a knife, had unfolded. I bent down and licked his bloody wound. Then we heard the voice of Brother Raphael, who had come to check what was taking us so long. I jumped to my feet like a spring, reaching out to help Arthur up. Fortunately, we were both behind boxes and fully clothed. But I often replayed those moments afterwards, always with the same intense pleasure."

I had seen everything he had described to me as if he had projected it onto the screen of my mind. When I turned my eyes towards him, he was looking at me with a strange smile, probably quite similar to the one that had come to him when he had stuck the tip of the knife in his friend's flesh. I shivered.

"Do I scare you?"

"A little."

"That's good. If I don't want Arthur as a slave 24/7 and don't see him very often, it's because he's not afraid of anything. As for me, it's his fearlessness that scares me most. Years later, I asked him to choose a security word, but he never used it. I doubt he'll ever use it. This inability to stop me is my hard limit, as they say in BDSM circles."

"It's a good limit, in my opinion."

He began to laugh out loud. Which made me smile, even though I didn't know what he found so funny.

"And what about piercings and playing with needles or blades: knives, scalpels and the like?" he asked me.

I swallowed my saliva, especially since he had gotten up to get something from the bathroom. I thought, "That'll teach me to turn on such a sadist!" He came back with a straight razor. I tensed up.

"If I told you that of all the things Arthur and I've tried, this is what fascinates me the most, would you let me use it on you?"

My fear and his obvious arousal had just combined to transport me into my subspace: that very special place where I don't always find enough presence of mind to stop the dom from doing whatever he wants to me. I didn't confide this fact to him at the time for fear of being rejected for crossing his hard limit, but I knew I would have to tell him sooner or later.

I reached out to him. He took my left hand in his. It was so hot! He brought the blade closer. Before using it, he looked straight into my eyes, and I saw that his were now just two black pools. He made three tiny cuts at the base of my wrist, just above my thumb. They intersected, forming a six-pointed star. A few drops of blood had trickled down.

"Open your mouth and stick out your tongue," he ordered.

I did so without a moment's hesitation. He laid the razor flat on my tongue, sliding it in first on one side, then on the other, washing it and letting me taste its metallic flavor and that of my blood. He then bent down, licked the tiny star, then kissed it. The softness of the gesture and of his lips made me shudder inside.

"Release it," he demanded, looking at his lower abdomen.

I obeyed, trying to put as much reverence into it as Arthur had to.

"Suck."

His half-erect cock was a real treat! I ran my tongue over it first. Yummy! I had licked several before his. Two of them had totally disgusted me, one because it needed a good wash and the second because of the too strong cum's taste. One of the others had a musky flavor, without being disgusting. I had enjoyed some of them, but never as much as that day. No doubt it was partly due to my great excitement. No one had ever cut me, and my fear mixed with my desire to serve my new master well had surely contributed to my "gustatory" pleasure.

But, even without doing anything to demonstrate to me his talents in breath control games, I had an experience of this kind. His erect cock was of average length, but so large that I had trouble getting it into my mouth and pumping it without scratching it; I had to cover my teeth with my lips and develop a whole new technique to give him pleasure without hurting him. As for shoving his big pacifier down my throat, it was almost impossible. Almost.

He gave me time to demonstrate my skills to him without coercion, either verbal or physical. Maybe he was trying to find out what I could do first. Or maybe he was already so excited by our discussions and our little blade game that he wanted nothing more than to let me pamper him and his feelings carry him away.

But when he was close to cum, he put his hand on my nape and pressed either to keep me from moving or to push his big log down my throat a little more. But I couldn't breathe. At one point, just before he came, my lack of air almost made me panic. I was stroking him under his clothes, but I pulled my hands away to… I'm not sure what I was going to do with them, but they were still floating in indecision when he started moaning his orgasm. I put them on his nipples over his shirt to graze them. He cried out so loudly that for a moment I thought I had hurt him. But no, it was due to the intensity of his pleasure. His vital fluid filled my throat. But since I was trying to inhale at that moment, his seed entered my nasal cavity and burned it as I swallowed all I could. He pulled on my hair at the back of my head to get his cock out. The grip of my suction was such that this sudden withdrawal produced a plop! I sucked loudly with great gulps as he squirted his cum all over my face. Some of it filled my nostrils and, taken by surprise, I opened my mouth to breathe, but only managed to drool and take a gulp of his hot elixir. I started coughing, which made him laugh. When I widened my eyes to watch him laugh at me, he aimed his last spray at them. Now they were burning, as was my nose, and he was laughing like a kid who just played a prank on his friend. But I liked the idea that I could amuse him, even at my own expense.

I had a raging hard-on and I was wetting the inside of my pants. I wondered if my master would let me suffer, as he had done to Arthur in the cabin in the forest. He zipped up his pants.

"Take it out," he ordered, pointing to my crotch with his foot.

I obeyed. I had a little trouble this time getting it out of my underwear, which seemed to stick to it. But as soon as I freed it, it started to drip on his beautiful Berber rug. I looked at the stain that was forming on it, embarrassed.

"You can clean that up later."

He ran the rough sole of his shoe over my cock, up and down, over and over. It was like he was stroking me with sandpaper, but I wasn't wiggling out, quite the opposite. Then he opened a drawer in the corner cabinet next to him and pulled out his cell phone and a condom.

"Here, put this on," he said, handing me the condom.

I obeyed. Was he going to ask me to penetrate him?

"Whack off," he ordered me.

I've always had trouble coming when I jerk off under the watchful eye of an observer, especially for the first time, and even more so through a condom. But I did it while he was making phone calls. I felt this behavior was a show of contempt. Wasn't he clearly telling me how little interest he had in my jouissance?

First, he spoke in an Asian language, it seemed to me. He even yelled violently at someone. He was in such a rage, his yelling startled and scared me. He made a second phone call and talked in I don't know what language. Then he made several calls in French and English. At one point, his voice was so distorted that he sounded like he was in a lot of pain. Was he going to vomit or was he having some kind of seizure? When I looked up into his eyes, I saw that he was crying. Who was he talking to and about what? All I knew was that it was distracting me from my sexual pleasure. But when he hung up after transmitting something (a text, an HTML link, a file?), he slapped me with such vigor that I ended up on my butt. I must have had his hand stamped on my cheek.

"When I order you to masturbate, you masturbate, is that clear?"

"You looked so angry, then so unhappy, Master, that I couldn't remain indifferent and keep jerking off like nothing was wrong."

I felt bad, not so much because of his slap as because of his almost palpable pain. He stared at me absently. He didn't really seem to see me; it was as if I had become transparent or invisible and he had glimpsed something painful through me in the distance. But he seemed calmer.

"Masturbate," he repeated wearily.

My dick had gone down quite a bit, but I went back to work harder, replaying in my mind what he had told me about Arthur. I also replayed mentally the moment of the cut on my wrist and reheard his moans and howls of pleasure.

Meanwhile, he was calling other people, speaking to them in French. At one point, he laughed heartily, and I wondered who could have this happy influence on him. He made an appointment with some of them for tonight and said he would bring his new slave. The thought of perhaps having to demonstrate my submission in front of strangers stressed me, but also excited me. I was imagining Master Mendel demanding all sorts of perversions from me to perform in the presence of these strangers when I ejaculated.

"Go wash up. There's a tube of antibiotic ointment in the bathroom cabinet, put some of it where you bled. Put your clothes back on. Oh yes, bring something to get all your cum off the rug."

"All my cum?"

Had I done that much? He must have seen from my furrowed brow that I was wondering about that, because he said, "The one you left when you were dripping and the ones you did while you were lying there flat on your back, and I was beating you and fucking you."

I didn't realize I had done so much damage. It's unsettling to find out that you've cummed without even realizing it.

"Oh. Okay, Sir."

I did everything he told me, then joined him in the kitchen. He was sitting at the table with his computer open in front of him.

Chapter 8

Master Mendel then ordered me to sit in a chair next to him. He wanted me to see something on his computer screen. It was a video of people shooting at each other, some of them falling to the ground, apparently dead. Then a dozen children between the ages of approximately nine and fifteen, mostly girls, and a young woman of rare beauty with a baby of no more than one year old in her arms emerged from the back of a delivery van. He then showed me a photo, no doubt taken from the video, of this woman and the group of children gathered in the back of the truck.

"These children and this woman have been kidnapped by human traffickers. They will probably be sold into prostitution, but they may also be forced to beg, to become smugglers of drugs, divers to clear the nets of industrial fishermen, domestic servants, workers in brick factories or textile mills, or soldiers. And in most cases, they won't get paid for their work."

"But they are only children!"

His face tightened into a painful expression.

"Yes, it's even possible that some of them will be killed for their organs," he added in a wavering voice.

"Oh, my God, no!"

"People in these networks are the most despicable and disgusting part of the human race. And they don't care if they're just kids. Young people sell better because they can work hard, long hours every day and for years. This woman's baby will probably even be bought by pedophiles."

All my hairs stood on end. I shook my head in an attempt to shake away the horrific images that were running through it. I felt like screaming.

"I was in Cambodia. I wanted to stop the traffickers and save this woman and her children. Someone had given me indications that could lead to the owners of a cargo delivery van. My informant had pointed out that in the back of the van there was a hiding place big enough to conceal a dozen people if they were packed tight together. The driver and his companion, who acted as a go-between, were paid to take them across the border between Cambodia and one of the neighboring countries, probably Thailand or Vietnam. Then, individuals as shady as the former were to take care of transporting them to their final destination. My informant had given me the description of the vehicle, the time and place where it'd stop to pick up one more child. But I couldn't go to the police, because I was told that there was a hack among them, someone who would turn a blind eye to this traffic for cash. And I was unarmed."

"Are you ever armed?"

"Never. When you travel a lot, you either have to apply for authorization to possess and use a weapon country by country, as you travel there, or you have to get an international permit, and that's complicated. Given the job I do, I could probably get one, but I don't want to. Especially since I've noticed that armed people are more likely to be killed than others, even when they aren't threatening. And until then, I never felt the need to own one. I told you, I can be considered a pacifist. But, in this case, I knew I couldn't free anyone without a gun or help."

"If the trucker and his partner went to get the children from their homes, wouldn't their families try to prevent the abductions?"

"No, quite the opposite. These people have little or no education and are extremely poor. It's easy to fool them with promises of a better life. All you have to do is give them an amount of money, insignificant in our eyes, but important in theirs, and convince them that their children will have a good job that will bring them nice sums of money, which will be sent to them on a regular basis, and that's it. The children sold and their parents are happy to be able to guarantee the survival of the rest of their family thanks to these 'benefactors' [Mendel made quotation marks in the air with his fingers as he said this last word]. But once there, the kidnapped youth never see the color of their money. They are led to believe that their wages are sent directly to their relatives; which is not true, of course. The only ones who get rich are the traffickers and oppressors, who profit from the hard work of their little victims. And these children are shackled a little more financially by telling them that they have to pay for their accommodation, their food and even the cost of the journey that brought them to their place of captivity. But how do you pay it all off when you never get a cent? Thus their debts accumulate and their forced labor carries on."

He looked at the image with such attention, as if he hoped to bring them across the screen to his home. Among them was a little boy with disheveled hair who was squinting a little. It made him look like a little elf. A cute little girl who was missing her upper incisors was smiling at us with all the baby teeth she had left. Poor innocent children! I shuddered with horror.

"And were you able to do anything for them?"

"I called the Human Trafficking Department, but they couldn't respond promptly enough in Tatai, the beautiful riverside village where our stilt hut was located, because the entire underfunded and understaffed HTD was already on another important case miles away. Anyway, given the fact that this department is under the national police jurisdiction and what I'd been told about police corruption, I was also afraid that I'd do more harm than good by calling them. But I just couldn't stand by and watch. So, I asked my informant if he knew of anyone who could help me stop the carrier, assuring him that I was willing to pay them handsomely. I offered him eighty baht, the local currency, for each person who would help me. After haggling, we agreed on one hundred baht each. I was sure that this amount would seem to be a lot to him, even if it was almost petty cash to me. So, he agreed to help me with his friends."

Master Mendel shook his head and smiled, surely at the memory of those poor devils who came to help him.

"Did it go well?"

"When they arrived and I saw that there were only four of them, including my informer, I wasn't sure if I should continue. They'd all wrapped their heads in scarves that left only their eyes visible. Three of them had knives and machetes. The last one had an old submachine gun so worn that it might blow up in his face if he used it. But I'd have to make do. We got to the location well ahead of time. We waited so long that I thought we'd missed them. I didn't know if I felt relieved or disappointed. But when the old truck appeared, I hoped it was the right one. My informer told me it was it. I was both scared and overloaded with adrenaline at the thought of what we were about to do. There were two men sitting in the front. One of the two traffickers remained behind the wheel while his partner went to the families to pick up the children from their homes. But they were both armed and as soon as the second man got out of the vehicle, he saw us. Then the driver got out and they threatened us with their guns. The guy with the machine gun shot them as they raised their guns to shoot at us. All the while, taking cover as best I could behind the van, I filmed everything."

"My God! Weren't you afraid of being killed or arrested by the police? Anyone could've recognized you!"

"I didn't think of that. I wasn't there to commit a crime, but to save people, children. And at that moment, I was just relieved that we were all alive except for the traffickers. Then, while the gunner was checking if the two crooks were dead and picking up their weapons, we opened the box of the van and looked to see if anyone was holed up in it. It was locked, but we found the key in the pocket of one of the two criminals. There was definitely a cache in the back behind all kinds of merchandise. We discovered the woman and children there, as expected, and helped them out. They were dazzled by the sun and disoriented. I'd have preferred to try to explain to them what was happening and reassure them, but without Celine, my new assistant, I couldn't. She hadn't wanted to accompany me or even stay at our hut. She was hiding in a shelter near the airport waiting to escape. Therefore, I had no choice but to film the whole scene myself to prove what had happened and for the article I'd eventually write."

"Celine? I know a journalist with that name. She is a woman with brown hair and eyes. She is almost as tall and stout as I am. What is her last name?"

"England."

"That's her. But why didn't she agree to follow you?"

"She was afraid. She knew this whole thing could go wrong. And when she learned that at least one important policeman knew about these sales and was in cahoots with the traffickers, she feared that he would come after us. Which, I guess, was quite possible, especially if he'd been warned about my desire to intervene."

"What happened to the woman and children you rescued?"

"After paying my four accomplices and asking them not to tell anyone about the money, I drove the kids and the woman in their kidnappers' truck to the consulate in Sihanoukville. It was the closest one and I didn't care what country it represented as long as they were all safe. I'd have preferred to stay and protect them until my contact at the human trafficking police was there to take care of them, but I had to leave quickly because Celine might fly off without me if she didn't see me coming soon enough."

"I guess that other children before them had already fallen into the same trap. When they realize their situation, don't they rebel, don't they try to escape?"

"Yes, there have been and there will be more, I'm afraid. This is what I want to highlight in my article. But for them, escape is almost impossible, because they're transported to countries where they don't speak the language. And their identity papers and passports, if they have them, are taken away. Then, if they rebel, they're locked up without food and beaten regularly until they give in. Or they're put on drugs that are so addictive that they'll do anything to get them. If by some miracle, they manage to keep their heads on their shoulders and escape, they end up on the street where their pimp easily recovers them, especially if he's implanted a microchip, like the ones that are put on pets so as not to lose them. Sometimes they even go back to their torturers to avoid suffering from withdrawal symptoms or starving any longer."

"It's horrible!"

I could imagine myself at their age in such a horrible situation. I would have been totally desperate and so unhappy!

"But the police aren't all corrupt, are they? Don't they ever intervene? If the children don't have IDs, the cops should know something is wrong, I assumed."

"Most of the poor people have no papers. Many times, parents don't even register their children after they give birth at home. So, they have no birth certificate, nothing at all. In the eyes of the state, they don't exist. You don't look for someone without a legal existence. If they escape and wander the streets, they may steal food and the police arrest them; but since they don't speak the same language, they can't defend themselves or explain who they are, where they come from, and why they're hanging around. They're either incarcerated in prisons that are often worse and more crowded than our industrial henhouses, or they run away from those who could've been their saviors."

"Are there ever raids on brothels?"

"Yes, but if the owners have accomplices at the police station, they're warned of the day and time when they are to take place. And anyway, the children are never in the foreground. They don't even work at the brothel itself most of the time. Rich clients don't want anyone to know they go to such places, let alone if they are pedophiles. So secret meetings are held elsewhere, in hotels selected for their discretion. So, when the police arrive at the brothel, they find only adult women who claim to be doing this work of their own free will and who complain about the harassment of the police."

"It seems almost hopeless for these poor kids. It's a good thing you were in Cambodia to investigate human trafficking and modern slavery."

"I wasn't even there for that. Not that I was unaware of the endemic situation of this trafficking in that region. I thought it was an important and interesting enough topic to have read about it. But, actually, Celine and I were there to do ecotourism in the Cardamom mountain chain. The nature there is beautiful and it seemed like a nice place to visit and ideal for one of my first outings with Celine. As she is interested in the environmental preservation, I wanted to offer her an exciting and newsworthy subject, but not as dangerous as human or drug trafficking. So, we were there to film the protected animals of Botum Sakor Park and the surrounding area such as the clouded leopard, the Irrawaddy dolphin, the coconut bear, the Siamese crocodile, and many others. It is a region where new species are regularly discovered, such as the sparrow that has been named Cambodian tailorbird; but many of them are threatened. We were about to leave for a hike in the mountains when someone informed me about these traffickers. That's often how my best stories start."

"And what happened to your friends and the little survivors?"

"Those who helped me ran away with the bodies of the two killed smugglers. They got rid of them afterwards, I don't know where or how. As for the woman and children…"

He swallowed and breathed hard. I wondered if he would be able to continue.

"I had to leave them in the care of the deputy consul, since the consul was absent that day. I'd called back Arun Sam, my contact at the Human Trafficking Department, to tell him where they were and to get there as soon as possible. I gave Mr. Sam's contact information to the deputy and explained to her that he'd pick up the woman and children that night or the next day at the latest, not to transfer them to anyone else. But she handed them over to the municipal police as soon as I left the consulate. And the officer I had been warned against quickly turned them back over to the traffickers. If she wasn't in cahoots with him, it was all the same. And at the police station, everyone pretended not to have noticed anything or were just careless."

"Weren't you afraid of being chased by this police officer or by the criminals?"

"I left the country too quickly for them to find me and come after me. After handing the children over to the deputy consul, I called a cab, and while waiting for it, I read my messages. There was one that Celine had just sent me that said she was at the airport from where we were supposed to fly back a few days later. She'd managed to advance the departure of the plane I'd chartered and was about to board it with my luggage. Fortunately, I usually keep money, my papers and my passport with me in a belly band, so I was able to get there right away. After getting through the boarding process in fourth gear, I ran to the runway where our plane was about to take off from. Celine wouldn't have waited for me, not even for a few minutes! If the air traffic controller hadn't signaled my presence in time to the pilot, who cut the engines and put on the brakes to allow me to board, I'd have been stuck there and could've been killed by the corrupt policeman or the traffickers. And she was the one who accused me in front of everybody in the local BDSM scene of abandoning her in a perilous situation!"

I thought that, if he'd wanted to, he could've easily exonerated himself from this slander.

"Won't you be charged with stealing the truck and being an accessory to murder?"

"First of all, I left the van at the consulate. So, I can say that I only borrowed it to save the children, which is the truth. Secondly, I didn't shoot, I wasn't even armed. And those who did were doing it in self-defense. And I confess to you that I don't feel much sympathy for those two bastards who were shot or remorse for what happened to them."

"Did the police find the bodies?"

"Not that I know of. Maybe the men who helped me fed them to the crocodiles. I don't know and I don't want to know the details."

"And if their wives or another relative reported them missing…"

"I don't think underpaid and understaffed authorities would go on an expensive search to find out what happened to these two notorious criminals. And if they were ever found, their deaths would probably be blamed on a gang war or something similar."

If I were him, I'd still be worried that I'd be charged with these killings and arrested, but he didn't seem too worried.

"The people you were talking to on the phone earlier…"

"I spoke to my informant, the consul and his deputy, the Phnom Penh police, Arun Sam from the Human Trafficking Department, and Interpol's International

Technical Cooperation Unit. I suggested to them that they check the surveillance camera at the entrance of the consulate, and I give them the day and time of my arrival with the children. This way they'd know who had left with them. I also sent them what little information I had about the children and the woman I thought I'd rescued and photos of them, asking them to quickly check on their whereabouts and do everything possible to help them. But I was told that they were probably all already out of Cambodia, and that, without knowing the names or at least the faces of the buyers and the rogue cops, very little could be done. I admit that my concern and sense of helplessness made me a little hysterical, which is why I was yelling at them. But the information they have will be passed on to the relevant authorities in Cambodia, Thailand, Vietnam and Laos. The problem is that even though they pride themselves on collaborating in the fight against human trafficking, there must still be more than eighty-five networks operating in these different countries and there are quite a few border disputes between them. So, I don't have much hope that they'll be found."

He was so tense and his voice...! It sounded like it was going to break. Or maybe it was his heart that would burst.

"Thank you!" he said to me.

I looked at him through the fog of my tears.

"What for?" I asked.

"For those tears, for not being indifferent to it all."

"How could one be?"

"Yet Celine, who knew that children's lives were at stake, was running away. She thought only of her own safety. Even mine didn't matter that much to her because she was ready to leave without me."

"I was told that you didn't say anything to defend yourself from her accusation of abandoning her, why?"

"I was... I'm still in shock over the failed rescue. I didn't want to talk about it. But, like it or not, I need to clear the air and set the record straight. I have a meeting for that tonight with the people in the BDSM Community. Would you like to accompany me? I'd like you to, but I won't force you to come if you'd rather stay here or go and sort out... whatever needs to be sorted out so you can become my assistant and slave."

"If you give me a few days from tomorrow to free myself from my commitments and to be able to change my life, I'll gladly go there with you."

I thought that this step to clear himself of this accusation must weigh on him. I wished to be able to give him my moral support if necessary.

"Thank you! And if you need any help or money to simplify or speed up your process of ending your job, breaking your lease, or anything else, let me know."

He seemed so relieved that I was going with him that I was glad I agreed. He probably didn't like to remember what had happened in Cambodia, let alone talk about his failure to save the lives of a dozen children and a young mother.

"Oh, and you can meet Arthur. He should be there too."

"So, it wasn't him who banned you from his bars."

"He used to own several bars, but he doesn't have any left now. He sold them all at a high price. He only has a very exclusive BDSM club now. And no, he didn't exclude me. I'm even a respected VIP member. Arthur knows me well enough to know that I'd never abandon my slave in a dangerous situation. Given that the social elite of the entire country pay a lot of money to be able to attend his club and have the opportunity to live out their wildest fantasies, and that Arthur investigates all of these people very thoroughly before admitting them, he has the power to put pressure on many powerful people. So, his power of persuasion is… formidable. Arthur, his employees and all members sign confidentiality agreements, but he still has considerable influence in this circle and many other. He is feared, and rightly so."

"Do you think his presence might be necessary?"

"No, I don't think so. Not really. But he knows the owner of the bars I was kicked out of, since he sold his bars to him. And I like to make it clear that I'm not a lamb going to the slaughter bleating stupidly and that I have support. That's something I learned from my father's lawyers. And Arthur always knows everything that happens to me almost before I do. In fact, he called me as soon as I got back from Cambodia to ask me how I was doing and if I needed a relief. I declined his offer. But tonight… I'd love to introduce you to him."

Oh, I couldn't say that the idea left me cold.

"You… He… Is that...?"

He gave a mocking little laugh.

"I quite like threesomes, especially with Arthur. He's more submissive and more dominant in another person's presence. I know he'd rather be alone with me, but he takes everything I offer."

"And you plan to share me with him for the evening?"

He tilts his head to the side with a smile.

"Possibly. How about it?"

He seemed to have so much fun tormenting me, the bastard. What he had told me about Arthur should have frightened me, but it made me like him instead. I wanted to meet him. And I didn't want to miss the opportunity to see these two funny sparrows together.

"If that's what you want, Master. I accept."

He laughed even harder.

"Don't try to make me think you're not excited about this," he said, looking down at the bulge in my pants.

I blushed, thus adding more evidence to what he had just said.

Chapter 9

It was getting close to dinner time and my new master decided that we would eat at a restaurant near where his meeting would be held. He handed me a white linen shirt and a classy jacket to wear with my leather pants and boots. Whose shirt and jacket were they? Did Celine or Arthur forget them? Whoever they belonged, everything would have been too small for my master, but they fit me as if they had been bought for me. He had dressed himself in an outfit that gave him the look of a pirate of ancient times with a white puffed-sleeve shirt showing the top of his chest, a black vest embroidered with gilding, a wide belt, a corsair pants molding his buttocks and thighs nicely and long boots folded under his knees. The only thing missing was the eye patch and the tricorn or the bandana.

We were only at soup when I saw a very handsome man enter. Like me, he was a little shorter than Master Mendel. He was slim, but one could see a powerful musculature under his smart midnight blue suit. His eyes, of the same blue, sparkled with intelligence and malice. His well-trimmed beard and small mustache were jet black, as was his slightly long and curly hair. In the latter, I noticed a few purple streaks. When he approached us, his mischievous look immediately set off a red flag in my mind. He extended his hand to my master, who didn't shake it, but the stranger took a seat at our table between him and me anyway.

"I don't believe I invited you to sit," Mendel commented dryly.

The newcomer stood up immediately, pushed the chair back into its place, and, with his eyes fixed on Mendel, waited in silence for as long as it took to figure out if he should leave or if he could stay while we continued to eat. It seemed to me that he was reveling in what he was seeing and could have waited for hours if it had been my master's wish.

"You haven't put a tracker or a bug on my car or anywhere else, have you, Arthur? If I find one, you'll regret it."

So that's who he was! If I had been asked at that moment which of the two men at my table I found more attractive, I would have been at a loss to choose, but I would probably have gone for Arthur.

"I hope so," he replied with a mischievous smile.

What was he hoping for exactly? To regret it?!

"I don't think you'd like to spend several months without any contact with me, no fun at your club, no phone conversations or even emails. How about that?"

As Arthur remained silent, Mendel insisted.

"So, did you put a tracker on or not?"

"I don't have to. I know you well enough to expect to find you here tonight without much risk of being wrong."

My new master examined his friend with a frown.

"What's with this red?

Arthur smiled as he ran a hand through his hair.

"Don't you like my highlights?"

"No, I don't. I prefer your natural color."

"Just a moment. I'll be right back."

He left in a hurry in the direction of the restroom. In his absence, Master Mendel ate casually, looking out the window. When Arthur came back, his hair was wet, but without any trace of dye. Our master did not comment, as if Arthur's reaction was only natural.

"Bend over," he then ordered, taking his napkin.

Arthur leaned towards him and master Mendel wiped away the blood-red drops dripping down his friend's neck. This bloody trickle and the stain on the napkin caused me to have a disturbing vision of teenage Arthur covered in the bloody marks left by young Zach. I looked up at the eyes of my fellow diners. What I saw there was confirmation that it was better for them never to have S&M sessions alone. I even wondered if it was safe to put my life in Mendel's hands. But then he gave me the brightest smile I'd ever seen. I touched the little star-shaped cut on my wrist. He looked at me with such intensity that I thought everything around us, except for us, was disappearing. I could no longer hear the clatter of plates and utensils or the buzz of conversation. For me, there was only him, whose soul was sucking mine. Have you ever experienced anything like this? No? I wish it could happen to you. Even if it is a brief experience, it transforms you. Anyway, I suddenly didn't care what he would do to me.

A waitress came to our table and asked if "Sir" would be joining us. Arthur turned his eyes to Mendel, who once again made him wait for his decision. I felt bad for Arty and worried that the lady would get impatient.

"Sit," my master finally ordered as if he were addressing his dog.

Arthur nodded to the waitress, who handed him a menu.

"No need for it. It'll be the same as his," he said, pointing to Mendel with his chin.

Mendel made a little grunt as the lady walked away.

"The last time you did this, do you remember what you ate?"

Arthur shuddered and grimaced in disgust. My master and Arthur laughed. I wondered what seemed so unappetizing to him, but I was amused to see their beautiful, but peculiar complicity in action.

"Arthur, this is Gabriel Jacob, my new assistant. Gabriel, this is Arthur Dubois, my oldest friend."

I held out my hand to this friend with a smile. He crossed his arms over his chest and examined me with a frown as if I were a horse bought at a village fair. I resented him at first, then remembered how my master had just greeted him. If he was amused by my inclusion in their sadistic games, I could submit to them willingly and show him what I was made of.

When, several long seconds later, I lowered my hand, he offered me his. I hesitated. I was afraid he would take it away again. But he squeezed it this time.

"Where did you find this one? Is he going to abandon you at the worst possible moment?"

"Certainly not!" I answered so vehemently that the customers at the neighboring tables jumped up, turned around and stared at me.

"He wasn't talking to you, slave!" my master commented harshly, pronouncing "slave" a little too loudly for my taste.

I looked around nervously, but everyone had gone back to eating, pretending not to have seen or heard anything, and I looked down at my plate.

"It wasn't me who found him, but the opposite. Apparently, all the bad things people say about me just made him want to meet me more."

"That's because he mustn't know everything and must doubt what little he has learned," Arthur surmised.

"Oh, he'd been pretty well informed. Too well, actually. I confirmed almost all of it for him. And as you can see, he's still here."

"Who are these people so well informed about you?"

"About us. Do you know Eva Valley and Alex Jules?"

"I played with Alex a few times."

"What?! Alex is not…," I began, more than a little surprised.

"Isn't what: gay, submissive, masochistic? He's all of those things," stated Arthur.

I shook my head in disbelief.

"Alex seems better at keeping his own secrets than those of others," my master commented with a stern expression."

Then, turning to Arthur, he asked, "Where did you play with him?"

"At my club. He had signed a confidentiality agreement if that's what you wanted to know. And this Eva, who is she?"

"A journalist," I replied.

My new master and Arthur looked at each other. After a brief moment of surprise, a glimmer of understanding lit up their faces.

"Celine?" exclaimed Arthur.

"Almost certainly. Celine must've emptied her heart on her return from Cambodia, not caring that her friends were also journalists, and she'd have said too much, even if I'd made her swear silence about my past," my master concluded.

"In my opinion, these three chatterboxes could use a good lesson, don't you think, Sir?"

"A lesson, I agree; but don't go too far to teach them to keep their promises and to respect the secrets entrusted to them. At least stay within the limits of legality and, if possible, legitimacy."

"Will Celine be at your meeting tonight?"

"Yes. We'll see what the bar owner and the new president of the BDSMers Association have to say about this."

The waitress then came over and brought Arthur his soup. We all ate silently for a few seconds. When I looked up, I saw that my two tablemates were staring at me. I didn't like the sharpness with which these two beasts were watching me.

"Did you huh…?" asked Arthur, tilting his head towards me.

I assumed Arthur wanted to know if his friend had been playing with me or testing me.

"A little bit."

I thought, "A little?! Ouch! What will it be like if he inflicts more than a little on me?"

"Besides, you can see for yourself later the marks I left on him. What do you think?"

"I was hoping that you and I'd be al…"

"Yes. I know what you like best, Arthur. But it's this or nothing. What do you say?"

"Okay, if I'm allowed to try to change his mind about his relationship with you, I'm willing to have the three of us have some fun together."

I said to myself, "God! Am I going to survive this day?" I was hot and almost wanted to run away like the proverbial hare or like Celine.

"I think you scare him more than I do."

Arthur laughed.

"He's probably right, Sir. Don't you think so?"

I looked at my master, who was sizing me up with an overly serious expression at that moment, probably deciding whether I was worth it or not. "No, I won't run away!" I said to myself with all the more conviction as my dick had flared up.

"Yes, but the main reason is that you don't care if I lose my assistant."

"Who can claim to have really possessed the one who abandons him or her? Anyway, if he runs away, he doesn't deserve you," Arthur decreed.

My master then changed the topic of conversation.

"Have you heard from your private investigator?"

Arthur looked at him with a smirk.

"You know me too well."

"Is it possible? Would you prefer I knew less about you?"

Arthur didn't answer his last two questions. Instead, he gave an account of the investigation.

"First, I don't have just one investigator, but two: one in Cambodia, the other in Thailand. The detective in Thailand traced a prostitution ring that is probably the one your children were sold to. But this network looks like ordinary brothels with no connection to each other or to human trafficking."

"What do you mean by 'ordinary brothels'?"

"Establishments that aren't part of a network and where adults voluntarily prostitute themselves. Minors are kept secretly elsewhere, and you have to pay a lot of money to have sex with them. I was told that normally, for the first two weeks, the kids don't meet any real clients, but they are forced from the wee hours of the morning until late at night to have sex with everyone, absolutely everyone, that the pimps can find to prepare them mentally for what awaits them and to… train them. If they refuse or are reluctant to do anything, they are locked in horrible dungeons with no clothes or food and beaten until they're ready to do what is asked of them, whatever that may be. Mouth, vagina, anus, no orifice is spared. And they have no respite, except for a few minutes to eat a bowl of rice twice a day. It is only after these two weeks of training that they're given appointments with real clients, like pedophiles known for their twisted minds and extreme perversions."

My master was so tense that his hand holding his fork was shaking! And he was looking out, away, somewhere else. It seemed to me that he was turning green and that he was going to vomit. I, too, couldn't swallow a single bite and didn't feel well.

"One of my employees pretended to be a pedophile. I gave him enough money to have a session with a girl. He asked me if he should make an appointment right away or a little later since your children aren't yet scheduled to meet the network's regular clientele. I told him to go right away. If he needed to, I'd deposit enough money so that he could get another appointment later. And my two detectives record all their interviews, whether it's with the local or the trafficking police, and with the pimps and the kids. They also take pictures when they can't film. But it's difficult, since they're searched before they see a prostitute and have their phones, computers, or anything else that might be used to keep "souvenirs" of the meetings taken away. But they know all this, so they hide miniature devices in the folds of their clothes, in their hair, in their mouths if necessary. We'll have proof, I guarantee it!"

"Tell your man to ask for a date with a very young child, let him claim that the younger they are, the more he likes it."

I shuddered. But I understood that the woman and her baby had probably been sold to pedophiles or would be soon. And if the baby could be met immediately, the investigation could move forward more quickly.

I found that even Arthur had his limits. When he heard my master make this suggestion, he was speechless. Then he shook his head positively.

"Yes, Sir. Good idea."

"What about your other detective?"

"He thinks he can get the dirty cop arrested. Besides, he wouldn't be the only one. There's one in Sihanoukville and maybe several in Phnom Penh. Politicians would also be involved. And they all help each other to hide their crimes and their network of human sales."

"And my accomplices, what happens to them?"

"I paid your informant a lot of money to take upon himself the release of the woman and the children. If he's arrested and questioned about you, he'll say that you were only there to film the whole thing and take the survivors to the consulate. So, if you speak to the press about it, I advise you to confirm his words."

"Did you investigate the consulate assistant?"

"You think she's in league with the dirty cops?"

"I can't be absolutely sure. She may be a complete idiot and a heartless person. But I prefer not to leave anything out. If she was a member of the network, I wouldn't feel right having ignored her."

"Fine. I'll have my detective look into it too."

"Thanks, Arthur. I don't know what I'd have done without your help."

"The same thing I'd have done, no doubt."

"You'll keep me posted on the investigation?"

"Of course, I will."

My master seemed a little relieved. So was I. Maybe this was all going to lead to arrests. Of course, by then, the kids would have had a hell of a time. God only knew what state they would be in when they were released, if they were ever found. Surely, they would be scarred for life.

We sat in silence for a long time, eating without much of an appetite. The waitress came to check if we liked the meal and if there was anything missing. We all answered that everything was perfect.

"Gabriel. Put your hands on the table and finish your soup by lapping it up, my master then ordered me."

I stared at him in disbelief, then glanced at the surrounding customers.

"So?" he insisted.

Staring him straight in the eye, I placed my hands on either side of my bowl, which was fortunately quite wide. At the periphery of my gaze, I saw that Arthur was examining me with a vicious smile. He must have been hoping that I would flinch, that I would not want to humiliate myself in public; that would allow him to keep Mendel to himself.

I bent down and started to suck up what little soup I had left, trying not to dip my nose or chin in it and not to make too much noise. Not easy at all! I was afraid that the waitress would come back. I felt like my stomach had knotted up, so much so that I was sure I would never be able to swallow. But I did. After licking the bottom of my bowl clean, I looked up. Arthur had become almost too serious. But my master was smiling kindly at me. I thought I even saw pride in his eyes. He offered me his napkin and told me to wipe myself. I did so as carefully as I could, adding greenish stains to those left by Arthur's red dye. When he reached out again, I thought he wanted his towel back and gave him mine, which was not stained. He put it next to his bowl, then raised his hand again, palm up. I put mine there. He gently stroked it with his thumb, brushing the star-shaped indentation while giving me a small nod of approval. It's silly, I know, but I was so relieved I almost wanted to cry.

Chapter 10

When my master released my hand after touching my little star, Arthur was quick to start a new topic of discussion.

"Can Max borrow your cabin in the middle of the Amazon rainforest?"

Arthur smiled, as if it were a long-standing joke between them. Did my master really have a second home in Amazonia?

"Max?"

"Master Lemay. Actually, it's not for him, but for Fausto and David. He wants David to believe that he has sold him to give him a more realistic idea of what it means to be a real slave: not being able to escape without risking his life and having to do whatever his new owner demands, even if he doesn't like it at all and would rather run away, being punished harshly for the slightest mistake..."

"Lord!" I thought. My master frowned.

"I don't know this Fausto well. Do you think he can be trusted?"

"Master Forrest has trained and tested him. He even gave him his signet ring as a mark of great achievement."

"I didn't know he trained dominators and gave them his ring if they excelled."

"He had already taught a few doms, but Fausto was the first to receive this honor. Master Lemay discussed Fausto with Master Forrest, but he still investigated this young dom. And everything confirmed what Master Forrest had told him. So, he wants to offer David the ultimate experience: a few months in a remote area with a dominator he doesn't know. Fausto was hesitant at first, but everyone told him so much good about David that he'll surely accept. He'd like to try to break him. That's the word he used: 'break'," Arthur finished with a smile.

"I see. And you envy him, don't you?"

"What makes you think that?"

"Since I've known you, you've wanted me to 'break' you, and I've always refused to get involved in that. It'd be too dangerous. And Max is ready to entrust the one he considers the man of his life to this dom he knew nothing about a few days ago?"

My master shook his head.

"The first time I saw Fausto, I was tempted to kneel before him and offer him my services, so intense is his aura of dignity, not to say nobility, and authority.

All the submissives present that evening, and there were many, seemed to react like me, but he didn't even seem to realize it. So, I admit I was tempted to ask Fausto to try to break me rather than David. But I can't stay away from the club for long and…," Arthur replied, before sinking into a silence from which he couldn't seem to escape.

My master stared at him.

"What would you say if I offered you to him?"

"Offer me? What do you mean? For how long?"

"An indeterminate period. You always assured me that I had every right to you. So, I have the right to give you to him as well as the right to forbid you to give yourself to him, right?"

Arthur stared at his master and friend, his Adam's apple bobbing up and down on his neck. He looked down. As his answer was delayed, our master turned to me.

"If you'd signed your 24/7 slavery contract, don't you think that would mean you give me the right to do whatever I want with you, Gabriel?"

I felt a wave of heat invade my insides. Theoretically, the answer to his question was "yes, Master," but would I really be willing to accept living with a stranger because my master offered me to him? I swallowed my saliva before saying, "Yes, Sir."

"So, you consider that I'll then have the right to sell you, to give you or to lend you to another master and you'll live with him if I demand it?" he insisted, his so intense look piercing me.

"I would do my best, Sir, but I'd suffer greatly from your rejection."

I felt my vision fogging up, but my master was smiling at me. He seemed very happy with my answer. Then he turned his eyes to his old friend.

"What about you, Arthur? You say you're too busy to have asked Fausto to break you, but you're actually afraid of him, aren't you?"

Arthur shook his head vigorously in impetuous denial.

"You know that, Sir, I submit to no one but you," he hastened to reply.

Mendel laughed.

"I'd never have believed that of you. Arthur Dubois, who is afraid! That young dom must've really made a strong impression on you."

Our master looked at his lifelong submissive for a long moment. He seemed to read much more in his face or in his attitude than I could see.

"Don't do it, Arthur: don't ask him to try to break you. Don't you dare!" his childhood friend then ordered him.

"Now you are the one who is afraid. You are afraid for me, aren't you?"

Arthur had an expression of pure delight.

Master Mendel frowned, squinted and clenched his jaw and lips. He was so tense and his face had hardened so much that I barely recognized him. I thought he must be tempted to show Arthur what it'd be like if he really tried to break him. I found this transformation frightening. Then he relaxed and his face softened.

"You don't have to be his guinea pig! It's up to the BDSMers to make sure that nothing bad happens to David or anyone else and to decide how to make sure he doesn't, not you. Putting your life in the hands of a stranger who believes that a D/s relationship is about the dominator breaking the submissive is taking too big a risk. In my opinion, Fausto would've to be in a controlled environment, under constant surveillance while he'd test a slave who had agreed to experience it with him. But Fausto wouldn't have to know that he was being watched at all times while his actions were scrutinized, analyzed and measured."

My gaze traveled between the two men as if watching an Olympic match between the two best tennis players. Finally, I saw a lot of affection, both in Master Mendel's eyes and in Arthur's.

"So, in conclusion, you refuse to lend them your bungalow?" insisted Arthur.

"The last time I went there, I didn't have time to clean it up before I left. I left it in a… messy state. And that's not just a metaphor."

I wondered who he was there with to make his house such a mess, literally. Had he gone there with someone or had he found a handsome Brazilian there? Arthur dared to ask him.

"Who were you with?"

My master hesitated before answering with a perverse, almost cruel expression and staring straight at Arthur.

"With Flávio."

Arthur suddenly looked as unhappy as the stones. I still didn't know who this Flávio was, but Arthur seemed to know him. I took a bite and when I looked at him again, he had the face of someone planning a murder. It was a little scary. My master must have interpreted that dark look the same way I did.

"When you don't want to hear the answer, don't ask the question. And don't you dare harm any of my friends! You'll regret it bitterly," my master threatened.

He ate a few mouthfuls, looking thoughtfully at Arthur, who again seemed more miserable than murderous. The waitress came to take our bowls and bring us the main course.

"You investigated Fausto, didn't you? You wouldn't be Arthur Dubois otherwise. What did you find out?" my master asked next.

"He signed up as a member of my club, so yes, I requested a full investigation. He could compete with you about his crappy childhood and adolescence. He ran away from his family as soon as he could, which was when he was fifteen. A dominatrix that nobody knows took him in, trained him and helped him financially to start and finish a PhD in psychology, which Fausto doubled with a master's degree in sociology. Now he teaches a few days a week at the university while continuing his studies. He's currently completing a thesis on eroticism through the ages and societies. He also gives demonstrations here and there, some abroad, of bullwhip handling and kinbaku. Like you, his difficult youth would have prompted him to be more moderate in matters of domination and sadism. But he'll probably not resist the temptation to live an experience like the one proposed by Master Lemay. Especially with a high-level slave like David."

I hardly knew any of these people they were talking about except by name and reputation. I knew that Master Lemay had been trained eons ago to submission and then to domination by a master who is now deceased, but who was considered first class in those distant days. Max and David have been in an intense power exchange relationship for some years now, and their love for each other has reportedly not waned, despite Max Lemay's proven severity and sadism. As for Fausto, I only knew what I had been told: he was in his early thirties, Jupiter-like and very good at everything he did. I could have seen him one evening when he was presenting a kinbaku workshop but I had to give up at the last moment and gave my ticket to a friend. Afterwards, she told me that she was very impressed by his presence, his charisma, the care he took in the execution of his work and the attention he gave to his sub.

"Fausto would've been taken in by a 'dominator that nobody knows'? You mean even you couldn't find out who he was?"

"I found someone with the same name that Fausto gave who took him in. But nobody knew this man was a dom or what he was worth as a dom."

"Ah."

"Yes, but you must admit, Sir, that he's certainly not the only person who practices BDSM without joining a club, frequenting SM bars or attending workshops or conferences in this field. In any case, if he participated in something, it wasn't officially; it must've been under an assumed name. Besides, how many people don't want to be known as sadists? I'd bet there are more than you'd think. This dom may be excellent, but he wants to keep his identity a secret. Fausto has done his best to inform us about him. He told us that he was sheltered by Yūshūna Masutā and that he was trained by an outstanding master. Is this Masutā the dominator in question? He didn't say so, but it's likely."

"Do you know that Yūshūna Masutā means 'excellent master'? Don't you think that's a bit suspicious?"

I saw Arthur blush at this point. So, my new master spoke Japanese.

"Are you serious?"

"Yes, I am."

"I'll do a better job of checking the background and reliability of this mysterious dom. And I'll mention it to Master Lemay before he turns David over to Fausto."

"Inform Rock Forrest as well. He might be a little more hesitant to give his ring to strangers, no matter how good they are at domination, in the future."

"Yes, Sir. I think I'll make an appointment with Masutā. I'm very anxious to unmask this guy."

"Check his real name, his background and how long he's been in the country. And send me the contact information for both men. I don't know if I'll contact them, but I like to be able to talk to people who ask me for a favor."

"It's natural, since Master Lemay wanted to use your cottage. You can count on me to tell you what's going on as I find out."

"Max has a tendency to be naive, in my humble opinion. If he wasn't, he'd never have entrusted his life to James Teka in the past without even knowing what the man was capable of."

"I would've put my life in Master Teka's hands at the same age."

"I'm sure you would. But in your case, it wouldn't have been out of naivety, but out of pride, temerity and masochism."

Arthur winced and lowered his eyes. Master Mendel probably knew him too well for his taste.

"Master Teka was an extraordinary master, even for his time," Arthur said.

Master Mendel sank into his thoughts.

"Yes, perhaps he was. Max was lucky. But he could've just as easily fallen into the hands of a monster who would've sold him into a human trafficking ring, like my children were," my master replied.

The two friends looked at each other so penetratingly that, if they'd been fucking on the table, it couldn't have been more carnal and ardent. My mouthful got stuck in my esophagus. I coughed. My two companions looked at me with a worried expression, as if they were afraid they'd have to perform the Heimlich maneuver on me, until I managed to swallow and breathe. I then gave them a small, piteous smile. Arthur shrugged and looked at Master Mendel.

"Are you all right?" my master asked me, apparently still a little worried.

"Yes, Sir. It's just a bite that went the wrong way."

Despite what my master had demanded of me earlier, throughout the meal both men had been quiet, speaking in hushed tones and remaining silent when the waitress approached to clear the table and bring the next course; the topics discussed were not those that one would usually address in public with a megaphone.

The dinner ended in discussions about the past, the present, the future. Sometimes my master and Arthur would talk about people I didn't know. But their conversation was always so colorful and fun that I could join in without even knowing exactly who they were talking about. And we laughed a lot.

For example, a newly admitted dominatrix to Arthur's club had wanted to show off her skill in using two bullwhips at once; but her whips, which were only supposed to crisscross in figure eights before hitting their target, got tangled up in front of a crowd of about fifty stunned people. As she had difficulty to untangle her straps, a young submissive on the spot hastened to go to help her, then he offered to divert the attention of the public by being used as a model for the bondage session which she was to hold later, but which she decided to do sooner. Again, no doubt stressed by her previous failure, she got tangled up in her knots. The only positive note: the nice submissive who came to rescue her became her full-time slave.

"A very brave young man," my master commented with a sarcastic smile that brought a laugh from me and Arthur.

"Before admitting this submissive to the club, I asked him if he was at least old enough to shave. He replied, 'Yes, Sir, I shave my balls,'" said Arthur, which made us all laugh.

The meal was coming to a pleasant end. We took our last sips of coffee before leaving for my master's meeting place.

Chapter 11

It was time to leave for the meeting place. My master paid for Arthur's meal and mine. We crossed the street and walked silently to meeting the place.

Two women and a man were there. I recognized the younger one. It was Celine. I greeted her. The stranger was Eric Francis, owner of the most popular bars in the area. He was in his forties, pleasant, but paunchy, and must have enjoyed his beer too much. The other woman, a lady in her fifties, who had the self-confident air of experienced dominatrixes, was Micheline Bishop, the new president of the local BDSMers' association. But I didn't know much about her other than that she was said to have played hard to get the job.

I knelt to the left of my master's chair, while Arthur took a seat to his right. Mrs. Bishop then jumped in and asked Celine to repeat what she was accusing Master Mendel of doing. To everyone's surprise, she declared that she was withdrawing her accusation.

Ms. Bishop and Mr. Francis still wanted to hear her explain why she had filed a complaint against him and why she was retracting it. Celine stammered an apology, saying that she had acted under emotional stress. She recounted the events from her perspective, not very knowledgeable about the overall situation.

The president and owner wanted to hear Master Mendel's side of the story, and Arthur's was added to it. I was even allowed to slip my opinion. I said how disturbed Master Mendel was about the abduction of the woman, her baby and the other children. I said I admired his kindness and courage in risking his life to save them. I also praised Mr. Dubois's efforts to find everyone and stop this horrible trafficking.

When I looked up at Celine at the end of my commentary, I saw how ashamed she seemed to be of her not-so-international-investigative journalist escape. She then confessed that she hadn't realized that this job was so dangerous, that she would be confronted with it so soon, and that she had panicked. Everyone said that given the situation and her lack of experience, it was understandable. I didn't agree. I was so angry that I was almost frothing at the mouth!

"You abandoned your master at the worst possible time; he could've been killed because of you. Then you couldn't think of anything better to do than to reveal Master Mendel's entire life to a journalist, who is now telling it everywhere!" I commented in one breath, clenching my teeth and fists.

"I hadn't allowed you to speak, slave! Remind me to punish you for that unwelcome remark."

"Yes, Master," I replied, my eyes fixed on the ugly, poop-colored industrial carpet of dubious cleanliness on which I was kneeling, but which reminded me of another one that I had stained with the fruit of my pleasure.

I did not feel at all repentant. But I told myself that my master and Arthur would soon make me regret not having kept silent. Besides, Celine then admitted that she should have waited until she had calmed down and thought better of it before she spoke as she had. Since she had withdrawn her accusation, Mr. Francis and Mrs. Bishop gave my master back his claim and his right of access everywhere.

"Did Miss England promise you not to tell anyone about your past?"

"Yes, she did."

The lady pressed her lips together as she looked at Celine, who looked away.

"It is one thing, Miss, to denounce your master. It's another to not respect your commitments to him. No one, especially in the journalistic world, needed to know his whole story."

"Everyone knows it anyway!" exclaimed Celine.

"That's not true. I didn't know anything about him until I became president of this association. And it doesn't matter if Mr. So-and-So is gossiping. We can't give credence to them. But you were his assistant and his slave. Everything you revealed had strong credibility with the people you spoke to."

"I made Eva promise to keep her mouth shut. It's not my fault she repeated everything."

"But it was your fault if you told her everything. She wouldn't have had anything to tell otherwise," Mrs. Bishop insisted.

I nodded in total agreement with her words. In fact, I would have liked to give the president a deep kiss, even though I am gay.

Everyone present, except me, then discussed human trafficking and what should be done to stop it around the world.

My master told us that on his first trip to Asia, he went out alone one night and asked his tuk-tuk driver to take him to a place where he could have fun. The driver led him without hesitation to the busiest "hostess" bars.

"Musicians were playing old rock tunes like Whiskey Bar, but with modified lyrics. Instead of singing, 'Show me the way to the next whiskey bar. Oh, don't ask why,' the singer would say, 'Show me the way to the next little girl. Oh, don't ask why.' And these are very popular places for Westerners."

I was shocked to discover that far from being ashamed of child sex slavery, it was celebrated! And travelers from Europe, America and elsewhere encouraged it by frequenting their brothels.

"Since we know about this situation, shouldn't the national and world authorities do something about it?"

"Oh, they're trying. There is Article 4 of the Universal Declaration of Human Rights, which states that 'slavery and the slave trade are prohibited in all their forms'; the Palermo Protocol, which aims to prevent, repress and punish the sale of people, especially women and children; several international treaties, which prohibit human trafficking; and legislation against this form of trade adopted by most nations. But in spite of all this, it seems to me that things are getting worse every day. Because even those countries that have adopted the law against forced labor and modern slavery don't put in place proper and sufficient means to enforce it. It's as if they believe that legislating against a problem is enough to solve it by itself."

"But what is missing to make it work?" asked Mrs. Bishop.

"It's complex. The fight against trafficking involves cooperation at the national and international levels between NGOs, social agencies, law enforcement and justice officials and immigration authorities. And if we manage to establish some collaboration and satisfactory mechanisms to achieve a result, corruption takes over. It's hard to get the worms out of the fruit when the whole basket is full of them, my master rightly replied."

I was also surprised to learn that in my own country, this traffic existed and that it was, as everywhere else, especially the poorest and most destitute who were victims. It seems that they even tattoo a barcode on the back of the neck of sex slaves, as if they were only consumable goods.

Then my master asked Mrs. Bishop what she knew about Fausto. She knew no more than we did. Mr. Francis said that the young dominator had only gone to one of his establishments once and that it was for a kinbaku demonstration.

"Actually, everything I learned about him is only rumors," replied the owner.

Everyone wanted to hear the rumors anyway.

"The man who took him in and trained him was a Japanese bondage master who had immigrated to this country illegally. This would be the reason for his pseudonym and the fact that nobody knows much about him. Fausto is said to have mentioned that his master once told him, *'Whoever makes us feel good binds us to them by this well-being; whoever makes us suffer pushes us to surpass ourselves and to break our fetters. For no one knows what they're made of without having faced their greatest fears and deepest loathing to get free from them.'* And oh yes, he'd also have said something like, *'The only way to move forward is to fight our way through it all.'* If anybody understands, I'd appreciate if they could explain it to me because I, anyway, have no idea what all this gibberish can mean."

Chapter 12

We then went to Arthur's Deliverance Club, where he also had a residence. I had only heard of it, as I was unable to pay the ruinous membership fee. But now that I was a VIP member's submissive, I would probably be admitted by proxy. The house was gigantic, palatial and isolated enough that neighbors wouldn't complain about loud music, screaming or carriages with strange horses outside, for example.

Perhaps Arthur wanted to show me around or he wanted to strut his stuff in front of everyone present, as we did not go through his private access. Instead, he led us through the large public room of his club amidst his inimitable, abundant and lavish clientele. Upon seeing us enter, everyone fell silent. The eyes did not focus on my little person, of course, but they did turn to Arthur and, more importantly, I could only notice, to my master. I could hear voices whispering his name with a mixture of fear and reverence. It seemed to me that his presence was even more commanding and compelling than that of the owner of the place. Besides, Arthur had let him pass before him, as he would have walked respectfully behind his king. As for me, I humbly followed them, eyes lowered (not so much, since I was looking out of the corner of my eye at everything I could). I caught a glimpse of more dominators in outfits likely to fuel the most perverse fantasies of their submissives, all on their knees or in humiliating or painful accoutrements and postures, than I had seen in my whole life. But I couldn't help but feel proud to accompany these two representatives of the craziest and freest universe over here, if not anywhere else.

When we arrived at the residential part of his huge house, two white wolves charged at us. I wasn't expecting it and I tensed up. My master crouched down, and the beasts rushed to lick him and show their joy at his presence while he cooed, "Hello my beautiful babies!" and petted them. "Impressive 'babies'," I thought. But I was pleasantly surprised at the seemingly shared affection between my master and these two big dogs. They then greeted their owner, who petted them and chirped sweet nothings. Then they surrounded me to smell me. I held out my hand, palm down towards their nose, to allow them to sniff me better. Satisfied, they let me pet them.

"They are impressive. They really look like white wolves."

"They are wolfdogs. A cross between a female Swiss White Shepherd and a wolf. I gave them to Arthur on his next-to-last birthday. He'd have preferred a hard BDSM session, but I was sure he'd still like the gift," my master explained.

"I didn't want them!" replied Arthur with a sulky pout.

"When he saw what I'd brought him, he told me I could return them to their owner. But as soon as I put a puppy in his arms and that little wolf licked him and squeaked, he became very fond of them and has been spoiling them as if they were his beloved children."

"You convinced me to accept them as an alarm system," said Arthur.

"He doesn't have an alarm system for his home, only on the club side. He claims he's too feared to be robbed. I'm not so sure. But he has too much confidential information about important people not to protect himself," my master criticized.

"If robbers come in and these two wolves lash out at them, I hope these thieves aren't armed. It'd be a shame if they shot such beautiful animals," I commented.

"I wouldn't advise anyone to harm them," Arthur growled, as if he were a big white wolf himself.

He seemed very protective of his dogs for someone who didn't want them. Anyway, I had no doubt that the thieves would regret their actions if they hurt his "babies".

A very pretty young woman in a man's outfit including suit, tie and Lacoste shoes approached. Everything about her screamed "lesbian".

"Prince, Princess, here!"

The two "sovereigns" went towards her, with their tails between their legs and their heads down, as if remorseful.

"Sorry, Sir, I was getting ready to take them for a walk outside when you showed up. They smelled and heard you, and I couldn't hold them back."

She was giving me curious glances, but no one bothered to introduce me. Hence, I did it myself, holding out my hand.

"Chloe," she simply said, as if she didn't have a surname, grasping my fingers firmly, before leaving with the dogs.

As soon as I stepped into Arthur's vast, luxurious dungeon room, I understood why he had dyed strands of his hair red. Everything here was in various shades of red. He had to really love this color.

My master and Arthur stood by the door like Cerberus and the serpent, guardians of hell. For some reason, it was only at that moment that I realized that I was going to take the admission test to the club like no one before me had ever experienced. And their predatory stare gave me goosebumps and made my blood boil. I was scared like never before, but I was also more thrilled than I had been before.

My master then stepped forward, followed by Arthur. Smiling wickedly, they stripped me naked with such ardor that the clothes I had been loaned were in tatters except for my leather pants, which they ripped off as if the skin were my own and they were skinning me alive. They seemed to have a lot of fun, both with this brutal stripping of their prey and with the fear thus provoked and maintained. And, I was sure, they were already enjoying what they were preparing to inflict on me. But with each piece removed, my mind lit up a little more and my dick got harder.

When I was naked, the two men stood still and silent for a moment, waiting for I didn't know what. But every second spent in anticipation intensified my fear and ignited my desire. Then I understood.

"Sir, I must ask you to punish me for speaking out of turn."

"Does he look repentant to you, Arthur?"

"Um, not so much, Master."

"I assure you that…"

My master then forced me backwards until my calves touched the foot of the bed. Then he pushed me with enough force that I fell back on the mattress. Then the two men pulled me together onto the bed until I was completely lying on it.

"You're going to learn silence tonight," my master said in a tone so harsh that I thought a giant, burning hand was grabbing and twisting my insides.

"May I go to the bathroom first, Sir?" I asked, afraid to wet the beautiful quilt.

He and Arthur laughed at my obvious fear; despite this, my master showed me where the toilet was. In addition to relieving myself there, I washed both my sex and my anus as well as I could. When I returned to the room, my legs were shaking. I saw that the two men had laid face to face on the bed and that Arthur had unzipped his fly and released his half-erect cock. This vision, more obscene than the most total nudity, rekindled my desire. Shuddering, I stretched out between them, exactly as I had settled before I got up.

"Normally, I'd show you mercy by tying you up to immobilize you and make you feel a little more at our mercy, but tonight, I want to see if you can obey your master perfectly. I order you to keep this position: on your back, head straight, arms and legs spread, eyes open, and try to remain silent. And don't ejaculate without my permission."

I knew it wouldn't be easy to stay still and not make any sound. And when we are in pain or orgasming, we often tend to close our eyes, as if to avoid seeing what is in store for us or to concentrate on our sensations. I couldn't even do that.

Given the prohibitions, I could not respond with words or gestures. But they started without delay. They began to graze and caress me with infinite gentleness, giving all their attention to my most sensitive, erogenous areas except for my glans. They brushed my neck, my shoulders, my armpits and the inside of my arms and thighs, the valleys between my belly and my hips, the crease of my elbows and knees, the soles of my feet and the palms of my hands, even my nipples and my anus. Soon, I couldn't stand it anymore and I tensed up.

"He moved, didn't he, Arthur?"

"Yes, Sir."

"Then I'll have to add that to his slate. We'll make him pay for his mistakes later."

Ouch! I just tensed up a little and quite involuntarily. I wanted to beg him not to count this mistake and to swear that I wouldn't do it again. But I would probably commit perjury, for I was not at all sure that I could stand still. Anyway, I suspected that my plea would be ignored. Since he had ordered me to remain silent, I tried to relax as much as possible by breathing slowly and deeply while they continued their stroking and touching.

At one point, I felt so good that I closed my eyes to better surrender to my pleasure. Then I remembered that I had to keep them open. I looked at my master, who had a smirk on his face, because, of course, he had noticed this lapse. He had certainly just added it to my slate.

Then they started licking me, tickling me, scratching me, nipping me, biting me, but without insisting too much. I seemed to be bursting into flames like a human torch, even though I was sometimes covered in goose bumps, and I was vibrating from the inside, as if I had a weak, but constant electric current running through me.

Even my struggle to keep my eyes open and remain still and silent contributed to the pleasure of feeling so dominated by them, for it satisfied my submissive and masochistic nature. The harder it became to obey, the harder I tried and the more I enjoyed it, especially if I succeeded. I loved it! So much so that my cock was rock hard and dripping, my tight balls felt like they wanted to go inside me. I thought if I didn't do something right away, I would cum without permission.

"No, don't grab the covers, leave your hands open and flat on the bed. I'll add that to your slate too."

I wanted to cry so much what they were doing to me was exquisite and my growing need to cum became urgent and irresistible.

When they started stroking me again, one of them pushing a few lubricated fingers inside me and the other rubbing my shaft, but only the shaft, of my penis, without touching its tip, I shook my head from side to side in an instinctive refusal to endure any more without being allowed to cum.

"You moved again, commented my master."

I gave them a pleading look. But then I noticed that their dicks were almost as hard as mine. I could see the neat edges of a bulge in my master's pants and a few tears were dripping from the eye of Arthur's erect penis. And I had done nothing more than try to comply with impossible demands. No one had even touched them. Were they so pleased with my impending orgasm and my stubborn efforts to submit?

"On all fours," my master ordered me.

"Oh, no! They're not going to do it again on the other side," I thought as I assumed the requested posture.

My master reached into a drawer and took out some ropes. He offered one to Arthur. They then tied my knees to my elbows, but kept my legs wide apart. With my body now following the shape of the Greek letter Ω (omega), all parts of it had become accessible to them.

"He made one mistake when we were on our date and four more here. I'll leave it to you to carry out his punishment, Arthur. But undress first."

Arthur looked at him quizzically, as if he was convinced there must be some catch behind this requirement of complete nudity or as if he had something to hide. But he obeyed while I admired his athletic body, with its powerful thighs, muscular chest and belly, which a T of black hair ran through, connecting his most erogenous zones, his nicely sized member which sprang from a curly fleece so dense that it almost completely hid his bursa, and his markings which only added to his wild charm.

"Show me that. You recorded us?" asked in a reproachful tone my master, pointing to the watch Arthur was taking off.

A spy's watch! Did this guy think he was James Bond or what?

"I thought that if Celine or someone else was trying to trick you into making trouble, maybe it would be better to keep evidence of what happened during the meeting. You never know… But in the end, it all worked out," Arthur replied.

"Did you stop it?" my master asked, looking at the watch now sitting on a cabinet.

"Yes, Sir."

My master, like me, looked at Arthur with his eyebrows furrowed. He didn't seem to know what to make of this recording. Were there really any situations that would make such a recording useful?

"Why didn't you tell me about this?"

"I didn't think it was necessary."

"Not necessary?! You know you have to inform me of everything you do that is directly or even indirectly related to me."

"Sorry, Master. I hadn't thought of that."

I didn't see the slightest regret in his eyes until he looked away. Had he only sought to be harshly punished by provoking his dominator?

"Go get us each a riding crop," my master finally ordered him.

Arthur returned quickly and handed him the requested instrument.

"Have they been disinfected?"

"Of course, Master, surgically, as always."

"Gabriel, you can whine, scream, even move, as long as you don't take away our target, my master allowed."

As soon as Arthur started hitting me, I knew what I had fallen into. Anything he would do to me, Zac would do to him. Arthur, the Masochist with a capital M, wanted to suffer. So, the harder he was on me, the more he would get. And in his eyes, more is better.

So, he continued to whip me without mercy over the marks left today by Mendel. I was wincing, I clutched at the bedspread and bit it, and grunted as I glared at my master who inflicted as much if not more on his old lover with his crop. Ah, the beautiful wild animal! His hair, which had undoubtedly come loose because of the intensity of the blows, was flying in all directions. The feline grace of his movements and the ferocious look on his face as he twirled his wand before bringing it down with fury sent shivers up my spine all the way over my head, bristling my hair along the way. I felt bad for Arthur, but he didn't even moan. He must have enjoyed what his favorite torturer was doing to him, because he was still doing it to me.

But if you had seen my master, you would understand why I continued to admire him while he whipped his friend and his friend tortured me. Of the three of us, Master Mendel was the only one with his clothes on. I liked this fact, because his pirate outfit gave him a conquering look and a dignity that we, his slaves, had lost.

When Arthur started hitting my feet, the pain was so severe, so unbearable that I sat up screaming. Anyone who has ever been hit on the soles of their feet with a cane or a stick will tell you, it's just horrible! And he was having the time of his life. Since Arthur was standing, my master couldn't do the same to him. But believe it or not, he didn't let the situation bother him for a fraction of a second; he went after Arthur's nipples, ankles, cock, balls, wherever it was most sensitive, in order to inflict on him pain comparable to mine. When I was in too much pain, I would instinctively move my feet, but Arthur would immediately order me in a sharp tone to put them back in place and he would continue to hit them as soon as I obeyed. But Arthur's pain must have been as intense as mine, for he would sometimes make a shrill hissing or squealing sound. Sometimes he would even hiccup, as if he was choking, and he would interrupt my torment for a brief moment. He would then take his revenge on me, the bastard, by doubling the harshness of his blows, until my master, judging that my punishment had been sufficient, ordered him to stop.

I was dizzy with pain and endorphins. But my erection had decreased. I'm masochistic, but obviously not as much as Arthur, because he was as hard as ever.

"Undress me," my master ordered us, dropping his crop to the floor.

I got up and hobbled over to him. I pushed his wand away with a painful foot so I could stand closer to him and began to unbutton his shirt. Meanwhile, Arthur was skimming him, unbuckling his belt and unzipping his fly so sensually that the very sight of his gestures was like a vaporous touch on my sex. Every move he made was executed with such delicacy and respect that everything seemed to glide along, like the lightest of caresses. Everything he did was so perfect! I realized that I would never, ever, be able to compete with him in masochism, passion, worship, anything worthwhile for a sadistic dominator. And I felt like crying, because like every submissive on the planet, I hoped to be my master's favorite slave, and the conviction that I could never become THE one was more painful than all the blows Arthur had inflicted on me.

My master turned to me and, holding my chin between thumb and forefinger, lifted my head, forcing me to look at him.

"What's wrong?" he asked.

"I…"

I didn't want to lie to him, but to tell him the truth was to admit my imperfection.

"I'm jealous, Master."

"Jealous?"

"Yes, he is too perfect. He knows everything about you. How can I compete with him?"

He laughed.

"Arthur, perfect?"

He chuckled. I gave him a miserable little smile.

"All I want from you, Gabriel, is that you strive to be as perfect as you can be at every moment. Don't try to outdo him. You won't succeed. As you've figured out, he knows me too well. Anyway, I don't want you to outshine him in my eyes, nor do I want you to be like him. He wants more than I'm willing to give. And I like variety; I prefer to have two slaves that are as different as possible. But you can take your cues from him in what he does best to improve yourself, while striving to please me in YOUR own way. Alright?"

I nodded. He placed a wet peck on my mouth. His words and that light kiss reassured me; I felt more valued and capable of being even more so.

I continued to undress him with all my skill, reverence and need for love, not caring about Arthur except to see that he was folding and neatly storing our pirate's clothes on the nearby dresser and to figure out how to get my master's shoes off.

He sat on the edge of the bed and Arthur, with his back to him, placed a boot between his thighs and pulled it off while Master Mendel pushed him with his other foot on his buttocks. I imitated him with the second boot. His foot on my marks was a new torment. The boot came free so suddenly that I went forward and almost fell. When I turned around, I found that my master was giggling. He was paying much more attention to me than to Arthur, who seemed sad to have to share this man he had loved all his life. I felt bad for him and touched his arm. He made a reflexive gesture of rejection at first, then pulled himself together. His lower lip between his clenched teeth was bleeding a little because he had bitten it so hard.

"No!" I exclaimed.

I approached him and kissed him passionately, savoring his blood, like a vampire feasting on that life-giving drink. When I pulled away from him, I saw a tear running down his cheek and… oh my God! I felt so sorry for him that I almost wanted to walk away and leave them both alone. But I had no right to do that; it wasn't my decision to make, was it?

Our master, far more sadistic than I will ever be, was watching Arthur with a smile. He seemed to savor this moment of intense pain, this moment of giving. As Arthur knelt and laid his head on the ground in front of our master, my master looked at me, then reached out to stroke the hair of his old lover. He also had his eyes misty by the emotion generated by this so particular encounter. Ah, how beautiful they were both! Whatever the nature of the feeling they felt for each other, it was so deep, lasting and unique!

"If you prefer, I can leave you alone," I suggested, my voice hoarse, almost choked.

Arthur's flesh was covered with shivers. Were they due to his beloved's caresses or his desire to see me go… for good perhaps?

"No! Stay. You'll join forces to give me pleasure," our master demanded as he lay back on the bed.

Arthur and I worked together to lead him to nirvana. We replicated the gestures they had made sooner to drive me wild with pleasure and raise my dick.

When I saw that my master couldn't take it anymore, I let Arthur give him a blow job. While watching him at work, stroking my master's perineum and anus with a few fingers, I brushed my other hand over Arthur's back. He was really good. He wanted so much to make his old friend and dominator happy that it soon became obvious to me that he still loved him passionately. When he opened his eyes, I could see the longing and pain of not being able to belong to him absolutely every moment. I felt that he would offer his life to him without any hesitation. And again, I wondered how I could compete with him and with that.

"Arthur," whispered my master.

"Yes, Sir," Arthur replied plaintively.

"I still love you! You have nothing to fear. I'll never forget you or forsake you. Never!" said my master in a voice breathless and hoarse with pleasure.

Arthur let out a long, high-pitched, painful moan, like that of a child who would have dreaded losing the only parent he had left.

I wanted to hug him tightly. I understood too well how my master felt about him. They were two abandoned angels on earth: one ejected from heaven, the other straight off of hell. And yet, they had fallen in love with each other the moment they met.

"I'm madly in love with you!" whined Arthur.

On hearing his complaint and his words so full of pain and passion, my master cummed with an exaltation such as I had never seen. I was glad to have participated, though I had no doubt that his feeling for Arthur and the intensity of his friend's heartbreak were, far more than our most voluptuous gestures, responsible for this erotic ecstasy.

After he had recovered his breath, our master ordered us to give each other pleasure, without worrying about him. So, I tried to prove to Arthur that what he was feeling mattered a lot to me. We hugged and caressed for a while. Then, after switching to the sixty-nine position, we both used our mouths to bring each other to orgasm. Arthur was as good with his tongue as he was with his hands, and I soon came close to cumming. His cock, longer but not as wide as his old friend's, throbbed in my throat. All the while, our master, lying on his side, looked at us pensively. Was he satisfied with me, with us? I sincerely hoped so. When Arthur's moans mixed with mine, our master allowed us to cum. He smiled when he heard us screaming in unison with pleasure.

Chapter 13

I was away for several days to take care of most of my personal business concerning my home, furniture and so on. I took the opportunity to notify my family and friends of my change of address and job, telling them that I would be traveling a lot and would probably not be as available or easily accessible. Those who had heard about Mendel's sadism seemed concerned.

"Are you sure you made the right decision?"

"Yes," I said firmly.

But, in fact, I wasn't quite sure yet. Only time and experience would tell if I was right or wrong to trust my new boss and dominator. And for now, I was covered in bruises proving that my life with him would not always be easy.

"One of my acquaintances had been at the Deliverance Club recently. She told me that Master Mendel had made a quick appearance there with the owner and a man she had never seen before. Was that you?" asked Fanny, a cute little submissive who must have "tried" every straight dom in the area.

"Yes, it was. Why did she say that?"

"She told me that someone would've let out an awful scream shortly after your arrival and that it came from the residential part of this well-soundproofed house. If she could hear it, it must've been very loud. She even thought of calling the police."

Perhaps it was Arthur's lament after our master assured him that he still loved him and would never let him down. This cry must have contributed to Master Mendel's reputation for cruelty.

"What was the name of this acquaintance?"

She hesitated for a moment.

"It didn't matter. But what does matter is what Mendel did to make you or Dubois scream like he was ripping out your soul."

"No one is supposed to discuss outside the club what's going on there. Everyone signs an agreement that includes a confidentiality clause."

Which reminded me, I didn't sign it.

"If he didn't do anything wrong to you, then there's nothing to hide, right? I, for one, am not afraid to talk about my sessions with the doms I date."

The line between what is acceptable and what is not, between pleasure and pain, for the uninitiated and even for those who are, is quite thin and blurred.

And it's not the same for all SM enthusiasts and it's certainly not the same for the common man.

"You tell everything to anyone?"

"Yes, why not? I don't hide the fact that I'm a submissive. And I don't do anything illegal."

"Do these doms know that you talk about all this to everyone?"

She shrugged. How could she be so naive as to not understand the harm she could cause by revealing everything to everybody? I looked at her, eyebrows furrowed, wondering if I should shake her or slap her to wake her up, to get her out of her fantasy world where everyone is beautiful, unprejudiced and kind.

"A confidentiality agreement is like a promise of silence. If you signed one, would you then still tell anyone about everything you experienced there?"

She shook her head no without much conviction.

"I wouldn't sign one anyway," she concluded.

We then dropped the subject.

When I returned to my master's house, I was heavily laden with my entire wardrobe and my most precious belongings such as my computer, my tablet, my iPod and its base, my SLR camera with two thirty-two gigabyte memory cards, one of which was almost empty, and two batteries, one of which was full, my telephoto and wide-angle lenses, my important papers: birth certificate, passport, financial information, etc.

I also had a recent medical certificate attesting that I was one hundred percent healthy. When I had put everything else away and showed it to my master, he reached into a drawer in his filing cabinet and handed me a similar paper certifying his perfect health. We could fuck raw from now on.

"Speaking of documents, Sir, shouldn't I have signed a confidentiality agreement to get into Mr. Dubois's club?"

"I have it on my hard drive. Just change the name and date, print it out, initial all the pages, put your signature on the last one and mail it to Arthur. But I'm sure he's not worried. If I hadn't insisted that he treat me no differently than any other member, I'd never have seen this NDA. He knew I wouldn't discuss what was going on there unless our lives depended on it. As for you, you promised not to reveal what we go through together and you won't set foot in the club without me, so… But you're right to make me think about it. It's better to do these things by the book."

I also shared with him what Fanny told me.

"I'll say a word about it to Arthur. Shortly after the members sign up, he checks to see if they can hold their tongue and respect all the clauses of this agreement. Don't ask me how he does it, he didn't tell me, but it seems to be effective. And from time to time, he does some sort of purge at the club. Those who don't meet his very strict criteria are kicked out. So this chatterbox must be a new member."

He tells me that he took advantage of my absence to research the human trafficking case and start writing an article. But he was waiting for more news from Arthur to finalize his writing. He received some while I was settling in at his house. He made sure I could hear the conversation.

The investigation into the deputy consulate was ongoing, but you can't incarcerate a member of a consulate or embassy as if they were citizens of the host country. There has to be sufficient evidence of guilt and then the procedure is to repatriate them. But a Cambodian lieutenant and police officer had just been arrested. Senior officials from three of the four neighboring states, who had been suspected for some time of complicity, were reportedly followed wherever they went in the hope of catching them in the act. Interpol reportedly provided support and technical resources to local authorities and victim assistance agencies.

"The human trafficking police have an interesting lead in Thailand for your children, Sir. I'm confident they'll be found soon," Arthur said with great enthusiasm.

He believed that they and many other abductees would soon regain their freedom and return to their families. My master was staring at the picture of "his" children while talking to his friend and he was very tense; he must have doubted the realness of such a quick and total outcome of this case. I was moved to see all the sadness on his face every time he looked at those pictures. I think he felt guilty for children's current misfortunes and, until they were liberated, he would blame himself for not being more effective in his attempt to free them.

Hearing my master's labored breathing, Arthur added, "I know how you feel, Sir. But at least you can tell yourself that you're one of the good guys. You're one of the ones trying to help them. And the police have made it clear to me that if these children hadn't been returned to their buyers, it'd have been more difficult to find out where they were to be taken and who these traffickers were. It was your intervention and their exit from the country that allowed them to follow the trail between the transporters and the buyers. By sending all the information you had to Interpol and by suggesting that they view the videos recorded by the consulate's surveillance camera, you collaborated in the arrest of corrupt police officers and the dismantling of this network."

I don't know if Arthur was just saying this to comfort his friend or if it was all true, but my master didn't seem completely convinced or relieved.

"Yes, but while we follow their trail, these children suffer."

It was Arthur's turn to remain silent.

"But others who would've suffered the same fate will remain free," he finally added.

"Do you think I'll be able to talk to them when we find them? I'd like to make sure they're okay and can go home."

"There's not really a formal rehabilitation center for victims of trafficking, but the police gave me the name of a contact at AFESIP, an independent organization that helps women or girls in difficult situations. She also has to connect my partners with counselors and psychologists who are familiar with the Cambodians' particular way of thinking. All of these therapists and other specialists will talk to the survivors and decide what kinds of interventions with them and their loved ones would be most appropriate to help them overcome possible post-traumatic stress. But, Sir, I'm afraid they want to avoid meetings with the press. And… you're one of them. Unless you are given the benefit of the doubt since you were the one who got them released."

"No, forget it. You're right, these kids won't be ready to confide in us right away. We need to give them time to recover. And I hope the police don't get overzealous in questioning them as if they were criminals."

"That's why I asked that a therapist interview them rather than police officers. The children may be more terrorized by the cops than by their captors and traffickers. While trying to reassure and help, the therapist may still be able to gather information useful in dismantling the network."

"That's very good thinking, Arthur, and excellent work. But if I can set up a meeting with some of the survivors of this kind of trafficking who would like to confide in me so that others don't have to go through the same thing, I'd love to talk to them. Do you think there is a way to put me in contact with some of them?"

"I'll see what I can do. And if your desire is mainly to make sure that the ones you tried to free are okay, I'll try to get you a copy of the videos or the minutes of the meetings with the therapist. Normally, this is protected by the seal of confidentiality, but if the identity and location of these children are crossed out, perhaps they'll agree to provide it to you. But you may have to sign an agreement that prohibits you from using those documents for an article or a TV report."

"That's fine with me. Thank you so much, Arthur!"

"I'm always happy to help you, Sir. And, oh yeah, I met Masutā yesterday. He confessed to entering the country illegally and living under an assumed name. His name is Hiro Shishaku. But shortly after immigrating, he applied for political asylum and has now been naturalized. He was admitted because of rivalries between mafia syndicates that put his life in danger."

"Is he a criminal?" my master asked.

"No, but he's the son of an important yakuza. They were afraid that he'd come of age and claim his rightful place as heir to his clan, so someone wanted to eliminate him before that happened. He fled at eighteen thanks to his father, who was then murdered. As for his mother, nobody knows what happened to her. Maybe she died, too, or emigrated elsewhere."

"Or she lives here under an assumed name too. But are you sure of this information?"

"Yes, I'm sure. As sure as one can be when it comes to illegal immigrants, foreign countries and their mafia."

"But how does all this make him a BDSM master?"

"For one thing, he thinks he's more sadistic and domineering than most BDSM practitioners he knows. In addition, his investigators must be more talented, experienced, and better connected than mine; he knows more about everyone than I do. He told me all the good things he thought of you."

"Ah. He has talent indeed, but to touch the heartstrings of the people he's talking to."

Arthur remained silent at the end of the line.

"But even if he knew all the BDSMers in this country, that wouldn't make him a master, it seems to me," insists mine.

"Actually, his family is part of the ancient Japanese nobility. He learned bondage and the art of interrogation when he was just a kid. He was also taught the values and qualities that would've made him a true shogun. But he never had the opportunity to put all his knowledge into practice before leaving Japan. He claims to have attended every major BDSM symposium, conference and workshop given in the country since his arrival, but under false identities. I checked to see if many of these events had participants with Japanese names. Of course, I found several, which doesn't prove anything. But, Sir, he told me things about you and your family, your background, your experience in the BDSM scene that no one but me and you should know."

My master remained thoughtful for a moment.

"I'm not sure I like the idea that someone I didn't know anything about a few days ago knows so much about me and that it's so easy to find out everything about my life. I already have journalists gossiping about me…"

"I don't think it's that easy, Sir. But he is sufficiently interested in certain dominators and submissives in our community that he's willing to devote more energy, time and probably money to getting to know them well. In your case, his respect comes not only from your dominating skills, but mostly from the fact that you travel the world seeking to help people in need whenever possible."

My master tensed up. Perhaps he doubted his own worth as a rescuer of the needy people, or he suspected Masutā had other reasons for wanting to learn more about him.

"I confess, Arthur, that I still don't know what to make of this Masutā or Fausto, for that matter."

"Perhaps you should meet them. If they seem trustworthy, you might agree to let Fausto stay in your bungalow. As for me, I could do some tests to find a reliable surveillance system and install it nearby to check on things from time to time."

My master gave a hoarse little laugh.

"How typical of you. You do what you need to do to find out if you can trust someone, and then what you need to do to spy on them in case you're wrong."

Arthur grunted, no doubt at his friend's insight into his behaviors and motivations.

Chapter 14

For the next few days, my master and I settled into a sort of routine. Every morning, as soon as we got up, we would work out, either inside in his gym or running outside. Then we would take a shower, together or separately, depending on his mood. And after preparing and eating breakfast, we would read the newspapers, not only local, but international, including, of course, the press of Cambodia and its neighboring countries. After that, we would answer our emails. Then we would check the Internet to find new subjects for investigation here or elsewhere. I had to explain to him why the ones I had selected seemed interesting to me. He would tell me why he didn't think any editor would buy a story on a certain topic and why another one might have several takers. Sometimes I tried to convince him of the value of my choice, but it was a waste of time, because he always agreed with me.

"I agree. It's very interesting. But again, they won't buy it because, among other things, they'll get sued for libel."

"Oh, so in order to spare the susceptibility of some personalities, we won't work on it?"

"Of course, we'll work on it!" he replied with a smile, his eyes glinting with pure malice.

I didn't understand anything anymore.

"All I'm saying is that all the newspapers and magazines will be reluctant to buy an article from you on this subject, unless you can prove conclusively to them that what you're revealing is true. In such a case, it would no longer be defamation, it'd be an accusation in due form. And that way, newspaper owners love it! They're willing to pay a lot of money for that. Do you understand?"

I smiled.

"Except that the investigation would be longer, more difficult and risky. No public figure likes to have their name tarnished and to be arrested. If people find out that you're investigating them and you already have evidence of their crimes…," he explained.

His eyes were always bright; he loved it too. Framing crooks is fun. But the more powerful they are, the more dangerous it is.

"But whatever the time and risk, I prefer you to be passionate about your subject of investigation. That's what makes our work compelling," he concluded.

"Thank you."

"For what?"

I thought for a moment.

"I don't know."

He laughed and went back to his Internet search. But I think my thanks were about the fact that he valued what I was most passionate about and was willing to follow me into something that could take time, money, and even put his life in danger, as long as it was for the right cause.

He encouraged me to let my instincts guide me, especially if I was going for a humanitarian or environmental issue that he liked. From what I could see, his favorite topics were very diverse and could take us on a lot of trips to absolutely anywhere in the world. But what he liked most was to choose something that would make a difference to a lot of people or to the whole planet.

He would also sometimes ask me to look up crucial information for him to finish writing his current article. He would often call one or another of his contacts from everywhere to find out what the situation was with this and that here and there on the globe. Each time, he made sure I could hear what he was saying so that I could be as informed as he was and come to understand his work better and be able to help him more effectively.

He asked me, "Which of your contacts could be a reliable source of information on local or international events?"

"As you know, there are some journalists among my acquaintances. My mother is a member of a wealthy ladies' club. I think she was only admitted because of her long-standing friendship with the mayor's wife. But I personally have never met any influential people. I do have a good friend who is a geek with a capital 'G'. He says he has managed to get into secret government files, especially the national police. When I asked him how he managed to do this without getting caught, he winked and said that he left no trace of himself. I'm not sure that's true or even possible.

"If you interview other reporters, you'll tip them off to something you'd probably rather keep to yourself, but occasionally they might give you useful information, sometimes without even knowing it. And you're right about the mayor's wife and this club. If she was your friend instead of your mom's, it'd be even better, but you work with what you have. And geeks are usually very competitive and quick to prove themselves. If you ever need computer support to solve a mystery, it could be very helpful. As for influential people, most of them tell us that they have nothing to declare, lie to us or hide important things from us. Their relatives, friends, assistants, colleagues and other business contacts often tell us much more. But you have to maintain a good and constant relationship with all these informants. To do this, you need to call them or meet them regularly, for example at the restaurant, even if you don't have anything to ask them at that moment. So, to help you develop your network, I'll make you my spokesperson. This way, you'll at least become familiar with my main contacts, who will get used to you, whether in person or on the phone, and you'll make new connections."

"But if you're calling and meeting with possible informants often without even needing their help, that's got to take quite a bit of time and money, right?"

"Yes, but, trust me, it's worth it. Some of them will become great friends and those meals together won't seem like a chore anymore. As for the costs, you can keep your bills and other invoices and add them to your business or self-employed expenses; this will reduce your current year's taxes a bit."

Sometimes he would ask me questions to find out how much I knew about this or that subject, this or that regional, national or world event, current or historical. I already had a good general knowledge, but his was much more extensive and, above all, more authentic and practical, because he had had the opportunity to go and work from a few days to several months in many of the countries where these events had taken place. His experience was more real and close to the local population than mine, which was only theoretical. But I would have the chance to confront theory and practice in the future if he kept me in his service; I was sure of it.

Besides, he often tested me, asking me about some point or other that might or should have been part of my knowledge, warning me with a teasing expression that he would question me again the next day or so, and that if I still didn't know the answer, he would spank me.

"A spanking, huh? Just that," I said to myself with a half-smile. He laughed, then asked me what I had just thought of.

"That a simple spanking probably wouldn't be enough for you. That doesn't sound like you."

When he had given me this warning, we were just finishing breakfast. He was in his pajama pants and I was in my very short shorts.

"Strip," he ordered me.

I stood up and undressed. He turned his chair around.

"On your stomach on my thighs. I'll give you a demonstration."

I obeyed. He barely tapped me. It was more symbolic than real.

"So, how do you like it?" he asked me.

"Eeeh!"

I didn't know what to say. One thing was certain, neither he nor I were more excited by that than by the thought of eating toast without butter. He laughed again.

"Go get me the smaller cutting board, the one with the handle," he ordered.

I got up and rummaged through the drawer where it was and offered it to him. He patted his thighs. I lay back down on my stomach. He started hitting me with such energy that I soon felt my ass catch fire and I started to look forward to him stopping as I was in more and more pain. That thick, stiff plastic board, smooth on one side but ridged on the other like a gnocchi board, made a formidable paddle. He flipped it over to continue hitting me with the grooved side. Ouch! I was at the point of wiggling my buttocks to try to protect the overly sensitive areas.

"Do you see now that even a simple spanking can be a deterrent?"

He hadn't stopped hitting me for a moment while talking.

"Oww! I see, I see very well! I can see so well that I'd rather not see at all," I said, wiggling my buttocks.

He burst out laughing. But I loved the frank and playful sound.

"Do you know that when your cute butt wiggles that way, it gets me excited, and the more excited I am, the rougher I get?"

Oh! But he was probably right. Usually, the more we let our pain show, the more the sadist's cock hardens and the crueler he gets. I froze, which made him laugh again. He definitely had a perverse sense of humor.

After several more strokes, not enough to allow me to escape into my masospace, he stopped.

"So, will you try to enrich your general culture?"

"Yes, Master," I answered with great conviction.

"Go to bed."

As I got up, I saw that the front of his pajamas had a revealing bulge. I laughed again.

"Don't make fun of me, or I may well be tempted to use something crueler than this board on your lovely red bottom," he threatened with a smile.

"I wasn't laughing, Sir. I assure you!" I hurried to say, but made a face at him.

My sudden chuckle caused him to change his plans.

"Damn masochist! Come on, try to escape me."

"What?!"

"Run, run like I'm your jailer and I've come to get you beheaded because you're a homosexual pervert," he added, making a face at me.

I looked at him with a haggard expression, not quite sure of his seriousness.

"Are you going to run away or not? Come on, run away as if your life depended on it. Now!"

I leaped out and ran through the whole house, trying not to fall into a possible trap. I had just opened the door to a room I had never been in, but which had all the makings of a torture chamber with its motley but fearsome and certainly painful instruments hanging on every wall, its punishment bench, its cupboard with lots of drawers whose contents I preferred not to know, its rings on the ceiling and much more. I froze for a moment. One moment too many. With a crunch and a shove, he dropped me to his rubberized tile floor, then pounced on me and held me in a martial arts expert's submission hold. He wasn't decapitating me, but he was well and truly choking me, the bastard. The more I struggled to free myself, the tighter he tightened his grip and the more I choked. He only released his arm lock around my neck when I started to see stars. But I was on my stomach, and he took the opportunity to penetrate me dry, grunting his pleasure at having dominated me physically. While he was ruthlessly fucking me, he told me that I should learn to defend myself better than that.

"And when I order you… to run away…, don't pretend…, run away… as if… you were really… risking your life. One day…, it could be… true."

He huffed and puffed between his instructions. This gave them a tone of urgency and truth.

"I… don't want to… run. I need to… stay to… save you," I managed to answer between several sharp penetrations.

He stopped, pulled his cock out of me and started kicking me. Fortunately, he was not wearing shoes. But as he kicked me, he explained that, without weapons against heavily armed opponents, I would have to go for help if I hoped to be able to rescue him. Then he threw himself on top of me and kissed me passionately. He literally chewed my lips and tongue and sucked them into his mouth, almost swallowing them. My head was spinning again, this time with pleasure. I had one of the most magnificent men I'd ever been lucky enough to meet on top of me and he seemed just as crazy about me as I was about him. And he was obviously very aroused.

"Blow me now," he ordered after the burning kiss.

But I hadn't had time to wash up and his cock was a little covered in my shit. I'm not a fan of scat. The smell was enough to make my stomach churn. But he had given me an order, was I going to disobey him for the first time? And would this also be the last time I would have the opportunity to do so?

He lay on his back on the floor and spread his legs, waiting for me to make a move one way or the other. I knelt between his thighs and leaned in. Once over his cock, the smell invaded my nostrils. I gagged but stuck my tongue out.

"That's okay. Fetch a wet wipe and two condoms. There are some in the first drawer of the cupboard, right there," he said, pointing.

"Thank you, Sir," I replied, relieved, as I stood up.

"Don't think you'll always get off that easy," he scolded.

I hurriedly brought the necessary supplies to clean us up properly. They were odorless, hypoallergenic wipes like the ones for infants. I was about to put the condom on him when he ordered me to put it on and lay on my back. He then fucked himself on my dick. No doubt he had reason to fear that he would dirty me as well.

Even though I was still under him, he was still in total control of the situation. While I was brushing his nipples and stroking him everywhere I could reach, he was cruelly pinching mine, clawing and biting me, sliding a hand behind him to grab my balls and squeezing them tighter and tighter until I screamed in pain.

"Hummm! That scream rings in my ears like a sacred song, beautiful and disturbing. And every time you're in real pain, your cock jerks, as if it's beating the rhythm inside me, and the rubbing against my prostate becomes…

distressing. Come on, sing for me again," he demanded, cruelly twisting my nipples between his nails.

I squealed and sobbed as he released them.

"Mmmm!" he said as he bent down to lick my tears and kiss me tenderly.

He then pulled me out of his belly, slipped on the other condom and penetrated me again, this time from the front. Then he started his torture again, adding a new torment. He began to scrape the frenulum of my cock with his thumbnail. I tensed and twisted to get away from it, because it was very painful. He slapped me, hard.

"Don't ever try to evade what I ask or inflict on you again. Only when I command you to run away should you run away," he growled, clearly angry.

I forced myself to surrender to his will, to accept everything he did to me, even the worst, without stopping to caress him. This order and my effort to obey it opened the doors of my mind wide to my desire for submission and intensified my pleasure.

"Mmmm! When you're in a lot of pain, you contract your anus and it accentuates the friction on my cock. It feels… so good!"

At least I could do that! But he wouldn't let go. In between penetrations, he would scratch one of my nipples and my penis or squeeze my balls in his fist. I only had a few seconds to breathe between torments and my screams.

"Mmmm! So good!" he hummed.

I tried to grab hold of something, but I couldn't find anything with a bit of a grip, and I shook my head, so hard was it to take what he was doing to me.

"No! Open your hands, don't struggle anymore and look me in the eyes. Your whole body belongs to me; give it all to me, not just by letting me scratch your cock or squeeze your balls, not just by stretching them out to me, but by offering them to me mentally, with your whole mind and all your heart."

At the time, it seemed quite unfeasible: to desire this pain so intensely that I would spiritually offer it to him!? Then I tried to obey him. I looked at his eyes with pupils dilated by his pleasure, I heard his "mmm!" of pleasure, I felt his cock so wide and hard inside me, and I began to accept everything, to desire everything, to abandon myself to the intoxicating pain and to fly away.

"I'm yours, Master. All yours!" I screamed, because he was still hurting me badly.

"This is just the beginning. This is nothing at all. I'll make you suffer a little more every day, Gabriel. If this is already too much for you, run away from me, faster than you did earlier. I'm not just giving you permission, I'm demanding it."

Even though all this was more gasped than spoken, I still understood what it implied. But while this announcement of greater torment frightened me, it also excited me terribly. My spine and skull tingled with pleasure and I screamed while cumming. He gave a few more thrusts and cummed in turn. After waiting a few minutes to catch our breath and come to our senses, we went back to showering together and then getting dressed.

We often ate lunch at home, but sometimes at the restaurant. Somebody had to go and buy food to cook good meals and all the other things necessary for domestic life. If he had time, he would go with me and put in the cart or basket what he wanted or what he knew was missing from his fridge, pantry or elsewhere. Every morning when I got up, he was up and about, and more often than not, breakfast was ready, which made me feel guilty, unworthy of being considered a good slave. But we prepared all other meals together. On the other hand, I almost always did the laundry and cleaning by myself while he played the piano, violin or guitar. He was a wonderful, creative musician who could make any piece inspiring and improvise countless original variations, melodious or surprising, to anything he played or composed. Sometimes he played rock, blues, folk or ballads, mostly on his guitar. But he liked to sit at his piano and let himself be carried away by classical pieces or Latin jazz. No matter what the instrument or song, I loved listening to him. It made me want to sing; not the way he had been forcing me to sing lately, but to use my voice to accompany his music. In the evenings, we read historical novels, spy novels, futuristic novels, adventure stories, biographies… He is interested in everything, in humanities and pure sciences, in technological inventions and arts. Sometimes we watched a movie or an episode of a TV show. And quite often, we would fuck before falling asleep in each other's arms for the night. It was a lifestyle that suited me perfectly. But I knew that one of these days he would find a cause he believes in and that he cared about, and we would have to go on an adventure somewhere far away, where we might get killed. So, I enjoyed the calm before the storm.

Chapter 15

Although our daily activities were similar, they were never quite the same. But what differed most each time was the way he took and gave pleasure and the places on his beautiful property, even outside, where he wanted to fuck. He was just as inventive in finding new ways to provoke my screams of pain or blushes of shame. You'd think that at my age, nothing could get to me enough to make me blush and that there was a limit to the perverse imagination of a dominator, but if you think that, you certainly don't know Zach Mendel.

However, he did not forget about the kidnapped children. One morning, he called several of his contacts in Cambodia and its neighboring countries to get news on arrests related to human trafficking.

A Sihanoukville police lieutenant had been arrested, two senior officials had just been formally charged with corruption and various crimes, and a third, fearing for his life, had fled when he learned that clear evidence of his homosexual pedophilia and involvement in the drug trade had been passed on to the appropriate authorities in his country, where such crimes are never joked about. One of the accused was a senator in Cambodia who owned several massage parlors, prostitution establishments, bars and numerous casinos. The other was a Thai parliamentarian. The fugitive was a Vietnamese minister who was also the head of a major drug trafficking network. If one of his brothels became the target of the authorities, he would temporarily relocate anyone who could get him into trouble to a different location. Since he was connected to the arrested police officer, he was warned of what was about to happen. Interpol's national headquarters had had him in their sights for quite some time, as he operated as far away as Europe. Everyone was happy to have finally caught two big fish and gotten rid of a third. And if the runaway was caught, he would be repatriated to his country where he would almost certainly be sentenced to death.

When Arthur called, after discussing what we already knew about the corruption of the various governments and the arrests, he added a few details we didn't know. Among other things, a second Phnom Penh police officer, who knew and helped the one who had been imprisoned, was to be indicted shortly. Then my master came to the most burning issue.

"What about my children?"

I was touched to hear him speak in a voice that was still vibrant with emotion about these children as his own.

"They are in good care and a psychologist makes sure that nothing is done to them that could make them feel worse."

"And… how are they? Have they been… raped, beaten?" my master asked, his hesitation indicating his concern.

As Arthur remained silent, we understood that the answer was "yes", they were mistreated and abused.

"Everything is being done to help them, Sir. A doctor and a gynecologist have examined them and those who need it are being treated right now. Then we will make sure that they go back home and can go to school."

"Have they all been found? No one's missing?" I asked, emphasizing the word "all".

"Several children, who weren't among those we were looking for, have also been freed and are being provided with the necessary medical treatment. The only ones missing are the young woman and her baby. The police are still trying to locate them."

"Someone powerful must've taken them. She may even be at another crooked high official's home. Or maybe a rich client, probably bald and paunchy man, who thought she was too beautiful to leave in the hands of pimps, bought her for his personal needs. If this is the case, the baby must've been teared away from its mother, sold to an international adoption broker and offered at a high price to local or foreign pedophiles or auctioned off on the Deep Web."

Ah, Lord! How could such a horror exist? To think that this child was barely one year old. I saw my master's discomfited expression. Mine and Arthur's must not have been much happier.

"Thank you, Arthur, for your help. It is much appreciated."

"You're welcome, Sir. I'm always happy to be of service to you and to help these children. I'll get back to you as soon as I hear anything."

He then said goodbye and hung up. My master thought for a moment, then worked on his paper, adding what he had just learned, but keeping it open enough to incorporate what we might still discover. After he had me review it and his synopsis, he smilingly made the few corrections and improvements I had suggested. There weren't many, because what he had written was overwhelming, as was everything else I had read from him. And what I would call the core paragraph was always breathtaking. As for his summary, even without spoilers, it gave enough interesting details that publishers were tempted to pay for the full text. Like Arthur, I was happy to have been helpful, in a small way, but I still wondered if those typographical errors and small structural flaws had been left there on purpose to see if I could spot them.

Then he sent his synopsis to all the magazines and newspapers that might buy this article, telling them that another one would probably be added to it, since they were expecting to receive additional information about the children abducted by the traffickers, and that if they wanted to buy it, they should get this one. He also specified that if they wanted exclusivity, the price would increase accordingly, and that they should discuss this with him (he always gave them his detailed contact information).

"Don't you attach your portfolio or resume?"

"I used to do it when they didn't know me yet. But now, my name is somewhere at the top of the journalists' list of several media consortiums. Sometimes they even ask me for something on topics of interest. So, I just send them a summary and tell them what they can expect: one or more articles, a photo essay or a TV report, and if they need to know more or have any proposition to make, they say so. They all have my business card or at least my phone number and email address."

I thought, "Ah, fame!"

After I finished all that, he was walking around the house in circles and looking as miserable as sin. I felt so sorry for him that I took him by the hand and dragged him to his room. He started to refuse as I slowly began to undress him while stroking him.

"I'm not in the mood for this," he said.

I didn't care. I kissed his beautiful chest as it was revealed to my eyes and hands. I covered him with idolatrous looks and gestures. I was drooling with desire so much his raw sensitivity seemed desirable, charming, admirable even to me. What an exceptional man I had as a master! He deserved all my attention and my adoration. And I wanted to offer them to him at this moment.

"I love you so much!"

"You hardly know me, Gabriel."

"What I've seen of you is enough to make me crazy about you. I've a better grasp of the depth and indefectibility of Arthur's feelings for you."

He gave a hoarse, doubt-filled little laugh.

"'If you really understood him, you'd leave me so that he could've me all to himself, as he has always wanted."

"I'm possessive, but not jealous," I replied.

"Interesting assertion. How can you be possessive without wanting to possess?"

He seemed amused by this discussion. Anyway, he was smiling now.

"Your happiness is the most important thing to me. If that means you screwing other men, I have no objection; as long as you don't reject me, I'm happy with it."

"So, you're not that disinterested?"

"Of course not! No one is quite so."

His smile widened.

"I think I like you, too, my little psychologist submissive."

"Your feelings for me make me love you more and your happiness intensifies mine."

During all this time, I had not stopped caressing him. And although he said that it was necessary for him to cause pain to cum, he was getting hard.

"And if, so that I reach the seventh sky, you had to suffer more than you ever did?" he asked as he was pinching one of my nipples between his claws, much too long.

He squeezed and twisted ever harder, his nails digging into the tender flesh already sensitized by his previous erotic games. I threw my head back and closed my eyes.

"Mmm!" he uttered.

"Aaaaah!"

"Is that all you have to say, slave?"

I looked him square in the face. His proudly raised chin and half-closed eyelids almost hid his dilated pupils. I looked down, not out of embarrassment or humility, but to admire the newly emerging manly form that seemed to come alive in his pajamas.

"Mmm!" I said, too, at that sight.

I was proud of myself, of my success in getting the children out of his mind. Maybe he hadn't forgotten them, but he was suffering a little less because of me.

"Take this off," he said, stretching and releasing the elastic of my boxers.

"Ouch!"

It stung! He laughed as I obeyed him.

"Let me examine you."

And he inspected me from every angle. It seemed as if he was making a detailed survey of my every mark, all those that were his direct work and those that he had caused me by Arthur's hand. For his friend had only been his instrument that evening. Or was it the other way around? Hard to say.

He sat down at the edge of the bed and signaled me to turn around. While I was still standing with my back to him, he grabbed one of my ankles and lifted it onto his tight thighs. He looked at the soles of my feet, one after the other.

"He didn't spare you, did he?"

"It was the only way he could get as much from you as he wanted."

"No. To get as much as he wanted, he'd have had to put you in a state that I'd have found unacceptable, especially from him. He knew that. Believe it or not, he held back."

I shuddered at the thought of what I would have suffered if he hadn't controlled his sadistic or masochistic urges; it was hard to tell in Arthur's case.

The inventory of my marks had not diminished my master's erection, far from it. He relished the sight of them.

"Will you… will you ever do to me what you did to Arthur the first time?"

"Never!" he exclaimed, clearly shocked.

One would have sworn that I had seriously insulted him, believing him still capable of such brutality. But I, who had said I was not jealous, was. It was as if he had just affirmed with a strong conviction that he would never feel for me a love as passionate and unbridled as for his childhood friend.

He forced me to face him and kneel before him.

"What's wrong?" he asked, seeing my pitiful face.

"Nothing's wrong."

"Gaby, don't play games with me!" he growled like a hungry lion, ready to devour me.

He grabbed my hair and, pulling it back, forced me to raise my head and look at him.

"Swear that you'll never lie to me again, never hide anything from me, never try to deceive me in any way!"

I promised him. And when he asked me again what was wrong, I explained how I felt. He tilted his head to the side. His cock gave several jerks. Why? What was it about what I'd just told him that excited him: the possibility of inflicting as much on me as he had on Arthur one day or, on the contrary, the certainty of my constant torment at the idea of never being entitled to as much crazy love as his friend? Damn sadist!

"Do you think you'll ever love me enough to accept that I feel something this strong for someone else, Gabriel?"

"I… I already love you so much!"

I barely recognized my voice, my tight throat making it squeaky.

"Not that much. If my feelings for Arthur hurt you, if you suffer because of them, and if you hope I'll push him away…"

"I may hurt even more as mine for you grow, Sir."

"No. If you loved me as fervently as he does, you'd accept my happiness, even if it were in his arms. At the diner, Arthur started to say that he'd have preferred to be alone with me. I interrupted him, not out of cruelty to him, but out of pity for you both. If he'd expressed everything he felt, you both would've suffered. And my refusal to keep you out would've hurt him. He obeyed me; he kept quiet and accepted your presence, however painful it was for him. You have no idea what it costs him to admit that another man stays with me. He begged me in middle school to live alone with me. We lived in the student residence where I made sure we each had our own room. And with the poorly insulated walls, it was almost impossible to do anything together. Then he stayed in the army for five years and we hardly saw each other during that time. When he returned, I already had a full-time slave. Arthur still started taking journalism classes in the hope that he could one day be my assistant and thus become a bigger part of my life. I offered to make him my submissive 24/7 on the condition that he'd stay with us as a threesome. He turned my offer down. He dreamed of forming a couple with me, not a trio. I told him, 'No way.' I knew too well where that would lead us. He's submitted to this demand all these years, however cruel it may be to him. But these few hours between the three of us have been a torment for him, much more because you were there than because of the hardness of my blows. Especially since at the restaurant, he saw your resolution to stay with me, and in the bedroom, he understood that you were sincere, and that if you weren't his equal in terms of masochism, you were close enough to satisfy me. All this worries him a lot. You scare him a lot, Gabriel."

"If you loved me as fervently as he does," he said. His words were like a sharp, burning blade that he was slowly plunging into my heart. So, he believed Arthur's feeling for him to be greater and stronger than mine, sincere enough to agree to never share his life.

They would die for each other, I had no doubt about that. So how could I dream of finding my place between these two men? It was like the three of us were sitting on a loveseat.

I began to beg to all the powers of the universe to give me the strength to inspire and the chance to feel what they felt for each other. But don't they say, "Be careful what you wish for, it might just come true"?

Chapter 16

My master told me that he would leave tomorrow for a few days with Arthur and Celine in Cambodia to interview child survivors of trafficking, to photograph his own children, if possible, and to gather all the information he could find on the recent arrests.

"Arthur and his gang will serve as my bodyguards. As for Celine, she was ejected by the local BDSMers community association for accusing me without good reason. She applied for readmission, but was required to show proof of her good faith. When she called me to help her, I was quite hesitant. But when Arthur told me that I could talk with little survivors, I decided to give Celine this opportunity to right her wrongs. So don't worry, I'll be careful and we'll be gone only a few days: two or three, at most. As for you, while I'm gone, you'll have to write a paper on a topic of your choice. But it'd better be captivating!"

I wish I didn't seem so sulky, but I must admit I was very disappointed, and it showed. I felt like he didn't trust me enough to assist and protect him, if necessary. I was afraid that he would start thinking that Celine wasn't such a bad employee after all, and that he would resume his relationship with her. I envied Arthur for being able to leave with him and help him if things went wrong. And this stupid story he wanted me to write was just a way to keep me busy in his absence; nothing else! It seemed to me that he was depriving me of my right to do my duty as a submissive and an assistant to him.

He made me pay dearly for this reaction. Or is it I who punish myself?

"Get naked!" he ordered me.

"But…"

"Now!"

He barked so harshly that I didn't dare argue. I undressed.

"Run away!"

So I ran around in the house, and at one point I had no choice if I wanted to escape him but to go outside into the chilly late spring air. I went outside thinking that, anyway, we were in a secluded spot surrounded by trees and groves, that no one would see me and I would just have to wait for the right moment to go back. But he foresaw my reaction; he locked all the doors. Of course, all the windows were locked too. I couldn't get back inside without his help. I stood on the stoop, huddled in the corner shivering for at least an hour before he deigned to open the door.

"You'd make a lousy fighter. If you had to rely on your ability to save your own ass, things could go very badly for you," he said as he watched me walk in with my teeth chattering.

He led me to his room where he found a blanket and wrapped me in it.

"What could I do? I was locked out."

He stared at me, eyebrows furrowed, as if I were an alien whose language he didn't understand.

"I was the one locked in the house, I remind you. And 'locked out' is a contradiction in terms; unless you were bound outside, and even then you should say you were tied up or chained out."

That's what happens when you live with someone whose job is writing: your mistakes get corrected at the worst times. But at least he rubbed me all over to keep me warm.

"But I was naked. Where could I go, dressed like that?"

"Were you naked or dressed?"

"God," I thought. I was beginning to wonder if I would get an answer to my question one of these days or just some linguistic comments.

"Naked," I finally admitted when I realized he would wait, arms crossed over his chest, until the end of time if I didn't say anything.

"It felt like an episode of Tarzan. Although the apeman must've had a less white ass than yours. Besides, you look pretty much like Weissmuller with your curly brown hair and green eyes," he added with a mocking smile.

"Weissmuller? Who is this guy?" I thought as I watched him laugh at me. At that moment, I wished I could have forced him to go outside with his ass in the air, too. I would have followed him with a whip to make him run faster. I thought that was a pretty funny idea.

"What's so funny?" he asked me.

I shook my head, not sure if telling him the truth would not get me in trouble.

"Answer me, slave!"

I described to him what I had imagined. He looked at me with that infinitely serious air he sometimes adopted when he was disconcerted.

"I like this idea. Not for me, of course, but for you. Maybe I can certainly use it one day."

"Shit! I knew that confessing these kinds of fantasies to him would get me in trouble," I thought. But he finally answered me.

"There's the garage and a shed filled with all kinds of junk you could have hidden behind to escape me. I've stored some blankets you could have covered yourself with. You would have been relatively warm. And for lack of a better word, even though the little shed at the back of the yard is full of gardening tools, you could have made room for yourself there. In any of those shelters, you'd have found tools you could have used to defend yourself."

"What?! You wanted me to hit you with a shovel or a rake or to attack you with shears?"

Now I was the one who was baffled. He was still smiling from ear to ear.

"Try it, and you'll see what happens to my prisoner if he attacks me."

"Your 'prisoner'?"

"Didn't I ask you to act like a prisoner sentenced to beheading who tries to escape from his jailer?"

Yes, that's what he told me the first time he ordered me to run away. I couldn't deny it, so I nodded.

"What would you do if you were really being held against your will somewhere? Would you not take advantage of any opportunity to escape or would you just sit by the prison door, chattering your teeth, waiting to be let in?"

I would run as far away as possible, of course. His last question was really stupid, but maybe it was my behavior that had been stupid. I hadn't really tried to do what he asked. It was just role-playing, but meant to prepare me for a very possible danger, given where he practiced his craft. So I shook my head piteously.

"Are you feeling better? Are you less cold?"

"Yes, thank you."

"Run away," he ordered mercilessly.

This time, I didn't hesitate for a moment. I left, taking my blanket and pushing a chair out of the way to slow him down. I grabbed his keys from the shelf near the exit and went to the garage and opened the sliding door. It contained a lot of miscellaneous stuff, the kind you pile up in these places, plus a big motorcycle and his car. Since I didn't know how to drive a motorcycle, I got into the car and just had time to start it when I saw him coming. He was standing in the driveway with his arms crossed over his chest and smiling at me. I pressed the gas pedal very lightly and the front bumper brushed his legs. I wasn't going to run over him! But he didn't move a muscle, that too cheerful bastard. What could I do now?

I lost sight of him for a moment. I wondered where he was and what evil trick he was up to. I looked around through the windows and in the mirrors, but he was invisible. Then the electric door closed. He must have pressed a button or used a remote control nearby. I was startled when I suddenly saw him standing next to me. He was mimicking a gun with his hand firing imaginary bullets at me and saying, "Bang! Bang!" He opened my car door. I didn't even think to lock it.

"Do you understand now why I never carry a gun?"

I didn't see what that had to do with my situation. I frowned and shook my head "no".

"Never use an instrument, gun or whatever, if you are not determined to use it to the end. As Cândido Rondon said, 'Die if you must, but never kill.' I know I wouldn't use my gun, even if I had one. So, what's the point of carrying one?"

I realized that there was no point in getting into a vehicle if all he had to do was block my escape path. "Don't use something you're not determined to use all the way," he had said.

"Could you hit your jailer or drive over him if he was trying to kill you?"

The thought of feeling a man's body under the wheels of my car gave me a strong sense of guilt and nausea. If I did that, I would have nightmares about it for the rest of my life. I was not at all sure of the answer to his question. Then I imagined him, my master, in mortal danger…

"To save me, perhaps not. But to rescue you, I would. I would!" I said with great passion in my heart and voice.

He went out the little side door and started in the direction of the house. Since I had gotten out of the car while he was talking to me and had taken a few steps towards him when he walked away, he probably thought I was following him. Why didn't I get back in the car and drive away? Maybe I was afraid he would come back and block my way. I don't know, but I ran off into the nearby woods.

Actually, it was little more than a long grove bordering a small stream. But I ran as fast as I could down the first path I found, hoping to save the soles of my bare feet a bit. Then I thought that if I stayed in that alley, it would be too easy to find me. So, I took a dive through the woods. My blanket was clinging to every branch and twig, and was strewn with twigs, thistles and burdocks. I had to pull it off a bushy and thorny shrub. I got to the creek and walked a good distance in it, hoping that, like in the detective movies, a pursuer would lose my trail. I thought to myself, "They must not have dogs." Then I realized that I had wandered in all directions without paying attention to where I was going. I was lost, shivering and panting. My feet were frozen. I sat down at the foot of a big tree to think: should I go back to my master's house or go anywhere to call a cab and… go where next? To a friend's house or my parents', to the police?

I wondered if I should accuse Master Mendel of abuse, as Celine had done. I was in danger of getting sick outside half naked in this weather. I was already not feeling well. But who was responsible: him or me? The first time, I waited foolishly on the stoop instead of seeking shelter. The second time, he had thought I was going home with him, right? At least, that's what it seemed to me. But instead of following him, I took off without warning him. And I had been stupid enough to run away on naked feet without looking where I was going.

I tried to retrace my steps. When you're moving through the woods, you don't judge distances well. Especially if you're running. I started walking and walking to find the trail, but I couldn't. I looked around for a way back and for a house, any house, but all I could see were trees, in front, behind, on one side and on the other. The branches scratched my skin and the rocks scraped my feet.

"You'd make a lousy fighter," he said. I was seriously beginning to believe him and to doubt my ability to survive and rescue him if anything happened to us. Maybe he wasn't wrong after all to leave me here while he went back to Cambodia. This idea hurt me more than all my little wounds put together or the cold that was making me colder and colder. I was ashamed of my inability to get out of this small wood. It shouldn't have been that hard.

I walked in all directions for a long time. Several hours probably. Then I wondered in which direction the trail went: east to west or north to south. I was pretty sure that the front door of my master's house faced south. I had gone the other way, so north. I started looking at the solar shift, the moss at the base of the trees, the kind of stuff they teach you at scout or summer camp when you're a kid. But it didn't help me much. To observe the movement of the sun, you have to stay still long enough and have a reference point. I stood still for several minutes and I still wasn't sure which way it was going. And it seemed to me that there was no moss anywhere or everywhere. Nothing really revealing.

Then I saw what looked like a trail. I went over to it and walked along it. In the wrong direction. I realized it when I got to the creek. I retraced my steps. It wasn't the trail I had taken to get away, but another one. And it led to an unknown dwelling. I came out of the woods anyway. It was windy. I wrapped myself better in my torn blanket, thinking that maybe I should knock on the door and ask to use the phone. Then I wandered off down a dirt road hoping to find my master's residence. The more I walked, the more I was convinced I was going the wrong way. Could I really have walked so many miles?

Then, finally, I was home! I felt both happy to finally be there and afraid of what my master's reaction would be. As I walked in, I heard him talking, probably on the phone. He must have been in the kitchen telling someone about his concern for me. He was asking for help in finding me. The panic in his voice! He was really worried.

When he caught sight of me, I saw the relief relax his face and light up his eyes. He seemed to start breathing again.

"He just got here. Forget about my request."

He hung up and came to me. He was tense as a bow and anger flared in his eyes. He slapped me. Hard! I put my hand on my cheek.

"Don't ever do that to me again! Do you understand me?"

For a moment, I was overcome with rebellion. I wanted to scream at him that it was all his fault, that he was the one who had told me to run away, and that he could consider himself lucky since I hadn't gone to the police or to the BDSMers association to file a complaint against him. But when I looked up at him, I understood that pain and relief were fighting in his mind, rearranging every feature of his face and the expression in his eyes.

I knelt before him and bowed my head.

"Sorry, Sir. I didn't mean to alarm you, but… I got lost."

As he remained silent, I glanced at him. He chuckled. But his laughter gradually became almost hysterical. It was as if all the nervous tension of the last few days, the fear of not being reunited with his children, the feeling of guilt towards them, the fear of having been the cause of their suffering and perhaps even of their death, and the anxiety at the idea of having risked his own life, the accusation of Celine, all that had just broken the locks holding back his anguish, and it was all pouring out now in that frenzied laugh.

I stood up and took him gently, tenderly in my arms. I held him close to me and rocked him as one comforts a toddler. We stayed hugged for a long time until I felt he had calmed down a bit. He put the back of his fingers against my forehead and cheek.

"You're boiling. If your temperature goes up, you'll need to take an antipyretic."

"What?!"

"A fever pill. I hope it's nothing serious."

"No, I just have a cold. I'm sure it's nothing."

"Since when are you a doctor?"

"I'm not, but I know myself. It wouldn't be the first time I've had a fever flare up and it would go down without anything serious happening."

He threw off my tattered blanket, led me to his bathtub, ran water hot enough to thaw me out, but not enough to make my fever worse, and told me to get in.

"Come bathe with me," I suggested with a smile after I got in.

As we soaked, he asked me what had possessed me to run away without warning like that.

"I could see that you were disappointed not to come with me. Does this have anything to do with it?" he asked.

"You said I was a so poor fighter that I'd never be able to save my own ass if I was in mortal danger. I wanted to prove to you that I wasn't as bad as you thought. That didn't work out so well, did it?"

"On the contrary, you showed me your willingness to try, even under adverse conditions. And you found your way back on your own, didn't you? People have gotten lost in this wood before and stayed there for days. It is not very wide, but it is long. You can walk without realizing how far you've come and still get lost. And of the two of us, if anyone made a mistake, it wasn't you. I should have put more specific boundaries on this role-playing."

"No, Sir. You were going home and I knew you thought I would follow you. I didn't. You had nothing to do with it. But I think I lost my mind at the thought of you abandoning me here when you might still be risking your life in Cambodia. I envied Celine and Arthur. I was sure that if you didn't want me there, it was because you didn't trust me. And this reportage that you gave me to do, I saw it as an occupation left to a child to entertain him and to prevent him from doing stupid things in the absence of his parent. I'm sorry for my reaction."

"Gabriel, you don't have a visa for Cambodia and Celine's is still valid. For you to get one, we'd have to wait at least ten days. Maybe Arthur could delay the appointment he made with the little survivors by a day or two, but not by almost two weeks. Do you understand?"

I hadn't thought of that. But I didn't doubt for a moment that Arthur would be pleased with the idea of preventing me from accompanying my master.

"Yes, Sir," I mumbled.

"Come on, Gaby, don't play the abused child."

I straightened up and tried to wipe the disappointment off my face, if not my mind.

"It's true that I don't have much faith in your unarmed gorilla skills. Not because you wouldn't try to save my life if it was necessary. You told me you'd do it in a very convincing tone of voice. I'm sure you wouldn't hesitate to protect me with your body if necessary. But you're not trained for this and you don't have Arthur's resources. He learned to fight in the army years ago and he'll be accompanied by some of his usual bullies, ex-military men like him, who will all be armed to the teeth. He's leaving with them in a few hours. They'll be there before me so they can meet me at the airport and make sure I'm safe, as soon as I arrive. I didn't ask him anything, but he insisted. He likes to play my guardian angel so much that it would've been useless to forbid him. Even if I'd threatened him with the worst, he would've come, I'm sure. But I've already ordered him to always ask my permission before doing anything that concerns me directly or indirectly and to keep me informed afterwards. So he told me about his plan to make sure I was safe while I was there. I can hardly blame him for looking after my safety, can I?"

"But if Arthur is following you around to protect you, why wasn't he with you the day you wanted to free the children?"

"First of all, he doesn't always come with me. He only comes when he thinks he has good reason to fear for my life. And if you remember, I was supposed to be on vacation with Celine. Secondly, he sometimes has to take care of his own business. While I was away, he had to finalize and participate in one of the most important activities of the year at his club. Especially since he gets a kick out of playing the king of the party in front of the rich and famous. Third, even if I'd called him when I got the information about the truck and those kids, he'd never have made it in time."

Of course, I had nothing against Arthur going out of his way to protect my master. If he had been just his bodyguard, I wouldn't have minded. But he was much more than that. And my new position with Zach Mendel was still not secure. After all, I had signed neither an employment nor a slavery contract yet. It was rather worrisome to know he was in the care of his old friend and lover. And if Celine ever regained her favor, she could go back to being his assistant and bye-bye, Gabriel!

While I was thinking about all this, my master continued to explain his reasons for keeping me away. He could have done like the dominators I had already spent a few days with and told me, "It's my decision, period!" But instead of imposing his will on me, he wanted me to understand the situation, and I was grateful for that.

"I wanted to hire a female translator, but we only found a male interpreter who knew Khmer and French. That's what convinced me to accept Celine's request; she has studied the basics of Khmer and I'm sure the girls will be much more comfortable talking to a woman than to any man. So we will prepare the questions and write them in the phonetic alphabet, then she will learn to pronounce them as best she can. She will wear an invisible earpiece so that I can correct her from a distance, help her answer if the children ask her questions, or point out other questions if necessary. One more person over there wouldn't help. That's why I'm asking you to stay here and write a story. And also because I like the idea of teaching you all the tricks of the trade and helping you improve. But first I need to know what you're capable of when you're doing everything from scratch without the assistance of an entire journalistic team, like at the daily paper where you worked. I've quizzed you a bit in the last few days and made you revise my article. But that's not enough; I need more insight into your talents. So I expect you to give it your all. Unless you'd rather be my enslaved cameraman, a silly little technician who just does what he's told without questioning, discussing, or even thinking."

It was stupid to have thought that he was rejecting me because he didn't trust me. Going with him there would have been worse than staying; I would have felt like the fifth wheel. Here, I could at least show him what I was worth as a journalist.

"I'd prefer you to teach me as much as possible, Sir. But I'd still like to learn how to shoot and fight so I can protect you if necessary. That way I can serve you better."

Maybe if I practiced all of this, my master would end up not needing Arthur on his dangerous overseas missions.

"Shooting? You mean with a gun?"

"You're not against self-defense, are you?"

"Of course not. But I couldn't bring myself to take a life."

He looked at me thoughtfully before continuing.

"I'm not a saint, Gabriel. I'm just a man who isn't comfortable with the idea of giving death, someone who is happy when he can, instead, save lives."

Yes, I understood him better. He probably would not have killed his father, even to avoid being stabbed by him. Without Karin's intervention, Zach would no longer be in this world. But he helped his sister and mother whenever necessary, risking his own life. His father was violent. Zach is a sadist, but he is peaceful. Sadism and violence are not motivated by the same impulses. Even when he had hired strangers to free the children, he had not carried a weapon. And if he was relieved that others had them, it was to ensure the kids' protection, not his own.

"So, are we good? You're going to stay here and work on a proper article."

"Yes, Sir. But what happens to me if you hate it?"

He remained silent for far too long not to jostle my psychological comfort. My throat tightened and I swallowed my saliva, suddenly too abundant.

"Put everything you have into it, and I'll like it."

And he added teasingly, "At least a little. And we'll see what to do next, what I should emphasize in your training."

The water was cold now. We got out of the bath and toweled each other off. I was kissing everything I scrubbed thinking, "He cared about me, he really cared about me!" as he stroked me with his towel and hands. I don't know what was on his mind, but he was smiling at me.

Then he became very serious and felt my forehead and cheeks again.

"You're still burning up! I'd better postpone my flight," he said.

"No! It's just the bathing heat that warmed me up. And anyway, I told you, I sometimes have fever flare-ups that disappear as suddenly as they appeared and without creating any problems. You'd be delaying your departure for nothing, I assure you."

"It wouldn't be right to leave you alone here if you were ill."

"Sir, please. Forget it. Everything will be back to normal before you even get to Cambodia."

To think I didn't want to be left alone here, and now I was begging him to go without me!

Fever or not, it didn't stop him from having fun with his submissive before his trip. He didn't whip me, but throughout the fuck, he described all the torture he would inflict on me when he returned if my report wasn't as good as he hoped.

"What are you trying to do here, Sir? Convince me to succeed or to screw up?"

We continued to have sex, but his descriptions of torment became frightening, much more frightening than exciting. For me, anyway, because he was more aroused than ever. I think the sight of the fear caused by his words contributed to his hard-on.

"So, are you going to give it your best shot or not?"

I answered as he bit me and I cummed.

"Yesssss!"

He could torment me in so many ways! But I would never leave him again, not even for all the riches in the world. I belonged to him now, more and more.

Chapter 17

While I was cooking breakfast for us the next day, he was finishing packing. Besides his journalistic equipment, he brought almost nothing. He seemed happier than worried about the trip. While he was still busy, I took the opportunity to apply an ice pack to my forehead, cheeks and neck to cool them down in case he felt them and my ever-present fever made him stay.

When I called him for dinner, he, of course, checked my temperature first. He seemed satisfied, so he would leave. Even though this was what I had wanted, I was disappointed. Then he put a finger under my chin to force me to look him in the face when I would have rather looked away.

"Not jealousy again, is it?"

I'd been dreaming all night that bad things were happening to him, and I perceived these nightmares as dark omens.

"No, I'm not. Just… worried."

He shook his head, as if to say, "What a baby you are!" Should I tell him about my bad dreams? I didn't; he would have blamed them on my apprehension when they were certainly caused by the fever. And what was the use of having cooled my face, if it was only to make him stay? But I have always been more inclined to trust my instincts than my logic. And they were giving me a glimpse of dark times ahead.

We had breakfast in almost complete silence.

"Call me sometime," I asked him as he hugged me before leaving.

No doubt the wives of sailors or soldiers felt the same way I did when their husbands went to sea or to war. To avoid ridicule, I restrained myself from telling him to be careful.

"Take care of yourself and this fever. You didn't fool me, you know, with your ice pack," he said with a mocking smile.

I felt myself blushing, like a child caught stealing cookies from the forbidden jar; which made him laugh, of course.

"Since you promised never to lie to me or hide anything from me, I'll have to punish you for that when I get back."

I knew I'd still be looking forward to his return.

"And if it gets worse, call me. I'll come home right away."

I nodded without much conviction.

"That's an order!" he added.

"I'll take care of myself, I promise, Sir, if you take care to stay safe and sound."

"I intend to," he said.

But his wrinkled forehead revealed that he was a little worried, too. Was he worried for me or for himself?

The cab honked and my master got in and left. He had left his car with me, because my old car was acting up and he knew that I would need a reliable vehicle to go and do my report. He didn't like parking his car at the airport anyway.

It hadn't been five minutes since he left me and I was already regretting not going with him. What a jerk I was!

My fever kept rising all day. I felt worse and worse. My breathing was becoming difficult. "Shit," I said to myself. I didn't want to force him to come home when he had probably just gotten there. And he was so excited to meet these kids! How could I have the heart to deprive him of that?

Even though I was feeling zombie-like, I swallowed two pills of… what did he call it again? Anti…something? Anyway, I took a couple of Advil and did an Internet search for article topics. But everything I found was boring, flat, political stuff. Maybe it was just me who couldn't see the point of anything anymore.

I felt nauseous. I went to vomit, then lay down with the intention of getting up in an hour. But I didn't wake up until I got a call from my master. He told me that the flight had gone well and that he was at his hotel.

"I have several other calls to make, but first I wanted to reassure you and, above all, to know how you were feeling."

I was happy to hear from him, but I just wanted to go back to sleep.

"I'm still having a bit of fever, but I took some pills and it's a little better," I lied.

I played it cool and said "yes" and "no" at the right times to everything he told me.

"You don't have to do this story or even write an article if you don't feel quite right, you know. We'll do this when I get back."

"Thanks for understanding, but I'm getting better and better. I should be able to produce something, if only I can find something worthwhile to write about."

"They're all over the place if you keep your eyes open. Go to bed now to give yourself a chance to fully recover."

"Yes, Sir. That's what I intend to do."

"Good night, little submissive! I can't wait to get home and punish you for your lies and sneaking around."

I heard a smile in his voice. What?! You don't believe me? I can tell when people are smiling at me on the phone, even if I can't see them.

I then wished him a good stay there and fruitful meetings before hanging up and going back to bed for the night.

When I woke up, if I could be called awake, I realized that I had to do something because my condition had only gotten worse. My breathing was extremely difficult, I was coughing, I had pain everywhere, but especially in my head, neck and chest, I was shivering and felt weak. Pneumonia? In any case, all the symptoms were there.

I wanted to get dressed and go to the clinic, but I was wobbly and dizzy. There was no way I was going to drive like this. I took some more pills, but an hour later I was no better. I decided to call my parents. No one was home on a Tuesday. I flagged Mom's cell phone number. I got her voicemail which said, "I'm in a meeting for an hour. Leave a message or call back later."

"Mom. I have a fever. My forehead is hot, and I don't feel well enough to drive. Could you take me… anywhere, as long as they give me an antibiotic or something to make me feel better? I think I have the beginnings of pneumonia."

I lay down and went back to sleep. When the phone rang, I couldn't find it. It was lost among the tangled blankets and my brain seemed to be the same: lost and tangled, I mean. My answering machine shipped before I managed to pick up. It was Mom. I called her back.

After making lame jokes linking my fever and sleeping with my butt naked, she said she'd come over even though she was pretty busy today.

"But you didn't give me your address, honey."

I hated it when she called me "honey", especially in public. I hoped no one in her office heard her affectionate words. At the restaurant, I always felt like everyone would think we were a mismatched couple: she, the cougar, and I, her gigolo.

"Eeeh…"

I couldn't remember the address; not the door number or the street name. I told her.

"I'll get it and call you back."

I hung up before the end of another one of her comments that only she thought was funny.

I searched everywhere for a piece of paper, a bill, a ticket, anything with the address on it. I found a binder in which all the financial documents were neatly arranged in order of suppliers, banks, or whatever, and date. "What a perfectionist!" I thought. As I uncovered several business contracts, I realized that I hadn't signed anything like this before, either for my assistant job or for my slavery. Did he still have doubts? The thought gave me a twinge of guilt.

But on an account statement, I found the address and texted it to my mother. She replied that she would be there in about half an hour. She rang the doorbell an hour later. These delays were her trademark. I had never seen her arrive on time once since I was born.

"Is he here?" she asked as she entered.

"No. He's in Cambodia."

"In Cambodia?! What is he doing there?"

She had come forward and began to tour the house with exclamations and admiring comments. Then she found on his beautiful upright piano two pictures of my master with his sister, one when they were children and the other probably taken last Christmas.

"Wow, he's really hot!"

I was tempted to tell her, "And you haven't seen anything yet; wait until you meet his friend Arthur." But I kept my mouth shut. My homosexuality had hardly been digested yet; I wasn't going to add to it if I could avoid it. She didn't take it too badly, but Dad… He sometimes asked me if I was still seeing that little bitch Annie with whom I sometimes had fun when we were kids. She was always playing tricks on me and we often bickered. She was my date at prom. But three years ago, she had to travel to Mexico and Peru. Since no one else could or would go with her, she offered to take me along on an all-expense paid trip. I accepted, of course. But Dad had built castles in the air for us and believed we were planning to move there. And now that I think about it, I wonder if it wasn't him who paid for my trip with Annie. But if there was a woman in the world I could fall in love with, it certainly wasn't her.

It's a good thing my master had locked up what he called the "playroom" before he left, because Mom was now trying to get in.

"What's in there?"

"A storage room. There's nothing but junk piled on top of each other. Anyway, do you think it's right to look around his house while he's away?"

"Isn't this your house too?"

"For such a short time. And I'd like the house to stay as it is. So would you please behave yourself, for once."

I finished my sentence with a coughing fit followed by a retching sound. She reached out and felt my forehead and burning cheeks.

"You'd better go to the emergency room at the hospital. Otherwise, you'll be waiting for hours to see a doctor."

"Ah-ah! That's a good one. Because you think it will be faster in the ER?" I coughed in a hoarse voice.

"Maybe not, but if there's an outbreak of something, they'll know and, if necessary, they'll run tests to make sure they get the right verdict."

"We say diagnosis, Mom, not verdict. This is not a court of law."

That was it. I had caught the zachomania, the mania for using the right word at the right time, and it's not treatable in a clinic.

As we drove to the hospital, I began to explain to her why my master, whom I called Zach, had gone to Cambodia. At the emergency room, after checking in at the front desk, we were kept waiting, as expected.

During this time, I continued to tell her everything through the mask that I had been forced to wear so as not to contaminate everyone with my cough. She responded with exclamations of horror about the treatment of the kidnapped children and admiring comments about my master. The only thing I didn't tell her was that he was the one who had asked for help from armed people to free the children.

"Who is this Arthur?"

"His long-time friend. He's also an ex-military man who has inherited a lot of money." I didn't tell her who the donor was. "And he's using it to protect his friend and to help him find the children."

My head hurt like hell and I coughed from time to time, but I managed to answer her not too stupidly.

"Have you met him before?"

"Yes. He's even more gorgeous than Zach."

She looked at me, speechless.

"How is it possible?"

After thinking for a moment, she added, "Is he gay, too?

"I've only seen him once at the restaurant, so I didn't ask. It's not exactly the first question you ask people after meeting them."

Did I know his sexual orientation? I had just pretended I didn't, but that was both true and false. Because I knew that Arthur really only loved one person: my master. But he would fuck anyone he liked: male or female. Technically, that made him a bisexual man.

"Do you have a picture?"

"Mooom! I'll remind you that I only saw him once at the restaurant. I certainly wasn't going to photograph him while he was eating."

"What's his last name?"

"Why do you want to know?"

"Just tell me?"

I didn't have enough energy or fight left to resist him. I just wanted to lie down on the benches and close my eyes.

"Arthur Dubois."

She took out her cell phone and started an Internet search. I had peace for at least a few minutes. But when she found him...!

"Holy wow! He is… breathtaking. Did you see him in princely clothes? I didn't know this activity: people who gather and dress up like in medieval times. There is even a guillotine!"

"No, I didn't see him at other places than the restaurant. This activity is called life-size role-playing or LARP for the regulars. By the way, the guillotine is an anachronism; I don't think it existed at that time. And I confess I'm not very interested in it. All I care about right now is having a bed to lie and sleep in."

Still, she showed me the picture of Arthur dressed as a medieval prince standing on the back of two horses at the same time. Oh, I understood her too well! Who wouldn't want to spend a night in the arms of someone like him? I was speechless, and it wasn't because of my pneumonia."

"Damn it!" she exclaimed a few minutes later.

"What now?"

"Do you know what he does for a living?"

"Ah. Yes, I do. Damn it," I said only to myself.

"No, and I don't want to know," I answered her.

"He owns the biggest BDSM club in the country. Do you have any idea what BDSM is?"

Despite my pain all over, I almost laughed out loud. My mom wasn't going to lecture me about it, was she? What could she possibly know about that anyway?

I had been silent too long; she concluded that I had no idea. And she leaned over to me to start explaining, while continuing to search the Web.

When she came across a picture of my master with Arthur kneeling at his feet, she choked up. I had to tap her on the back to help her breathe. She showed me the picture. Sublime! Simply sublime. I was almost drooling with yearning to see them together like that. They were dressed in their finest finery, and my master, with his most lordly, haughty air, did not even deign to give his lifelong slave a glance. Phew! I was very hot behind my mask. I felt my sex awaking and stirring. It must have been burning hotter than my forehead now.

I was still a little surprised. They didn't hang out together, not in that way. Arthur didn't want anyone to find out that he was someone's submissive. And my master preferred to protect his privacy. They must have had their picture taken without their knowledge. Or perhaps they felt they could indulge in it because it was part of a LARP where my master was the king and his friend played his manservant. Anyway, I would have to mention this picture to my master in case he wanted it removed from this website.

"Did you know about this?"

"Mom, please, not here."

"What do you mean 'not here'? Did you know about this?!"

"Mom! If you want an answer, you're gonna have to wait until we're alone. Okay?"

She looked at me like she didn't recognize me. I saw her blush for the first time in my life. She, whom nothing embarrasses, who always says everything openly, directly to people's faces, my very bold mother was troubled.

She sat upright and thoughtful on her uncomfortable plastic chair. She looked at everything and everyone but me.

"Mom?" I tried after a good twenty minutes of heavy silence.

"I need some time to… to come to terms with this."

"You're the truest, boldest woman I know, Mom. You'll get used to it."

"So, I'm right in thinking that you… you are… one of them."

I gave her a smile, pale no doubt as I felt worse and worse.

Then my name was called. I stood up and, in a daze, collapsed.

Chapter 18

I woke up on a stretcher bed. And I spent several days in the emergency room. The doctor who examined me for purpura and was preparing to do a spinal tap to confirm his prognosis saw the various wounds covering my body. He then asked me if someone had beaten me and who it was. He suggested that I file a complaint against my persecutor. And he added that he must report all documented cases of violence against a patient.

"Yes, I was hit, but there is nothing to report. I'll never tell you who did this to me and never press charges against that person because I consented to everything they did to me."

"How can anyone consent to such… brutality?!"

Fortunately, he and I were alone at the time, and even though I still had a horrible headache, a twinge in my neck, and nausea, I had recovered enough to try to explain.

"If I competed in combat sports and had come here covered in bruises and other injuries, would you have wanted to report my opponent?"

"Of course not."

"Why not?"

"It's not the same thing."

"Why not? They've fun hitting each other in the middle of the day and for you it's acceptable. But my boyfriend bites me or hits me during sex, and I love it, I ask for more, but to you it is unacceptable. In either case, everyone is consenting. So, what's wrong with my marks?"

He looks at me with a frown. He's obviously confused.

"I'm submissive and masochistic and my partner is dominant and sadistic. We're complementary and happy together. Did your training teach you how to treat people like us?"

I regularly stopped to cough and wondered if I would throw up in his face, but I had to explain.

"No, it didn't."

"It's a lack. I suggest that you seriously educate yourself about this. And if you want to have valid data, you can contact the local BDSMers association."

"BD what?"

"Do you know what the acronym BDSM stands for?"

"Eh, no, yes. I mean, I have an idea of… of…"

"Bondage, domination/submission, sadomasochism, does it mean anything to you?"

"Eh, yes. But I didn't know there was an association for that."

"If you give me your email address, I will forward it to the president, who will be able to send you more reliable information on this subject than what is usually found on the Web, be it on SM sites, on those of shrinks or in their DSM-5. Unfortunately, the latter always consider masochists as victims and sadists as heartless torturers. But few of them bother to interview the main people involved to find out what they think about it and what it really is. Or they rely only on the few who go to them because they feel guilty for being who they are. So shrinks have a distorted view of reality."

At this point, a stream of vomit erupted from my mouth. Fortunately, I had taken off my mask, otherwise I would have filled it and soiled my whole face. He helped me put my clothes back on and walk to the nearest bathroom, where I thought I might even evacuate my bowels, so powerful was the rush of vomit.

"I'll think about it," he concluded when I returned to my stretcher bed.

"So you don't really want to know the truth."

"It's just…"

"It's okay. Don't worry about anything. As long as you don't get me into trouble with your bullshit denunciations, I'd like nothing better than to forget about you, your ignorance and your indifference. Do we agree on that?"

"I don't think I have the right to not…"

"I'm sorry? Do you intend to talk about it or not?"

He looked at me, eyebrows furrowed, then away from my gaze.

"Um, no, no, I'll keep it to myself."

"Good. I'm counting on your discretion."

I wasn't sure he wouldn't rush to tell the authorities everything. But I would probably find out soon enough.

I was diagnosed with bacterial meningitis. It's rare to get it at my young age apparently, but it happens. And I was one of the lucky ones.

"We had a total of 15 cases in two weeks. Right now, there are three people with it in the ICU. Two of them didn't come fast enough and one of them might have died, the other one would certainly have had brain damages if the surgeon hadn't done a trepanning to decrease the intracranial pressure."

As for me, I was prescribed an antibiotic to get rid of the crap and I don't know what else for my blocked sinuses and irritated throat, which still made me sniffle and cough. But the specialist assured me that I would make a full recovery in a few days.

"Is it an epidemic?"

"No. Every year, we have a few cases. This year there have been more than usual, but still nothing exceptional for our population."

I asked if I shouldn't be vaccinated for all types of meningitis since I will soon be traveling around the world and meeting a lot of people, probably including aid workers and others who are in regular contact with the local population. I was told that this was possible, but that they needed to make sure I was fully recovered first. It was suggested that I make an appointment at a clinic as soon as I returned home. I had been vaccinated for all kinds of diseases when I went to Mexico and Peru with Annie, but not for meningitis unfortunately.

Mom came to the hospital as often as she could. Which I could have done without. I didn't need company, I needed to rest. But at least she had brought me pajamas, or rather pseudo-pajamas since they were fleece jogging pants and t-shirts. But they did the trick.

I had a urethral catheter installed so I wouldn't get up for two days after the spinal tap. I did my best not to imagine my master inserting it when they did it, because if I thought of him, I would have had a hard-on. They came to remove it the day after.

But I was surprised that I hadn't heard from him since my hospitalization. I had left my phone on my bedside cabinet to answer quickly, but not a single vibration. I was starting to get really worried when I finally got a call. But it was Arthur.

"He asked me to give you a call," he said by way of greeting.

"He" was our master, of course. And his comment must have meant that he wouldn't have called me if he hadn't been ordered to.

"What's wrong?!"

I was worried and you could hear it. Arthur took advantage of that. He left me hanging, the bastard! He was not only bi, but also sadomaso. And he exerted his sadism on me.

"He's just been arrested," he finally announced.

"What?!" I screamed.

"Don't scream in my ears," he barked.

I just waited for him to continue and explain, but he wouldn't say anything.

"I thought you were supposed to protect him," I yelled at him to get him to talk.

"Do you want me to hang up?"

I suspected that if our master had ordered him to call me, he had not told him what he should say or how long the conversation should last. And Arthur was quite capable of saying nothing, just for his own pleasure.

"No!" I yelled.

"I told you not to shout in my ears!"

"Stop it, Arthur. Why was he arrested?"

After a sigh and long seconds of silence, he explained the situation.

"They just want to ask him about the two guys who were carrying the children. People in the neighborhood reported seeing several men shooting at each other in the street and that the men in the truck appeared to be dead. The police are waiting to compare stories before deciding what to do."

"Compare stories?"

"Yes, the witnesses' story with that of Zach and his cronies, who were found despite their efforts to hide. But I don't think they have enough against him for a charge. After all, he wasn't armed and he didn't do anything other than film the scene. I'd get him a lawyer, just in case… Besides, I'm going to find out if he should be handed over to our consulate for extradition."

"Isn't the consul's assistant a suspect?"

"Investigators looked into this, but they found nothing concrete enough about her to risk causing a diplomatic incident. She said that since the children were Cambodian citizens, her duty was to turn them over to the police. But I understand that she'll still be closely monitored. If she isn't a complete idiot, she won't take unnecessary risks at this time. And if she's ever found to be actively involved in trafficking, either her diplomatic immunity will be lifted, and she'll be imprisoned or she'll be deported from Cambodia. Anyway, she'd no longer be able to cause harm."

I was only slightly more relieved. I hoped that my master would be released very soon.

"Thank you!" I told him despite my bad feelings.

He didn't answer. As if my thanks did not concern him or left him totally indifferent.

"Couldn't we sign a peace treaty, Arthur? I know you don't like me. But the reverse is also true. Wouldn't it be possible for us to…"

"Don't count on it!" he replied with rage in his voice before hanging up.

"Lord," I thought. My life would not be easy with this man between my master and me. But at least he was taking care of his friend. That was the most important thing to me. If I had to choose between leaving my master with Arthur and keeping him alive or losing him because he would be dead or imprisoned abroad for life, I would go with the first option.

I felt so helpless! This one discussion had been enough to exhaust me. So, after swallowing a mouthful and getting my antibiotic and other medication, I slept.

When I opened my eyes, a little girl was being carried to the next room. I didn't know what was wrong with her, but she looked unconscious and someone said she needed a ventilator. Her parents seemed almost desperate. I didn't envy them.

Several hours later, during the night shift, I heard the father screaming.

"I don't want a nigger touching my child!"

What? What! I couldn't believe it. Did people like that really live in my town? Could it be that there are some in the next room? Until now, I had never met any.

I learned the next morning that they were white supremacists. For them, everything that was not typically "Aryan" was to be banned. They had even submitted a document to the management of the institution stating that no member of the hospital team, be it a specialist, a doctor, a nurse or a paramedic, would participate in the curative treatment of their child if he or she was not officially identified as Caucasian. I thought that the principle of access to care, especially in emergency, was a priority and that a practitioner could not be rejected for sexist, racist or other discriminatory reasons! Would the hospital have accepted a waiver of these rules? If so, it must have been a first here.

I may not have been at my best yet, but I was recovering well enough to think "report!" But I didn't have my camera and my master had left with his. So, I called my mother to ask if she wouldn't mind coming here to get my key as soon as possible, then go get my camera from home.

"What are you going to do with it in the hospital?"

"Don't question it, Mom. I just need it."

She came over after work. I made her promise not to snoop around the house. She brought me my camera at breakfast time the next day. Fortunately for me, unfortunately for the child, she was still in the emergency room. I explained to Mom why I wanted to interview my next-room neighbors.

"What?! You have neo-Nazis in the next room!" she exclaimed.

I waved my hand and told her to keep her voice down.

"I don't know if they're neo-Nazis, but they're racist. And I can't believe it either. I didn't think I'd meet people like them here. And I'm amazed that they're trying to get their way."

"Gabriel, I was really saddened that you wanted another man to abuse you, but this is worse than anything. This is so...!"

"That has nothing to do with it, Mom!"

She at least had enough decency to look ashamed of what she had just said.

"The difference between them and us is that they want to get rid of or forcefully enslave anyone who is not Caucasian. I CHOSE to be Zach Mendel's slave," I whispered, so that only she could hear me, but with the emphasis on "chose".

"Come on, Honey! You can't be serious. You can't wish to become his slave."

I smiled at her.

"Mom, you don't know what you're talking about. Have you ever had a man like Zach in your bed, or have you ever had someone really willing to do your bidding kneeling at your feet?"

She looked at me, obviously stunned. She was a beautiful woman and, even at her age, she could have easily gotten either. But I couldn't imagine Dad taking on either of those roles or Mom going elsewhere to get it.

"I'm your mother! You're not going to ask me about my sexuality!" she reproached me, angry.

"I didn't. It was only rhetorical questions. You don't have to answer me. I just want you to question your prejudices. Because if you haven't experienced what you're talking about, it's nothing more than prejudice, right?"

Her gaze was lost in her thoughts. Was she imagining Arthur at her feet? Was she picturing herself flat on her stomach, bare-assed, in Zach's lap? What were her usual fantasies? I had never thought about it. What son wonders about his mother's erotic life? What parents really question their children's sexuality? As long as the evidence of a difference or a problem doesn't hit them hard, they don't usually think about it that much. I, for one, never imagined my parents in bed.

After Mom left, I wanted to go ask my neighbors about their racial choices and film them while they will answer. I had two good capacity memory cards. The one in my camera was blank, but the other had a few photos and a short video recorded on it. I could interview the girl's parents and the woman who had been called a nigger, but who didn't strike me as black or even mulatto. I would at least like to know her qualifications and if possible get a copy of the document prohibiting her from performing her job with this child.

But I had to delay my project, because Daddy was there. For the first time in my life, I saw in him who he really was: a serious and hard-working man, stuck in a banal and flat life. His worldview was as clear to him as my neighbors' was to them. And none of them questioned their values.

"How are you doing, my boy?"

"Not so bad. My health is improving. I'm in good hands."

"That's good! Monique told me that you fainted in the emergency room, that you had a high fever and that you had meningitis again."

Monique is my mother's name.

"What do you mean by 'again'?"

"Didn't we tell you? You had it when you were three or four years old. I don't know if it was exactly the same disease, but you were so sick that I was afraid to lose you. So much so that I threatened to sue the entire medical team if we didn't get you well soon and completely."

I smiled at this rare show of affection. My father, the introvert, was never very outgoing, unlike my mother. But he showed his feelings in action rather than words.

"Everyone does their best here. No need to threaten them," I assured him, with a teasing smile.

Had Mom told him about what she'd discovered about my sexuality? I doubted it, but…

"Your mother said something to me about the white supremacists in the next room."

"Yes. I was just about to ask them about it when you came in."

"Questioning them?! Are you sure that's a good idea?"

"For the common folk, maybe not, but for a journalist, it's a damn good idea, I think."

"Aren't you afraid of contaminating them? Not with your opinions, but with your meningitis."

"I've been told that unless I cough in people's faces or give them a deep, lingering kiss, I can't give them this disease. I'll wear my mask and I don't plan on kissing them," I joked.

"Your… friend, he's very… audacious. He doesn't hesitate to travel anywhere, even to the most dangerous places. And those are places where you have reasons to fear for your health and your life."

Typical. He didn't ask me if I was afraid to accompany my master abroad, but let me know that he thought we would be in danger there.

"Thank you, Dad."

"For what?"

"For worrying about me."

"Of course. I wish you'd live long enough to give me grandchildren. Then you'd know how much we feel for our offspring."

"Oh no! Not again," I thought. Would he ever understand?

"What if I never have any 'offspring', as you call it?"

When I saw how much that possibility pained him, I felt bad for him at the thought of depriving him of that joy. But I was not so sad enough to think of finding a wife.

We were silent for a while, then I asked him about his job. He launched into a vehement diatribe against "all the idiots" he encountered every day in the office, against their short-sighted planning and lack of vision and inspiration.

"I didn't manage to climb high enough in the hierarchy to have a real influence in the company and on all those people. And I doubt I'll be able to climb any higher. Sometimes I even feel like dropping everything and going on an RV adventure."

"Why don't you do that?"

"Your mother may look bold, but she's still very down to earth. I don't think I can convince her to come with me. And I don't see myself leaving her here alone."

"Have you discussed this with her?"

"Vaguely."

Which meant that he had talked about it as if it didn't concern him directly, to test the water, and the reaction hadn't been very positive."

"Why not tell her that this is your lifelong dream, that it's never left you, and that you'd be the happiest man in the world if she agreed to go with you? But first calculate how much it'd cost you to travel this way. If it's feasible, maybe she'll want to follow you. Anyway, it's worth a try, right?"

He didn't have time to answer; then we heard screams. The girl's mother was shouting insults at someone. A woman in a nurse's outfit came out of the child's room crying. She looked vaguely Hispanic.

I shook my head, disheartened at the thought of living in a world where no one could achieve their dreams, or be themselves without risking ostracism or losing what was most important to them. I almost wanted to scream back.

"I have to leave. I still have work to do at the office tonight."

"You always do. You've been a slave to this company your whole life. If only you'd gotten some happiness out of it."

I realized there are all kinds of slavery in this crazy world and not all of them are as exciting as mine.

"This job made me happy in the beginning when I was part of the new generation. Then I could take on challenges and move up the ladder. I felt I was making a difference, and I dreamed of doing much more. But somewhere along the line I got stuck in a rut and got trapped. Now the company is stagnant, and I'm stuck at my level. It's the same exhausting routine day after day."

"If you're not going on an adventure, maybe you should try to find a new, more challenging job elsewhere or start your own small business."

"I've thought about all of this before. Going into business at my age would be chaining myself to a ball and chain for maybe the rest of my life, with no guarantee that it wouldn't sink me financially. And another job would be both challenging and stressful at first, but wouldn't I find myself back at the same point in two or three years? But I'll think about it some more. Now I really need to get going."

Dad kissed me on the forehead before he left. His "I'll think about it some more" reminded me of the technician's, "I'll think about it". Often, people who are afraid of change pretend they will consider it, and sometimes they do, but then don't act on it. How does it feel to know that your life has been a fruitless routine and that you will not have offspring? I didn't know, but Dad looked unhappy, and I felt sorry for him.

Chapter 19

A few minutes after Dad left, I got up, pulled out my badge from the local newspaper. Even though I didn't work there anymore, it was still in my camera bag, and it was probably this paper that would buy my story if it was going to be published anyway. Then I went to interview my roommate. She was a beautiful woman, with big turquoise eyes and Venetian blonde hair. A few freckles marked the top of her cheekbones. She was slim and dressed in a tight dress that showed off her lovely curves. "Rich Caucasian," I thought. Was it possible that someone close to her was a member of the Deliverance Club? Maybe I could ask Arthur.

I introduced myself to her, explained why I wanted to talk to her, and asked her permission to shoot a video of our discussion. She was hesitant. I assured her that she could better communicate her views and beliefs to the public if they were widely reported in the newspapers. She agreed and allowed me to record.

When I started filming, I asked her to introduce herself, say what city she was from, say why she was in the hospital, and mention that she had allowed me to record. Andrea Hansen did so with the grace of high nobility. I asked her about her origins and those of her husband, Michel Meyer, about their daughter Arlet and her health, and, of course, about their beliefs. She answered with such conviction that, had I not been totally against racism, I could have agreed with her.

I then took some pictures of her daughter before going to interview the nurse who had come out of the room crying. She was understandably outraged by the mother's rejection.

I also asked her to introduce herself and describe what had just happened.

Her name was Alice Sossoyan. Contrary to what I had assumed, she was not Hispanic, but Native American. She told me that she was a Mohawk half-breed, but that she had not lived on the Native reservation with her family for years.

"Hadn't you been told about a document signed by the parents forbidding any staff who were not fully Caucasian from approaching their daughter?"

"No. I had just started my shift. And the child seemed to be in respiratory distress. So I rushed to see if there was anything I could do to help her as normal procedure requires. But there's nothing normal these days."

"And how is the child doing?"

"Neither better nor worse than since she arrived. She was born at twenty-six weeks of pregnancy and suffers from chronic lung failure. A simple flu could lead to her death. So, she ends up in the hospital at the slightest sign of respiratory distress."

"Were you able to help her?"

"No, her mother was dozing, but when she opened her eye, she started yelling at me like crazy. So, I went out. But fortunately, soon after, the little girl's vital signs seemed to have improved and they have now stabilized."

I asked her if we could look at the refusal of care form together. I had filmed the woman while she was answering me and when she demanded to see the document in question, of which I took a close-up photo of the two pages.

"It's revolting! There are no totally pure-bred people, if there ever were," she said.

"I understand your reaction. And you are right, there is no real basis for the concept of racial purity. But do you know if their document is legally valid?"

"I have no idea. This is the first time I've experienced such ostracism here. I thought that our laws forbade any form of discrimination based on race. And I also thought that it was the duty of the health care personnel to intervene if the patient's life was in danger. But I have to tell you that I'm not sure of anything anymore."

I thought I would have to check whether a staff member or certain categories of staff can be prohibited from treating a patient. But I remembered that Jehovah's Witnesses had once objected to the blood transfusion of their sick child, and that the child had died as a result. Yet it seemed to me that for a doctor to accept a refusal of treatment when a person's life is in danger was to go against the Hippocratic oath, which says that one must treat every patient without discrimination of any kind.

All I had to do was ask the father about his origins, his ideology and the famous segregationist document. I feared a rebuff from him, but I had already gathered quite a bit of data on this unusual situation.

I went back to bed and was thinking about what I had learned and what I had yet to discover when I fell into a sleep from which I was awakened by the phone.

"He's in the hospital," said Arthur without any preamble.

"Who's that?"

"Zach, of course."

"But… why?"

"He has meningitis. I had to get the lawyer and the embassy involved to convince the police to rush him to the hospital. They said that it was just a little fever and it'd pass, that it wasn't worth getting him out of jail for so little. I think they thought he was acting and they were afraid he'd run away. But there is an armed guard in front of the door of his room in the hospital."

I shuddered at the thought that I was the cause of his condition and that he might not have been treated or not quickly enough.

"And how is he? Do the doctors at this hospital know their stuff?"

"They told me that they had more cases of meningitis than we did, so they were specialists in this disease and that Zach would be back on his feet in no time."

Although the thought of him weak and feverish in a hospital bed broke my heart, I breathed a sigh of relief. At least he would be well taken care of.

"It's my fault," I admitted.

"What? How could his condition be your fault?"

"I'm in the hospital. I have meningitis. I had it before he left, but I didn't know it. I thought I had the flu."

"How can you confuse these two diseases?!"

"My throat and sinuses were sore, my nose was running and I was coughing. Apparently, a lot of people think it's the flu at first."

"You must have had other symptoms; you should have told him. If Zach doesn't make a full recovery, you'll pay for it!"

I didn't say anything because if they didn't get him to the hospital soon enough and he was left with some after-effects, I'd be the one blaming myself, and anything Arthur could do to me would seem trivial compared to what would have happened because of me.

"You should've talked to him about it," Arthur insisted.

"Yes, you're right. But if he had thought he was seriously ill, he'd have postponed his trip. That's what he told me. And I didn't want to force him to stay for a simple flu. He seemed so happy to be able to meet these children. I hope he gets better soon and makes a full recovery, because if he doesn't, I don't know what…"

My voice broke on the last words. As the silence stretched, I came to my senses.

"Arthur, can I ask you a favor?" I tried.

"What?! After what you just said, you dare to ask me for help!"

"All right, fine. Forget about it."

But his curiosity got the better of him.

"What is this all about?"

"I'd like you to find out if two people or people close to them are members of your club. The man's name is Michel Meyer and his wife is Andrea Hansen. Their little girl's name is Arlet."

I also gave him their address.

"Who are they? Why do you need to know this?"

I explained everything to him, but asked him to swear not to tell our master.

"I want to surprise him about my report."

"I promised Zach that I'd never lie to him or hide anything important from him. So, if he doesn't ask me about it, I'll keep my mouth shut, otherwise…"

I could understand that. But I was hoping that he would give me a chance to talk to him about it myself.

"So, do you think you can find out what I'm asking you?"

"I can do better than that. I can dig down and find out who they really are and who they have family, friends, business or social ties with. You say they are white supremacists. They may have pledged allegiance to the Ku Klux Klan, Blood and Honor, or one of the neo-Nazi groups called White Power or or Prison Bound."

I had only heard of the infamous KKK; I knew nothing about these other cliques.

"Thank you!"

"I said I could, not that I would. Besides, if I find something, that info will be mine and I'd rather give it to Zach than you."

If he told my master about this, he'd be forced to explain everything else. Damn it!

"Yes, but he's the one who demanded that I do this story, so…"

He was silent for so long that I wondered if he had hung up.

"I don't have access to my files from here. I'll see if I can still do something, but I can't promise you anything."

I hesitated to thank him again.

"Please keep me posted on our master's health."

"I have no choice: it's what he demands."

As friendly as ever, he hung up without even saying goodbye. But I still had a small chance to learn more about my neighbors. And I was left with a happy note: my master had not kissed him, or else he too would suffer from meningitis. And nothing very exciting would happen between them while he was in the hospital.

I was told that I would be kept for another day for observation, but that I was much better and could go home tomorrow. I was told that I would have to get the vaccinations I had requested as an outpatient.

In the early evening, several victims of a pile-up were taken to the emergency room. Most were then transferred to the intensive care unit, which was now overflowing with patients. I thought I could have also investigated the lack of space on these two wards for multiple serious accidents, but that would have been much more complicated and would have required investigation of other similar previous situations. Instead, I stuck with my racist neighbors.

Since I had to go out tomorrow, I only had a few hours left to interview Mr. Meyer here if he came to see his daughter. If not, I would have to find his phone number and make an appointment with him at his home or elsewhere.

He came by late in the evening. He must have been a busy man, like Dad. At first he was reluctant to answer me and blamed me for "taking advantage of his absence" to question his wife. And he was afraid that I would infect Arlet, who was already very sick.

"I was told that unless I gave a prolonged kiss or spit on someone, I could not infect anyone. And with this mask… Anyway, your daughter is on a respirator and I don't intend to go near her."

He looked at me like I was a big mosquito buzzing around him. So, I gave him my little speech about the importance of spreading his version of the "good news". He finally talked to me. But as I was walking back to my bed, Arlet began to grumble and fuss. The line pattern on her surveillance monitor made unusual spikes and then began to flatten out. The only person on duty at the time was

Alice, the nurse who wasn't white enough for the girl's parents. She wanted to intervene, but Mr. Meyer raised his hand to prevent her from approaching.

"She's going to die," she said, visibly worried as she looked alternately at the father, the daughter and her monitor.

She had already called the CPR team, who soon arrived. After checking the girl for throat blockages, they tried to revive her with their bare hands while someone prepared the defibrillator. Then they used it once, but it didn't work. After injecting her with something, they tried two more times with the device, but it didn't work. The team doctor declared Arlet dead at twenty-three forty-two.

I filmed everything. No one forbade me to do so since they were too busy trying to save her life. I returned to my room after the announcement of the death. I was shaken, but I still had the presence of mind to change the precious memory card of my SLR, because it must have been getting pretty full. I put it in the pocket of my pseudopyjamas before inserting my other card. I intended to go to bed with my phone nearby, but there was a lot of commotion in the next room. I peeked in and recorded a brief video with my iPhone while Alice explained that Monsieur Meyer had forbidden her to come near.

"That little girl could have lived if that racist had let me do my job!"

She was very upset and angry with Arlet's father. I realized that she was not the only one. Even though we had to witness deaths every day here, everyone was still feverish and talking at the same time. Then a relative calm gradually returned. Mr. Meyer collected his daughter's few possessions while her body was being unplugged for transport to the morgue. Everyone then went about their business. I took a few pictures of the next room, which was already empty, and of the nursing staff discussing and signing documents at the guardhouse before going to bed.

Once I was in bed, I began to think that my hospital room or my master's room could have been as empty as Arlet's if we had not been treated in time and properly. I wondered how my master was doing. I really wish I had received a call from Arthur at that time. Of course, the phone didn't vibrate. And I fell asleep. But my night was stirred by nightmares filled with children who were victims of mankind's madness.

Chapter 20

The next morning at breakfast, I heard that Mr. Meyer had filed a complaint because, according to him, his daughter had not been rescued fast enough. "What? What! Not fast enough!" I thought. He was the one who had forbidden the nurse to take care of his daughter. And she had already initiated the Code Blue anyway. In my opinion, the resuscitation unit could not have responded any faster. Even though it was explained to him that the ICU was full, that the entire team was busy saving other lives and had done their best to meet the needs of all the patients, he said that there should have been more than one person on duty at all times.

After lunch, I went to ask Alice what she thought about this accusation.

"All this is just to get me kicked out of the hospital. He only wants white people here," she replied, bitterly.

But I didn't disagree. Without trying to sound paranoid, I think that was probably what Mr. Meyer was trying to do. If he was really part of a local racist group, he must have taken every opportunity to harm anyone who wasn't white. However, it all seemed futile to me, because the hospital certainly wouldn't start hiring based on a Nazi ideology.

But was he right to think that there should have been more staff on duty?

"There were four of us. But Christine and Denise had gone to the cafeteria together and Francis was in the bathroom. Okay, Denise should've eaten at the nurse station or gone to eat after Christine, and Francis could surely have waited for them to come back to… If there was a lapse, it was not my fault. The emergency happened at the wrong time, that's all. Anyway, if that racist had let me intervene, maybe I could've done something to save his daughter. Maybe not, but we'll never know now."

I was told that I had to leave by lunchtime. They didn't specify if I had to do it before or after lunch, but I decided to leave before. I called Mom to ask if she could drive me home, since I had come with her. Otherwise, I'd have to take a cab home.

"Of course, darling. How about we have lunch together at the restaurant?"

I agreed. I wanted to pay her for the services she had rendered me.

While I was picking up what little I had in ICU, a member of the hospital administration staff came by and asked for the memory card from my camera.

"I don't think you have the right to ask me that," I said. "Or if you can, I don't have to give it to you."

"You shot videos of hospital activities without management's permission."

"Everyone I filmed gave me permission to do so, and I don't believe I recorded anything that would harm this facility. So why would I give you what is mine?"

He was very insistent and even threatened to call security guards to force me to give him my card.

"I'd like to see that!" I replied, shocked.

"You won't give it to me?"

"No, I won't. If you take my memory card away from me by force, I could charge you with assault and theft and have you jailed. Are you prepared to face arrest and trial?"

He didn't seem so sure about his intervention anymore. But someone in management must have really regretted agreeing to sign Mr. Meyer's denial of care document. In any case, they didn't want any publicity about it. That made me want to publish everything even more.

"You should come and talk to the director."

"I don't have the time for that. I'm expected elsewhere."

I finished collecting all my belongings and walked around the man, who hadn't even bothered to introduce himself. He grabbed my arm to hold me back. I looked at his hand resting on me, wondering how my master would react to such unauthorized physical contact. I could see him arching an eyebrow in thought, as if he couldn't believe his eyes that someone would dare try to hold him against his will. Then, I imagined his cold gaze slowly rising from the other man's hand to his eyes and staring at him, his expression clearly saying, "Let me go or else…"

In my case, I didn't have to force the guy to remove his hand. He could tell by the look on my face that I didn't like it at all. And he walked away. But after some thought, I pulled my memory card out of its slot in my camera and gave it to him, but told him he would have to give it back to me intact. When I gave it to him, I was almost certain that I would be able to leave the hospital without any trouble, and he would be none the wiser, because the card only contained a couple of old photos of me and my buddies at a boozy party and a video of a transvestite friend named Sasha, where he was playing the drag queen, singing and dancing in an eccentric way, to our enthusiastic applause and drunken laughter. I imagined with an amused smile what those who would see these images would think.

I then left to wait for my mother at the place she had indicated a few blocks away. She wanted to avoid going into the hospital parking lot, as it was difficult and expensive to get in.

I was still smiling at the thought of people looking at what was on my card when I got into Mom's car.

"What's so funny?"

I told her.

"And won't your friend Sasha be embarrassed to have been seen by them in that gear and that… state?"

"Do you think so? I can't wait to tell him. He'll choke from laughing so hard. Besides, it would be better if no one laughed at him; he's a black belt in I don't know what martial art, so it would be risky to tell him that he looked ridiculous."

She was probably thinking about all the fundamental differences between her world view, mine and Sasha's. She had certainly never thought that Sasha would be the kind to have a black belt. She certainly never thought that a drag queen could be a black belt in karate. Anyway, she remained silent and thoughtful while I started to smile again, imagining the flamboyant Sacha, apparently so fragile, hitting his aggressor on all his most sensitive parts and giving the coup de grace by knocking out his assailant with his glittering purse always full of blunt objects.

"Thank you for giving me more of your time, Mom? I appreciate it."

"It's the least I can do, my darling. I can't imagine not helping you when you could have been dying."

"You're exaggerating a little here."

"What do you know? What's the delay between the right time to intervene and waiting too long when you have meningitis? You could've been sicker than you thought and reached the hospital too late."

"The 'right time to intervene'? Mr. Meyer's lawyer will probably use this concept to get Alice fired."

"Alice?"

"Yes, the Native American nurse I told you about."

"Oh. He's going to try to convince everyone that it's her fault, not his. But you have a video of him keeping her away from his child, right?"

"Yeah."

"You should send that footage to Alice. She can give it to her lawyer to prove that she couldn't have done a better job than she did."

"You're right. I'll send it to her along with the copy of the care denial document."

"It's amazing that people still have such prejudices these days."

"But Mom, earlier, weren't you uncomfortable with the idea that Sasha would feel embarrassed to be seen dancing in his best clothes?"

"It's not the same!" she answered, scandalized by my criticism.

"Yes? How? In Mr. Meyer's case, it's a question of race, in your case, of sexual orientation. Sasha didn't choose to sit on the border between masculinity and femininity. It's what his genes and other biological or social factors made him. And I find him magnificent in all his eccentricity! I'm proud that he isn't ashamed to be who he is."

My throat tightened around the last words. Sasha was my friend and the idea that zie would be hurt revolted me. Even if it was my mother who hurt zim, I'd make her regret it!

My phone buzzed in my pocket. It was my master!

"Hello, my little slave!" he said so sweetly that I hiccupped with painful pleasure, so worried I had been for his health.

"Ah, my God! I'm so relieved to hear you, dear master."

My last words made my mother's head spin.

"Where are you? Are you alone?"

"I'm in Mom's car. We're going to have lunch together."

"Does she know about us?"

"Yes, but not Dad."

"Why not?"

"Because Mom guessed and didn't tell Dad. And I didn't really have a chance to tell him."

"He knows," my mother retorted.

"What?!"

"When I told him your new boyfriend's name, he looked him up on the Internet too and… he found the same pictures I did," Mom explained.

"Sir, apparently Dad found out too. But I don't know how he reacted."

"It's better that way anyway. I don't like to hide, at least not from my submissive's relatives. Arthur can try to fool the entire universe about his switch nature, it won't last forever."

"Speaking of which, there's a picture of him kneeling at your feet on the web, did you know that?"

"Yes. Arthur wanted to have it removed, I forbade him to do so to punish him for having hidden from me some of his unsavory associates."

"'Unsavory'?"

"Even reprehensible."

I was only half surprised. I found everything about Arthur quite inflammatory, much more so than about my master, who, apart from his sadism, or perhaps even because of it, was a good man.

"You seem to be doing better, Sir."

"Better and better. And you, I guess, if you're coming home, it means you're cured."

"Yes. And I can't wait to tell you about my story."

"Arthur slipped me a note. That sounds great. I knew I could count on you. Even in the hospital!"

"That dirty son of a...! I asked him not to tell you so I could surprise you myself."

"Did you?"

"Did you ask him about my report?"

"Not really. When he told me about the information you asked him about some people you met at the hospital, I wanted to know a little bit more about it, and then he gave me an idea of the situation."

A very good idea, I was convinced.

"I'm disappointed. I so wish I'd told you everything myself."

"I can offer you a chance to get back at Arthur when we are home," he suggested.

"I don't care about Arthur! It was having a chance to tell you, to surprise you and please you that mattered to me."

My throat tightened and my voice whined at the end of my sentence.

"Poor little slave!"

I wondered what I should think of his answer, especially since what I heard in his tone was a mixture of compassion and mockery. But I didn't see what was so funny about Arthur betraying me.

"Arthur knew it would hurt me and he did it for that reason, the bastard!"

"Arthur can be just as sadistic as he is masochistic. Especially towards someone he's jealous of. But tell yourself that if he reacts that way to your presence, it's because he understands that you're with me for good. He suffers from it and he envies you."

"Is that true, Master? Do you want to keep me?" I asked, smiling stupidly.

"Of course, silly! By the way, remind me to get you to sign your two contracts when I get back."

Yes!

"I'll do that, Sir," I replied, trying not to sound too excited. "When do you get out of the hospital?"

"Tomorrow. But I have to meet the kids. Arthur rescheduled our appointment. I'm so excited!"

Oh yes, he couldn't wait to see them. You could hear it in his throaty and tense voice. What a generous man! I would have loved to be there to witness his happiness.

"But they haven't found the young woman and her baby yet," he added with such sadness that I wished I could have hugged him.

"With all the people looking for them, they'll surely find out where they are."

"Alive or dead? And in what condition?"

"Ah, Master! If I believed in God, I'd pray for them to be found soon."

"I pray, even if I'm not a believer."

After a few seconds of silence, I added, "And you won't go back to prison, will you?"

"No, probably not. None of my accomplices talked about the money I gave them. So, the police don't have anything conclusive against me. To them, I'm just a well-informed journalist who was doing a story and rescued some kids. And they've already kept me under surveillance longer than prescribed."

"I'm relieved about that. But I hope you don't get arrested on your way home?"

"What?! Why would I be?"

I told him about the nurse who wanted me to report him for domestic violence. And I told him what I asked the nurse to keep his mouth shut.

"Well said. It's inevitable. At some point you'll be hospitalized again for something unrelated to our relationship, and they'll still want you to report me for the same reasons. Hopefully, you'll run into someone in the BDSM community who knows what it's all about, or someone you can convince again not to write a report. But if not, we'll do what we need to do at that time to fix this problem, if it still arises. I must leave you now. Give my regards to your parents. I look forward to seeing you again and giving you a hard time, little slave!"

And he hung up. I was relieved to know he was safe.

At the diner, I gave Mom an idea of the discussion, especially regarding the woman and her baby.

"It's infinitely sad!" she said.

"Yes. When he talks to me about it, I feel he's about to cry."

"Really? But they say he's very…"

"Mom, he wouldn't hurt a fly. His sexual orientation, his need to dominate and his sadism aren't all that he is. And he wouldn't touch me if I didn't want him to."

"Are you sure?"

"Absolutely! Stop imagining horrible things. Read about it. Get informed, please. If you want to understand me, don't just believe what you hear and see on porn sites."

"I'm not that stupid!" she said.

"It's not stupidity, it's ignorance. Even in our community, there are people who don't understand much about it. So, it's not surprising that you can't tell the difference."

Once at the restaurant, we looked at the menu. The waitress came over and we ordered.

"Your father…"

She had stopped in the middle of her sentences, as if to gather her wits. I was afraid of what she would say next.

"... seems less troubled than I am."

"Really?"

"Yes. That you were gay bothered him more than knowing you were a masochist. Sometimes it's hard for me to understand him."

I thought I did. The thing that bothered Dad most was the idea of never being a grandfather.

"He even talked to me recently about traveling around the world in a motorhome. He told me that as if it was someone else's project, not his. But I could see how excited he was about the possibility of such an adventure," she added.

"I think it's a great idea."

"What?! Not you too! But what would happen to us on the road? We're not that rich. Just the motorhome would cost a small fortune."

"Not if you buy it second-hand. There are people who think they are ready to go for good, and they try it out, then they realize it's not for them, and they sell all their camping gear and camper van for a low price. You should do your budgeting to see if it's feasible. If it isn't, well, too bad! I'm sure Dad would understand. If it is, why not? Wouldn't it be wonderful to go on an adventure with him? It'd be like a second honeymoon, wouldn't it?"

She looked at me as if I were a Martian, all green with antennae and suckers on my fingertips.

"I don't think so. I have obligations here and…"

She looked like she was on the verge of tears. I couldn't understand what was so confusing to her, who was usually so enthusiastic and daring, about traveling with Dad.

Then I thought about it. What if her "obligations" weren't just business, what if she had a lover? Could I venture to ask her? She had already taken offense because I had slipped in a word about her sex life, how would she react if I accused her of cheating on Dad? I took a chance.

"Is your work that important to you or do you have other reasons for not wanting to leave?"

She looked at me with a bewildered expression. Then she blushed. She must have understood that I had guessed.

"My relationship with your father is not what it once was. He has devoted far more of his time to his work than to me over the years. Almost from the beginning, it seems. I need… to feel loved, passionately. Do you understand?"

"Very well," I said, smiling and holding her gaze.

"But if this adventure was an opportunity to revive your relationship and rekindle the flame. Wouldn't that be worth a try?"

"Is it possible to resurrect a love? I'm not sure. And by leaving, I'd lose… everything."

I felt sorry for Dad. If Mom left him, it would destroy him, I was sure. Even though he spent too much time at work, he still loved her, his "darling little wife", as he sometimes called her.

"Shouldn't you explain to him how you feel? Doesn't he at least deserve you to be honest with him?"

She sank into her thoughts for a long moment before nodding positively. Me, I wondered what would come of this situation. Would my father go on a solo adventure? The thought seemed very sad, even a little scary. Maybe I would be traveling with my master soon, but I wouldn't be alone. If anything happened to me, he would be there to help me and vice versa. We would take care of each other.

"He deserves to be loved passionately too," I concluded sadly.

She nodded again. But there was nothing cheerful about her face.

Chapter 21

After our meal at the restaurant, Mom left me at my master's house, MY house. I took the car keys and went out to buy something to cook several meals, mostly vegetarian, since my master preferred them, which could be easily reheated when he returned. That way, we could occupy ourselves with more… stimulating activities.

When I got home after my shopping, I first made an appointment at a clinic to get my vaccines and at the passport office to renew mine urgently. For the necessary photos, I would ask my master to get them for me. I checked on the web to see if I needed a visa for Brazil and what documents would be needed if I did. They could all be filled out online. I asked for a police certificate, just in case it was required. But since I wasn't sure if Brazil would be my next destination, that was as far as I could go at this point. For travel insurance, I didn't know which one was preferable for a globetrotter. I would have liked to be ready to leave when my master came back home, but I decided to wait for him to finalize the preparations. I was sure he would tell me if I was missing anything and suggest me a good insurance company.

So I started writing my article and its summary and editing it for my story. I revised my text three times, including once after printing. I don't know if you're like me, but I always find mistakes once my text is on paper, no matter how many times I reread it on my computer screen. Then I sent the summary with a few pictures to the local TV station and the daily newspaper with my resume attached.

Since I had been interning and working for the paper for a few months, I thought I had a better chance of getting the editor's attention. He called me back about an hour later. He was eager to hear the whole story. But he wanted to see the finished product before he made a decision. I declined.

"Either you accept with what you already have, or I'll send the story to a larger, 'more serious newspaper'," I said, because I knew he was vain and I wanted to sting his pride.

He promised me much more than I expected to get the scoop. I told him I couldn't offer it to him because I wanted to hand over the broadcasting part to the local TV station, but I would give him priority: no one would get the news before him and he would get it quickly if he accepted my deal. I knew it wasn't customary for the newspaper to do this, but I was certain of the value of my story. To think that if I hadn't been ordered to produce something right away by my master, I probably wouldn't have done anything with this interesting story. I would have just recovered from my meningitis and sore throat, bored in my hospital bed.

The TV station called me back much less quickly. As soon as I started talking, I activated my voice recording software to keep track of what I would be told. The news editor was less enthusiastic than the newspaper editor, probably because he didn't know me. But it was enough for me to mention my master's name for him to perk up his metaphorical ear. But he wanted to see everything before signing an agreement.

"I'll send you everything if you guarantee not to use anything until you receive my written consent."

He hesitated, but finally agreed. I was thrilled! But I didn't know what my master would say, especially since his name had been the key to opening doors for me. And wasn't I supposed to show him all this first? But since his return was delayed, I couldn't risk waiting and having my scoop stolen. So I sent what I had to the newspaper's managing editor and the TV station's news editor, telling them I might have more information to bring to them later. I signed and sent back the TV station's agreement as soon as I received it.

I also called the hospital and asked to speak to Alice. I was told that HR had put her on indefinite paid leave. "Shit! Fucking bastards!" I thought.

"Could you give me her phone number?"

"I can't. It's confidential."

"Then, would you be so kind as to give her mine quickly? I have enough to completely clear her of this ridiculous accusation."

There was a long silence on the line.

"Okay, I'll do it. Give it to me."

I did so and Alice called me back almost immediately. I asked for her email address and forwarded the most compelling images to her. Sending her everything by email would probably not have worked; the file was too large. I offered to post her a USB key of the most striking moments of her meeting with Arlet's parents if she gave me her home address. She thanked me profusely. I told her to listen to the news and read the newspaper. I added that she would soon have something to look forward to.

As soon as I hung up, I recorded everything about her on a key, which I put in a padded envelope. I took the trouble to mail it to her by express mail immediately. I had just gotten home when my phone rang. It was Arthur.

"Zach is out of the hospital and he's no longer and won't go back in jail. Anyway, the maximum time for custody without evidence is seventy-two hours, and with the days under supervision in the hospital, they had exceeded that limit. They wanted his version of the facts; he gave it to them verbally and in writing. And he has already signed his statement. So, they have no reason to hold him any longer."

"Is he okay?"

"Yes. He met some of the little survivors. There were some of HIS children among them. If you'd seen his eyes when he recognized them. They were playing together in a psychiatric ward. But they were having fun like any other kids that age. Zach cried with relief at their pleasure."

"You bastard!" I thought. He certainly knew how much I would have loved to witness this and my master's relief and happiness; he was twisting the knife. But I was still very happy for my master and for the children.

"The woman and her baby, were they found?"

"No. It's a real mystery. The person who bought them must be someone important who has the means to leave no trace of their whereabouts and of the transaction."

"Isn't it possible that the baby was adopted by honest people?"

"I doubt it. The mother and the child disappeared at the same time. But who knows? That's the fairy tale I'm trying to sell to Zach without much success."

"What about the other information I asked you about?"

"The Meyers have ties to several racist groups, especially Blood and Honor, but they aren't among their leaders. And they aren't members of my club, but one of their very close relatives is. I'm sure he wouldn't like us to reveal that information. I heard that the Meyers are suing the hospital?"

"Yes. Mr. Meyer claims that the staff didn't intervene quickly enough to save his daughter's life. But he was the one who forbade Alice, the nurse on duty, to go near her. I sent pictures of this to her. They could be used in her defense and could prevent her from being permanently fired."

He grunted.

"What?"

"I hope her life won't be threatened."

"Ah, Arty, this is not an American thriller. Everybody isn't trying to kill everyone all the time," I commented.

"I forbid you, you hear me, I forbid you to call me Arty! Only Zach can use that nickname, and even then! He only does it when he's angry with me. So don't ever do it again!"

He was really mad. I was enjoying it! I felt like repeating, "Arty Arty Arty..." but I didn't. After all, Arty was the bastard, not me.

"She was temporarily kicked out," I added, referring to Alice.

"That way, if anything happens to her, the hospital's management will be able to claim that what happened to her had nothing to do with the hospital. Do you know who runs this institution? No? I do. One of them is very close to an old friend of mine, a leader of the Bandidos."

"The biker gang?!"

"That's right. You're not laughing so hard now, are you?"

Indeed!

"Is it because of this friend that our master doesn't want to remove the famous photo from the web?"

He hung up. Ah, ah! I was exultant. But I would have liked to know when they were all going to come home; he wouldn't tell me anyway. And I was also going to ask him to look up the name of Mr. Meyer's lawyer, and now I couldn't count on him for that either. So I resigned myself to finding the Meyer's phone number and asking them for the name of their lawyer, preferably before my article came out, because I doubted their goodwill when they read it. It's not easy to find out confidential information about people who want to keep their privacy. But from one call to another, I finally found it. And guess what? It was a friend of an old friend of Arthur's who pointed him out to me.

Mr. Meyer wasn't home and his wife didn't know if she should give me the name of their lawyer.

"Anyway, as soon as your action is made public, everyone will know it, right? So why not now?"

She gave it to me! I called the newspaper and the TV station and told them to add that information to what I had already given them.

I cooked the rest of the day. And when I listened to the evening news, I was surprised not to see my story on it.

The next morning, after breakfast, I went to buy the daily paper. Nothing. There was nothing there either! This time I was more than surprised, I was suspicious. What had happened that they didn't mention it anywhere?

My master phoned soon afterwards and told me that he was due to arrive the next evening. He had just left to catch his flight. Was he in a cab or was Arthur driving?

"I'm glad, Sir. I missed you very much."

"I miss you too, little slave. But maybe you won't be so excited about my return when I punish you for your lies and cover-ups."

Oops! Of course, he hadn't forgotten.

"I… I'm still looking forward to seeing you again, Master. But speaking of secrets… Since I didn't want to be robbed of my prime and your return was delayed, I sent my article and reportage to our city's daily newspaper and TV station. They bought them from me, but nothing has appeared anywhere yet. It's suspicious, don't you think? I'm not used to freelancing, but you are, so I wanted to ask your opinion."

He was silent for so long that I thought the line had been cut.

"Master, are you still there?"

"Yes, I was thinking. Yes, this is not normal. It can't be the work of racist groups, but it wouldn't serve their cause to cover it up. And I doubt that the hospital management is behind this, even though they would probably prefer it not to get out. I'll find out. I'll let you know as soon as I know more. What good are you doing waiting for me?"

I told him about my appointment for my vaccinations and passport renewal, about my efforts to learn Portuguese in case we go to Brazil, about the meals I'd prepared so I'd have more free time to spend with him when he came back, and about the fact that I'd jerked off thinking about him three times: two yesterday and another when I woke up this morning.

"I forbid you to touch yourself until I get back. Or rather, I have a better idea. You'll masturbate three times today and four times tomorrow before I'm home. Make sure you bring yourself to the verge of orgasm; you know that moment when your balls want to hide in your belly and your cock jerks as if you're going to eject all your sauce the next second. But you shouldn't cum. Do you hear me? If you come without my permission…"

Oh, I've always hated these vague threats. They often make me feel worse than what would really be done to me if I disobeyed.

"Yes, Master. I will obey. But if I imagine you punishing me, I think I'm going to have a hard time holding back. I'll be extremely frantic when you return."

"Mmm! I like that you're 'extremely frantic'," he said with a smile in his voice.

I groaned, as my cock was already hardening. I mentioned it to him.

"Are you dressed?"

"Yes, jeans with no underwear, t-shirt, bare feet."

"Get your dick out of your pants. Balls too. And masturbate. Tell me what you're thinking while you're doing it. But remember, you're not allowed to cum. And this time doesn't count as the three hand jobs you'll have to give yourself today."

I had to pull my jeans down a bit to get my balls out. The cool air enveloping my hot genitals made me realize what I was about to do at the request of my absent master. I was sitting alone in the living room. I leaned back comfortably and started to masturbate. I was not used to describing my fantasies while stroking myself. It was a bit of a disturbing experience, especially at first.

"You… you tie me naked to the big tree outside."

"To the oak tree?"

"Y… yes, I think so. It's cold and the wind makes me shiver. But you walk around me with a fierce look on your face, blaming me for my lies. You tell me how much you dislike being deceived. Then… you go back home. I wonder if you're going to leave me alone outside for long, but you don't stay away for more than a few minutes. You come back with a cane."

"Why a cane?"

Why indeed? It's typical of a sadistic dom to ask such a question.

"I find that's what hurts the most and that's what scares me the most."

"Okay. Good choice, then. Go on."

"You order me to confess all my faults, then demand my punishment. You want me to tell you how many strokes you'll give me. I… I never know how many… How many is not enough and how many would be too many?"

"Hummm! It won't be too much. Don't worry about it," he said.

And he laughed wickedly. I loved it!

"I tell you all my sins and humbly beg you to punish me with twenty strokes?"

"Only twenty?" asked the damn sadist with a disappointed tone of voice.

I was moaning now. Ah, he had managed to get me very hard with a laugh and some cruel words.

"How many?" he insisted harshly.

I whimpered a little louder. I felt feverish and truly ashamed that I had kept from him… what? I wasn't even calling back anymore and I didn't care. It was wrong to cheat on him, period.

"Thir… thirty-five, Master."

I let out another groan that sounded like a sob. I was afraid now that I would be hanging from that oak tree when he returned.

"Go on," he growled.

I wondered where he was right now and if he was masturbating and if his penis was as hard as mine. And knowing he was turned on by what I was saying turned me on more. I revealed these thoughts to him.

"How are you tied to the oak tree? Tied frontally against the trunk or with your wrists tied to a branch above your head?"

"Almost… almost hanging from the branch. Only my big toes touch the ground. You turn me around so that I'm back to you. And you walk behind me growling like a big predator, like you do sometimes when you're really excited."

He growled. I knew it wasn't just in response to what I'd just said or to titillate me. I was sure he was hard now too.

"You step back to gain momentum and slam me with the full force of your arm and even your shoulder on my butt. I scream. The pain is so sharp that it spreads to my back and thighs, but my belly swells and my cock stiffens. I'm very afraid now that I won't be able to take the thirty-five strokes if the others are as cruel as the first. I don't know what state I'll be in after all that."

"The rest will be hard, very hard, slave. You want to pay your debt so I'll forgive you, not that I'll feel sorry for you, don't you?" he asked me in a hoarse voice.

I shivered. I had a hard-on!

"No, Master. No, Master. Please be… ruthless," I grumbled.

Aaaah! It was as if my own words had sent an electric shock through my dick.

"Sir! I have to stop or I'll cum."

"Touch your nipples over your shirt. Brush them gently, but effectively."

He knew how sensitive my nipples were. He also knew that I found light caresses through a thin fabric, like the one of my shirt, even crazier. I obeyed him, but was afraid that these touches were enough to induce my orgasm. But they only kept me longer on the verge of orgasm.

"Ah, Master. This is… unbearable!"

"Is this a way of asking me to have pity on you?"

No! Yes. I can't take it anymore! Pity!

"Answer, slave!" he ordered me harshly.

"Yes, Master."

"I thought you were refusing my clemency."

My head was spinning as if I were very drunk. I was drunk, of him, of his madness, of mine.

"Aaaah!"

"What do you think? What do you prefer: that I allow you to stop or not?"

"I… I want… your will be done, Master. Forgive… my weakness."

"Come on, stroke your pretty little buttons. Are they spiky, sharp, like I like them?"

"Yes!"

"I'm going to hang up…, but you're going to keep… touching yourself for five minutes… You'll tell me… when I get back… how it was… And don't cheat… don't cum… Do you understand?"

He was panting. And it made me mad with pleasure to hear him and imagine his eyes rolling up with an orgasm I gave him. He is so beautiful, so desirable at the peak of his orgasm! It was as if I was transported to another dimension where carnal ecstasy was considered the supreme virtue.

He hung up the phone. I looked at the clock and continued as he had instructed. Images of everything he would do to me on his return swirled in my head. My half-opened mouth and cock were drooling. My balls couldn't go any further up in their pouch; they were sore. I felt like I was suffocating. Could I last five minutes?

Only four more… only three more minutes… only two more… only one more minute. I took my hands off my nipples. My heart was pounding and my breathing was just a rattle. A shiver ran up the back and top of my head. I had really been on the verge of cumming.

Had he come after I hung up? Was that why he had cut off the call so abruptly, so he could finish masturbating at his leisure?

How can you live with someone like him and not lose your mind with desire, pleasure and… pain?

Chapter 22

My master called me back a little later.

"Did you manage to go on for five minutes without ejaculating?"

"Hardly."

He laughed.

"You have to wank off seven more times before I return. Do them the same way. You only stop jerking off when you can't hold it any longer, then you stroke your nipples for five minutes through your shirt."

I groaned at the thought; which made him laugh again.

"You'll obey me as well as you can, won't you, little slave?"

"Yes, Master."

"Good. And about your report, I know who is behind its disappearance."

This way of stretching the suspense always annoyed me.

"Who?" I finally asked, since he didn't continue.

"You won't like it?"

I didn't care who it was, I could only hate the idea of my scoops being smothered.

"It's Arthur."

Ah! I was ranting. I wanted to throw my phone across the room. My hand clenched on the device and shook. The fucking bastard, the son of a bitch, the...!

"I'm going to kill him, this jealous jerk!"

"Don't scream in my ear, Gaby!"

Oh! Arthur said he only called him Arty when he was angry. Did that diminutive mean something?

"Sorry, Master, but…"

I felt like crying.

"I really put my heart into this story. I wanted to surprise you, to make you proud of me. And it was my first, my very first solo, done without the help of a whole journalistic team."

Tears were sliding down my cheeks now. I sniffled.

"Poor little mistreated slave!" he said in a tone that was half sympathetic and half mocking.

"Don't laugh at me. This is really not the time," I said dryly.

I was surprised that I had dared to speak to him that way. It wasn't very slave-like.

"Gaby, be careful, don't forget who I am and who you are," he said in a voice that was a little hoarse, but very soft, like a caress.

"From the beginning, every time he calls me, he makes it clear that he is only doing it because you make him. He hates me, that's obvious. And I hate him too now."

"I know."

"I didn't want it. Like him, I'd rather be the one and only in your eyes, but I was willing to do anything to make him my friend, even to give him pleasure, even… to be his bondage brother, if that was your wish. He once hit me with rage, but I didn't blame him; I understood him. I'm not like him, I am not vindictive. But now…"

"He says he only did it to help Mrs. Sossoyan, the nurse accused of not intervening in time."

"It's just an excuse to piss me off! I told him that I'd sent her the proof that she'd done the right thing."

"He hadn't told me that. It's good of you to have thought of helping her. By the way, Arthur got her readmitted; she's back to work, but they're keeping her out of the ER for now. Hospital management would like nothing better, of course, than to see this case tumble into non-existence."

"Did Mr. Meyer agree not to talk about it?"

"I believe Arthur told you that the Meyers had a close relative who was a member of his club. He threatened to expose them if they persisted in suing the hospital and the nurse."

Of course he did. How stupid I could be! It was obvious that even though he had signed a confidentiality agreement, it didn't stop Arthur from using what he knew to blackmail people into doing what he wanted. One day, maybe one of them will have enough of him, and Arty will kick himself for all his intimidation.

Why did the thought of Arthur's death make me feel so bad? Was it only because I knew my master would be so upset?

"If you want, I'll let you take your revenge the next time we meet," he offered.

"No, Sir. I repeat, I am not vindictive. If I were to act that way, I wouldn't do it out of a sense of justice, but out of revenge. If you believe that he deserves to be punished, I leave it to you to decide his punishment."

"Yet you said you wanted to kill him."

"It was just a way I expressed my rage and disappointment. But I'm still angry with him and very disappointed."

"I ordered Arthur to revert. Forbidding Mr. Meyer from suing the hospital and Ms. Sossoyan was fine, although I don't like the method. But preventing the public from being informed about the denial of care document is another matter. So, call the newspaper and TV station back and tell them that you know about the bribe they were offered, and if they don't want it to be known that they accepted it, to publish the news as you gave it to them. Tell them, however, that Mr. Meyer has withdrawn his threat of trial and that it should be mentioned in the article and the story. If you have a problem with any of them, I'll try to get them to agree to it."

"Thank you, Master."

"And, Gabriel, I'm sure this is an excellent piece. I didn't doubt it, but I still wanted to see what you were capable of, especially under the pressure of a limited production time. I also wanted to give you the opportunity to see that you had what it took to be my assistant and even more, much more. And you did it, not only in that short time, but while you were sick. I am really proud of you."

I was smiling from ear to ear now. Apparently, he had more faith in me than I did."

"I can't wait to show you everything."

"I'd also like to tell you that I approve of your decision regarding Arty. You could have used the opportunity I offered you to give him a hard time, but you prefer justice to revenge; that's fine."

"He'd like that too much!"

He laughed.

"Smart! Well, I must leave you now. See you tomorrow, little slave. And remember, seven times by the time I get back. And no ejaculation."

I winced.

"How could I forget that, Master?"

"See you tomorrow!" he said, hanging up without giving me time to say bye.

I immediately made the calls he had suggested. The people involved wanted to know who had told me about a bribe, obviously claiming that it was not true, that it was not what had caused them to forget the whole story.

"I have the proof of what I am saying. So, publish my story as soon as possible if you don't want people to know you can be bought."

They both replied that they would see what they could do. But my story was on the evening news and my article in the daily paper the next morning. I was still unhappy that it didn't go well. Despite what I had told my master about my accommodating nature, I was still very angry with Arthur.

~.~.~

I had jerked off seven times since the day before, if I counted my morning masturbation, the one I did on the phone, the three others he had asked me to do yesterday and the two already done today. I was not used to such a sexual regime. So I had a hard time not coming the last time. At the end, I said to myself, "Never mind! He's a sadist after all. He'll be glad to have one more excuse to punish me." And I almost convinced myself of this enough to continue until I ejaculated. Then I thought, "Yes, but, I'm a submissive and his slave. I'm supposed to obey him as best I can, right?" Despite this, I needed all my willpower and courage to stop.

I had to keep my mind occupied between this orgasm deprivation and the next. So I went to the room where the fitness equipment was located and used all these devices. I was thinking that if we were to go to Brazil together or anywhere else, I was going to have to walk around with a big bag on my back, lots of other useful things on my belt, in all my pockets and in my hands; I might not be able to keep up with him in my current physical shape, which my stay in the hospital hadn't improved.

When I started to feel really tired, I succeeded to go on by imagining my master whipping me to stimulate my ardor. But the only things I stimulated were my desire and my cock. I soon found myself sweating and my dick on fire. So I figured at this point I might as well go ahead and count this as the fulfillment of my third prescription of the day. So I went to lie down. I didn't have to jerk off for very long before I felt like my master had described the edge of orgasm. Then I gently rubbed my nipples over my shirt.

I've always preferred that way to rubbing over my bare nipples. It feels like the fabric is contributing to the light caress. As you touch the cloth, you wiggle it a bit and it then exquisitely grazes all over the top and around the spiky nipple's tip.

But my shirt was soaked with my sweat and the cotton no longer had the usual magical effect. So, I got up, went to the bathroom to towel off, then picked out a shirt thinned by wear that I kept almost solely for this purpose. Its slightly stiff fabric is even more effective than a t-shirt. I put it on without bothering to button it up and went back to lying down. Then I resumed fondling my nipples, counting the minutes: five… four… three… two… one. Phew! I was going to go crazy if my master didn't come home soon.

I then took a cool shower, hoping to calm down. But I put my old shirt back on. What a mistake! My nipples were still a little prickly and with every movement the fabric scratched the tip. It was enough to make me lose my mind. I ended up as hard as before the shower. So, I took another one, but only running cold water. It soon became almost icy. I still twirled under the spray until I lost my hard-on. Then I got out, dried off, and put on a pair of loose-fitting elastic waist pants with no underwear. What a mistake! My cock, not completely limp, was rubbing against the rough cloth, making it harden again! So, I undressed completely. But the air against my naked flesh awakened memories of bondage, of submission to other dominators and to Master Mendel. With all these obscene thoughts, my cock, of course, became fully erect again.

I didn't know what to do. Was it better to masturbate for the fourth and final time immediately or postpone it in case the desire aroused me in all its intensity before my master's arrival? If I didn't wait, I wouldn't be allowed to touch myself afterwards. Maybe it was better not to have the option of doing it anymore since I was not allowed to ejaculate anyway. To solve my dilemma, I was tempted to call my master and beg him to let me cum. But I was sure he would refuse. It would only serve to give him a negative image of me: that of a submissive who is not able to control himself and is not very eager to please him, a slave unable to obey. So, I gave it up.

I waited as long as I could, which wasn't very long, before I started to masturbate again. I had turned on the TV to see if my report was still on. But I didn't see anything like that since it wasn't news time. However, there was a film about a journalist who had been taken prisoner by the Taliban and had been questioned under torture for days. Normally, I would have watched brief excerpts of these interrogations, completely appalled at the idea of such cruelty. I am not attracted to real abuse. BDSM is not that way; it is subtle domination, voluntary submission, enjoyment of one's power over another, even to the point of pain and humiliation. But in my physical and mind states, the more the journalist was mistreated, the more I got a hard-on. It was not like me to react in this way!

I turned off the TV and masturbated with unusual ardor, almost forgetting to stop before I came. Almost… The five minutes of touching my nipples was a living hell. I was screaming pleas, pleas for mercy to the living room ceiling. I even cried in frustration. Sometimes pleasure is more of a torment than the worst torment. And my master, in all his sadism, knew this all too well.

Afterwards, I kept myself busy as best I could during the hours of waiting before his return. I rummaged through his library looking for a French/Portuguese dictionary. There was one that showed the pronunciation in the international alphabet. I had already read the traveler's guide from cover to cover, which gave typical phrases like, "Where is the bathroom?" But I found a second, more comprehensive one, which I flipped through, imagining what I would need to say once I got there. There was also a Portuguese grammar book, which was helpful in understanding the syntax. I even listened to Brazilians on the web saying typical sentences and repeated them as best I could.

When I got tired of studying this language, I looked on the Internet at sites about the flora and fauna of Brazil, especially the Amazon. There were plants and animals of rare beauty. But everything was exceptional, even the "monstrosity" of some of the beasts. I hoped that my master knew where we were going and that it would not be in the mouth of a jaguar or thousands of carnivorous ants. I wasn't sure if we were going to travel anywhere soon and if it were there! But what the hell? No knowledge is superfluous and the ones I had just acquired would be very useful to me some day.

I also read my master's camera and camcorder guides, hoping to understand them enough to use them well if necessary. But it was difficult to do this without the cameras themselves, which my master had brought with him.

Chapter 23

He arrived late at night. When I heard a car pull up in the yard, I ran over and opened the door. After dropping his bag, he immediately kissed me frantically. Then he took my head in his hands and looked at me as if he had just discovered a treasure.

"Ah, my little Tarzan. I am so happy to have you back!"

He looked very happy to be home, indeed. And I felt like my lungs were opening wide with relief. Only in his bubble could I breathe well. But it only lasted a few minutes; Arthur was with him. When he entered, my master turned to him and said,

"Get naked and go lie on your back on the living room rug. We will join you in a few seconds."

He had ordered all this in a very authoritative, almost harsh tone. But when he turned back to me, he was smiling. I wanted to kiss him again. I couldn't resist it and snuggled up to him. He let me wrap my arms around him and he began to gently stroke my hair and back. Mmm! He smelled so good! He smelled like HIM!

"We have to punish Arty for his jealousy. Even though you said you didn't want to do it, I expect you to cooperate. Okay?" he asked me in a whisper.

"Whatever you wish, Master."

I would have thrown myself off the roof if he had demanded it at that moment, I had missed him so much; so, punishing Arty was the lesser evil, I thought to myself, smiling inwardly.

We went to the living room where Arthur was waiting, lying on the rug, his legs sticking out. He looked miserable. And I didn't know if it was from displeasing his master, from hurting my feelings, from being stupidly jealous, or from having to take his punishment in my presence for all this. But I didn't care.

"Take off your pants," my master ordered me.

I obeyed without hesitation. Then he stood behind me.

"Touch your nipples."

I knew that since he had not asked me to take off my shirt, I had to do it over it. I started to brush against them. When my cock started to get hard, he took hold of it and stroked it with such skill and delectable subtlety that I was on the verge of orgasm within seconds.

"Mmm! You are really sensitive tonight," he noticed.

"I can't take it anymore, Sir!" I complained.

"But Arthur isn't the only one to whom I owe a punishment, right?"

"Yes, Master," I admitted, almost as unhappy as Arthur.

"So, you'll wait a little longer," he said, releasing my cock.

"Aaaah!" I said, already suffering from the prolonged wait.

He laughed. It seemed to me that he was the most beautiful sadist the Earth had ever borne. And to me, his laughter was like a chime announcing happiness, not just his, but mine.

He approached Arthur and crouched down beside him. He asked him if he knew why he was being punished.

"Yes, Master. I have displeased you by interfering with Gabriel's reporting."

"Right. And it's not that you didn't have good intentions in doing so, but because you also had very bad ones."

The master reached out and twisted one of Arthur's nipples, who closed her eyes and let out a hiss of pain that made my cock twitch as if it were the one being tortured.

"You know I don't like my slaves to be jealous of each other, right? You even reacted badly to the idea of my meeting Flávio while I was in Brazil. I hate it when you behave that way. You should be happy that I can find pleasure or happiness, whatever the source or the way, right?"

"Flávio! He's way too… You love him way too much!" replied Arthur huffily.

"Too, what? Handsome? Intelligent? Submissive? Masochistic? He is all of these things and more!"

"I hate him!" spat Arthur, like a dangerous snake ejecting its venom.

I would have liked to see the face of this Flávio. What my master said about him was almost enough to make me hate him too.

"Arty! Stop it!"

Arthur began to cry.

"Why am I always the last one you ask to serve you?"

"You cheated me, you deserved to be punished. You're a masochist, and my encounters with other subs hurt you far more than anything I could inflict on you," Master Mendel rightly said.

Arthur let out a heart-wrenching moan. Tears welled up in the corners of his eyes.

"I'm sorry, I'm so sorry," he said in the voice of a wounded child.

If I hadn't been so angry at him for his jealousy and treachery, I would have felt sad for him.

He and my master looked at each other for a long time. I envied them. There was a magical current traveling between them that I felt excluded from.

My master straightened up and came back to stand behind me, very close, so close that his very hard dick was making a dent in the top of my buttocks. I knew I wasn't the cause of this stiffness and I suffered from it. I should have been lying there on the floor instead of Arthur, because I was perhaps the more jealous of the two of them at the moment.

"Caress yourself again," my master ordered.

I did so as he grabbed my cock and stroked it. It hardened less quickly. My grief at not being the only man in his life, at not even being his favorite, was dampening my pleasure. But he was far too skilled; my member couldn't stay flaccid for long, not after two days of orgasm deprivation. I would have liked to cum, just to be done with Arthur's punishment and to be alone with him.

"Tell me how those two days of waiting went," he demanded, keeping me on the verge of orgasm.

I described to him the hell of not being able to cum, especially during my final masturbation. I told him I thought that being a sadist, he would find pleasure in punishing me if I disobeyed him. He didn't react well to this idea.

"What?! You think that's submission? Doing the exact opposite of what is required of you to be punished? I call it topping from the bottom. You get pleasure from me and you try to force me to be severe, which will excite you even more. I want real submission. And if you fail in REALLY trying to bend to my will, I will be disappointed in your failure, of course, but satisfied with your effort. I will punish you for not finding a way to obey me, but I will be happy that you really want to please me. If you want to fill me with happiness, if you want me to love you more than anything else, offer yourself to me totally, and forget about the others and everything else, think only of submitting yourself and serving me well."

I didn't know if he was talking to me or to Arthur. Maybe it was to both of us. Without ceasing to caress myself, I knelt down, spread my thighs and bent down to kiss Arthur on the mouth. My master followed me in my movement; he did not let me go for a moment. Arthur responded tenderly to my kiss. My tears mingled with his. We both wanted the same man, but neither of us could have him all to ourselves.

I stood up.

"When you cum, make sure your semen drenches his chest and face. Then rub it on his skin so that it soaks in."

"Yes, Master."

I understood the symbolism of the gesture. For Arthur, it must have meant that I was taking possession of him, more surely and completely than if I penetrated him. It must have been humiliating to become the property of a slave. But how could he continue to be haughty, dismissive of me after that?

When I came, I positioned myself so I could ejaculate on Arthur as requested. He had closed his eyes. I then spread my cum all over him, on his face and chest, while stroking and kissing him. He was so beautiful! His tears, his sadness and pain at being held at a distance despite his deep, faithful and impetuous love made him even more beautiful to me.

I imagined myself in his place: knowing that my master was living with a stranger and sometimes meeting other men, all of them beautiful, and me, waiting for a call, hoping for anything if it came from him, from my beloved… Wouldn't I take every opportunity to approach him? Wouldn't I also be ready to bring us together by any means?

I whispered in his ear, "Arthur, if I could, I'd offer him to you."

He looked at me first with incomprehension in his eyes, then anger, as if he didn't believe in my sincerity, then his expression softened.

"Easy to say. But if you loved him as much as I do, you wouldn't be able to do it," he huffed.

I felt him on the verge of sobbing. He turned his head away, perhaps to hide the intensity of his emotion from me.

Our master walked around the rug to face Arthur, who was lying uncomfortably on the hard floor, and then knelt down at shoulder height. He smiled at us one after the other and leaned over and kissed Arthur while I was still stroking him. Then he slid his mouth over Arthur's chest and bit him so viciously that Arthur wriggled like a suffocating fish on the beach, but gritted his teeth, no doubt to silence his pain. But he couldn't hold it in for long: he let out a horrible scream, like a whinny. By this gesture, I knew, our master regained possession of him, but it was also Arthur's reward for having forgotten his jealousy for a moment. When our master raised his head, I saw the blood-red pattern of his teeth on Arthur's chest.

"Go get some ointment from the bathroom cabinet," he said to me.

I went there without hurrying. I wanted to give them some time alone. When I came back, my master was whispering affectionate words in Arthur's ear, while squeezing his balls. The combination of the cruelty of the gesture and the tenderness of his words excited me to the point where I thought I would cum without being touched, without being looked at, almost without even existing for them.

As I applied the ointment to the jagged wound, I saw Arthur's whole body become covered with goose bumps. He must have been lost somewhere between pleasure and pain, between happiness and distress at the thought of losing the man he had always loved.

I watched the scene between master and slave, as we witness a miracle. I didn't know if I should have left, leaving them alone together in their secret universe, or stayed and tried to add a touch of my own madness.

"Go fetch us a drink," my master ordered.

I got up and found a bottle of port. I poured us each a small glass.

When I returned, Arthur was huddled with my master on the couch. I sat down beside them and handed them their wine.

"Thank you, sweet submissive."

I sensed he was thanking me for more than just the port. I could have been angry with Arthur, blaming him for his actions, insulting him, but I had kissed him. I had said the only words that came to my mind to show him my understanding. I was proud of myself. And I think my master was too.

We stayed in each other's arms, sipping our wine in silence.

"Arthur told me that you saw YOUR children?"

"Yes, a few," he replied, smiling broadly.

The memory lit up his face.

"Were you able to talk to them?"

"I didn't dare. But Celine did. And very well, too. Remind me to write her a good comment for that. If we could've found the woman and her baby, I'd really be in heaven," he finished in a choked voice.

I hugged him a little tighter on his right, while Arthur did the same on his left.

"Consider that the world is a better and happier place because of you, Master," Arthur said.

I shuddered, for those were almost the exact words I was about to say.

"That's right, Sir. Without you…," I began.

"Now, be quiet, little submissives. Both of you. I know you want to comfort me. I appreciate it."

I took his empty glass from him and put it on the table between the armchair and the sofa. He leaned back more comfortably and closed his eyes. He seemed to be enjoying the moment. Arthur looked at him smiling lovingly. I was happy. More than I had ever been.

Chapter 24

Arthur left us alone for a short time afterwards, without being asked. Although I was aware of all the love to our master that this silent departure must have demanded of him, I was glad that he did not hold it back.

I endeavored to give him the best blowjob of his life. Protecting my teeth with my lips, I slid gently along his penis, pressing with my tongue the big blue vein that ran through it to the meatus that I tingled. I sometimes sucked so hard that even with his large glans in my mouth, my cheeks would hollow out. In rhythm with my back and forth moves, I would strangle and release the base of his shaft between my right index finger and thumb, while with my other hand, I brushed his balls and perineum. When he started to tense up, to continuously moan and groan and I felt his heartbeat in his penis, I gently inserted a finger inside him to graze his prostate as he loved it so much. Then I sped up the in and out, pushing his member as far down my throat as possible. As he screamed with pleasure, I tried to swallow all of his copious and tasty seminal liquor, but a few drops dripped down the corner of my mouth and got lost in his thick pubic hair.

After cumming, he dozed off on the couch. If he hadn't been able to sleep on the plane, he must have been exhausted. I helped him into bed and lay down beside him. I watched him sleep, trying to match my breathing to his before I too fell asleep.

~.~.~

The next morning, after training, shaving and showering, we made breakfast together. In the past, I had temporary masters whom I stayed with for a few days on occasion, but they all let me do all the housework and never lifted a finger to help me. It was a nice change to share these chores like a regular couple while talking.

"Sir?"

"Yes."

"You don't live with Arthur just because you're afraid of going too far with him if you ever…, right?"

"No."

"Are you intentionally hurting him by keeping him away?"

He stared at me in such a way! As the saying goes, a look can pierce you. I had never felt anything like that before.

"Yes," he finally replied.

As he explained his motives, I saw in his eyes something icy: the magnitude of his sadism.

"This exile is his hell and the acceptance of this hell is his heaven. Remember that he is more of a masochist than anyone else. My blows, my bites, all my cruelest tortures are only pleasures for him. Didn't you see what a mixture of tormenting pain and bliss he was in when he was clutching me yesterday? It wasn't just the pain of my bite or the pleasure of my touch, you can be sure. He knew he'd have to leave and he was preparing himself to accept it, even though he was almost suffocating from the thought. His submission to my will is his offering, his testimony of love. By forcing him to endure the most intense torment, this gift elevates him spiritually and gives him the greatest happiness. He once told me that he dreamed that I'd keep him prisoner in a dark and cold dungeon and that I'd kill him slowly by starving and torturing him in all the cruelest ways for days, weeks, months…"

"Oh, my God!"

"You're not going to take his life, that way or any other way, but you still want him to suffer… a lot and constantly," I assumed.

"He likes to be held at the very edge of the abyss, knowing that I'd only have to blow on him to make him fall."

"But… he misses you so much!"

I remembered seeing Arthur shiver and cry. I was sure that being kept away from his master was a real torment, a constant torture for him.

"Yes, he does. If not, what's the point?" he murmured.

I was hot and cold at the same time. I understood that he had such a complete and intimate knowledge of his long-time friend that, out of love for him, he continued to inflict on him what was most painful to him: his absence.

What would he do to me when he knew everything about me? How much would I suffer then? Would I put up with the hell that he had tailored for me, would I lose my mind, or would I choose to leave him before it's too late?

"Arthur once told me that if I rejected him completely, forcing him to stay away without ever seeing or hearing from me, he wouldn't have the strength to endure it and he'd kill himself. I know he was telling the truth."

I was speechless, short of breath, my head spinning and my stomach as sore as if I had been hit there.

"I ordered him not to. I told him that his life belonged to me and, whether by his own means or with the help of another, he had no right to kill himself. I made him promise to stay alive and healthy, because if anyone was to destroy him, it could be no one else but me."

How cruel! He did everything to make Arthur suffer as much as possible, but he forbade him to let himself sink into despair, otherwise his health would be affected, or to shorten his torment, because he had no right to take his own life. I began to cry. My master walked away, while I was visualizing the horror of the situation.

I imagined myself not being able to look at him from a distance in the street, not being able to hear him speak or laugh and, despite my immeasurable and unbearable pain, continuing to exist and act as if everything was fine in the best of all worlds! Out of submission, would I obey him by staying away, would I force myself to do the impossible: to forget him? For love of him, would I manage to live like this or would I just survive as best I could?

I heard him doing God knows what in the living room. I joined him there after wiping my tear-soaked face. He had found a pen and a small notebook where he had started to write something down.

"He loves you more than anyone or anything!"

"Yes, he does. I also love him more than anything and more than anyone. I wanted you to know that and understand why. But don't expect me to ever feel for you more than I do for him. Swear to me that you won't tell him what I just told you."

"Oh, the SADIST!!!" I thought.

"I promise not to tell him, Master," I replied, trying hard not to start crying again.

Maybe he already knew me too well. He figured out what would hurt me the most: being the perpetual number two for him.

He accompanied me to the kitchen where we finished the breakfast preparations together in silence. Then we talked while we ate.

"After the meal, you'll read your two contracts, the employment and the slave contract. Before you sign them, if you need to think about it, if you need to check if we should change some clauses, don't hesitate to take as much time as you need. Then we'll discuss it and I'll see if your requests are reasonable. By the way, I reread your list of BDSM activities while I was in the hospital in Cambodia and I realized that you didn't put any limits on them. You must've some. You'll have to put them in. You don't have to sign anything today. You'll have a few days before our trip to think about it. But I'd like you to have it done before we leave."

"Other than the fact that I prefer to stay alive and sane, at least as much as I am now, I don't know what limitation to add, Master."

"Oh, so you're okay with me shitting in your mouth the next time I feel like it?"

I almost choked on the piece of mushroom omelet I had just swallowed. Shaken, I looked at him to see if he was serious. But he burst out laughing.

"If you could see your face!" he said, pointing at it and laughing again.

I crossed my arms over my chest, pretending to be offended and pouting. He understood that I was playing into his hands.

"You see now that you have boundaries other than the ones you just mentioned. And consider that I'll eventually go through all the doors you have left open. And, if you're lost alone with me in the middle of nowhere at that time, you might regret it. Do you understand?"

His words sounded strangely like a threat.

"Yes, Master," I said in a small, fearful voice that triggered another round of laughter.

I couldn't help but smile. He was so beautiful when he laughed! And I loved knowing he was happy.

"When you read the contracts, if you want to discuss them right away, we will. Otherwise, we'll wait until you're ready."

"Did Arthur sign one?"

"No, he didn't. First, because we started our relationship long before we knew such a thing existed and because I'm sure he would leave all his doors wide open."

"And I guess he doesn't have a list of activities either."

My master smiled sadly.

"Once, out of curiosity, I asked him to answer such a questionnaire and comment on each item so that I'd know what he liked best, what he hated, and what scared him. He gave me a detailed and very honest inventory of what he had and hadn't experienced. But his comments...! He convincingly, but disturbingly, indicated why he'd thoroughly enjoy everything as long as I'd be the one to make him experience it; even and especially what he hated and what scared him the most. The only hard limit he wrote was that he didn't want me to give up on him. After reading all of this, I looked at him. He was crying. I asked him the reason for his tears. He admitted to me that he thought I'd only demanded this list from him to give him the hope of experiencing all of this together, he and I, and then to take that hope away from him by denying myself to him completely."

"Wasn't he a bit right?"

My master looked at me with that icy expression that made me shiver.

"Actually, I was genuinely curious to see if what I knew about him would be confirmed and if there had been activities he had tried without me or others he would have liked to experience more than anything that I didn't know about. But yes, I thought it'd give him futile hope. And I admit that the idea of him dreaming of going through all this with me alone suspecting that it'd never come true turned me on."

"Wouldn't you be able to… control yourself enough to give him a night alone every year on his birthday, for example?"

He smiled and put his hand on my cheek, which he gently stroked.

"Every year on his birthday, I invite him here. He always hopes that he and I will be alone. Sometimes we are, but nothing erotic or S&M happens then. We eat a delicious meal and have a few glasses of my best wine. Then we have a good time together talking about our past, present and future lives, the people we know and anything else that interests us. We've even danced together on those nights. But if I want to have sex with him, I invite someone he likes, we don't drink alcohol and the three of us play together."

"That's not what he…"

"It's not what he wants. Yes, I know. But it's his karma."

His "karma"? A karma named Zach Mendel. I didn't envy Arthur; I really didn't.

Then we talked about our next trip. My master agreed to go to his home in the Amazon rainforest on the border of so-called civilized lands and wildlife and Native reservations. He wanted to tidy up the place and intended to photograph or film as many indigenous animals and plants as possible in a territory of about seventy-two square kilometers surrounded by three river branches. He had already started to take pictures of them during his previous stay in Brazil; but he felt that it was insufficient considering the quantity and variety of species, even in such a small territory.

"You told me that you did what was necessary to get the police certificate for the Brazilian visa and that you filled out the application form for this visa?"

"Yes, I have to pick it up tomorrow."

"Then we can go to the Brazilian consulate to finalize your application. But it'll still be impossible for us to leave for about ten days; that's the usual time it takes to get it if we pick it up at the consulate instead of having it mailed to us. As for me, since I have a residence and a job in Brazil, I was able to get a temporary residence visa which is still valid."

He ate a few bites while thinking.

"Do you have what is needed to go trekking?"

"I've waterproof clothes, some old hiking boots that are pretty worn and a small tent that gets soaked as soon as it rains."

"So, put on your sneakers or these boots, because we're going to be doing a lot of walking today. We'll go and sort out your travel insurance. I've a long-term insurance policy that covers every imaginable medical expense, lost luggage, and car or other accidents. We'll get you the same. We could do it online, but I prefer to stop by my regular travel agent. She knows what I need, so it'll be faster. I'll take the opportunity to discuss hotel reservations."

"We won't be going to your cottage?"

"Not when we arrived. We'll have spent a day on the plane, then made a stopover overnight in Manaus. The next day we'll probably fly to Leticia in Colombia or go directly to Tabatinga in Brazil, where we can take advantage of our brief stay to do our last shopping before going by cab or tuk-tuk to friends' houses where I left my dugout canoe, in which we'll finally sail to my house. It's located in a tiny village with an unpronounceable Kanamari name on the Sirão Dikumaru River. As soon as we have a clearer idea of when we can leave, I'll ask my travel agent to make all the necessary reservations for you and me. She knows my habits and my tastes well. She knows, for example, that I prefer four-wheel-drive off-roaders to luxury cars and rustic cabins to big hotels. And she always gets me the best value for money wherever I go.

Leticia? Tabatinga? Sirão whatever the name? Tuk-tuk? Journey by dugout? Holy cow! I had never heard of any of this. And this nameless village seemed really lost in the middle of nowhere.

"But wouldn't we need a visa to stay in Colombia?"

"No. And Tabatinga is only five kilometers across the border with no customs post. So, stopping in Leticia or Tabatinga won't make much difference to our journey. And there is more choice of… everything you might want to buy in Leticia."

"If you have to drive a long way and even travel by dugout to get to your cottage, it has to be far from town."

"When Arthur spoke of my thatched cottage lost in the middle of the Amazon forest, he was hardly exaggerating."

This was probably why my master insisted so much that I sign my two contracts before leaving. This would not be the time to panic and get lost in the forest. And I didn't want to follow Celine's lead. It was better for me to make a firm decision right away.

"We'll go shopping today to outfit you for the hike. And, since some of my gear is falling apart, I'll take the opportunity to renew it. That way, when you get your documents, we'll be ready to go," he said.

He was as excited as a kid who was promised a trip to the amusement park and a big ice cream. He was smiling at me in such a childish and contagious way that I couldn't help but catch his good mood as if it was a virus.

"Do you think I have time to renew my passport?"

"Until when is it valid?"

"January… No, February, next year. But I made an appointment for a biometric passport anyway."

"There's no rush to get it, but if you prefer to do it, since we'll have to wait for the visa, you'll have plenty of time to get it. Or you can apply for it when we come back from our trip."

As he finished eating, he made a list of items to buy on the notebook he found in the living room. Then he showed it to me.

"Check to see if anything is missing."

It must have had at least 40 items on it, including topographical maps, toiletries, various clothing, gaiters and shoes, hiking and camping supplies and equipment such as a Silva compass and freeze-dried meals; health and safety kits such as first aid kits with, in addition to the usual contents, malaria medicine, antibiotics, general antivenom and water purification tablets, as well as distress signaling kits including whistles and a pocket foghorn; miscellaneous materials such as Ziploc bags of various sizes, rope, a mini sewing kit, biting insect repellent, fishing hooks and lines, snare wire and more.

There was even a bear repellent spray with a holster to carry it on our waist!

"Do you think you'll meet bears in the Amazon?" I asked with a sly smile.

"Of course not, you silly man! But there are jaguars, pumas, wild boars and many other animals you'd rather see only from a distance, though. And none of them like to get cayenne pepper in their eyes."

No, they surely don't. And the foghorn was probably not for a boat, but to scare off unwanted animals if necessary or to call for help.

And with all that, he thought he might be missing something and expected me to see what it was!

"Don't you need a tent?" I asked, thinking that maybe he had one big enough for two.

"No."

"Do you have one?"

"Yes, but it won't be necessary."

"We won't be walking more than a day?"

"Of course, we will; otherwise I wouldn't call it trekking."

"But…"

"Don't worry. I've been there before, and not just in my cottage. I was accompanied by experienced Brazilian guides and Natives: Matis, Korubos and Kanamaris. I know what I'm doing."

"And do you have a GPS?"

"I have two. The first one includes the Brazilian road network and the second is a forest GPS, which shows the topography of a large area of the northern Amazon. But the problem with this second GPS is that it is impossible to receive our position when we are under a dense canopy, which is often the case in the rainforest. Oh, and by the way, remind me to buy a mini front camera and a small underwater video camera."

"An underwater video camera? You think we'll be diving?"

He smiled.

"You can swim, can't you?"

"Yes, but I've never done it with oxygen tanks and all that stuff."

"All that stuff?" he asked mockingly.

"Yes, you know, the whole shebang," I replied, amused.

"I could teach you the whole shebang. But you'll probably just have to snorkel a few feet away. You can do that, can't you?"

"Yes, as long as I don't have to do it in the middle of caimans and piranhas or hold my breath for more than three minutes."

"The bad reputation of piranhas is overrated. You can swim in their midst without any problem as long as you don't have an open and bleeding wound, because blood attracts them. Otherwise, the worst thing you risk with them is to choke to death by eating a mouthful of their hard flesh filled with their too many bones. And for caimans, the only ones potentially dangerous to humans in the Amazon are black caimans. But 'potentially' means 'not necessarily'."

"Yes, but I don't speak Caiman, so I can't ask them if they have murderous intentions towards me."

He gave me a funny look that was halfway between amusement and doubt about my assistant skills and adventurous nature.

"The black caiman is endangered. So, you won't meet many of them. And you'll dive where and when I tell you and for as long as I want, right?"

I tilted my head sideways. I must have looked funny then too.

"Yes, Master."

"Well. Anything else to add to the list?"

"No, I don't think so. But why a lighter and matches, rather than a flint?"

"Because they're easier to use and faster than the prehistoric version. But I already have a survival kit at the bungalow with, among other things, everything I need to start and maintain a fire, and I'm constantly renewing its contents. But you need one too. It's better to have your own."

"Okay."

"We'll find out what's missing, if anything, as we shop. And, anyway, we'll have to shop in Leticia or Tabatinga. I hardly see us trying to pass a machete or a cutlass in the shoulder belt at the airport or even liters of water in bottles. That way, if we forgot anything else, we could find it there."

We finished eating and he handed me the two contracts. They weren't very long, neither of them. The one for work was a classic agreement, except that it stated that I had to be willing to travel to any country at any time of the year and for indefinite periods. The slavery agreement stated that I agreed to serve Zach Mendel twenty-four hours a day, every day of the year for the rest of my life, unless we mutually agreed to break the contract. It also said that my master had the right to demand anything of me at any time except that which would put my physical and mental health, safety, and life in serious danger, in which case I could either agree to continue or unilaterally choose to end my D/s relationship. He also indicated that he would not require anything illegal of me.

"Isn't running around naked outside illegal?" I asked with a smile.

"Only if you're caught," he replied with a falsely serious look.

"Is that your idea of legality: as long as you're sure you won't be caught, it's legal?"

"But in the case of nudity, what is illegal is exhibitionism. In other words, it's to display oneself naked publicly. For that, you need an audience, right? And there was no one else around but me. No one but me saw you. On the other hand, wasn't it you who chose to go out naked and go outside the boundaries of my property? I only ordered you to run away, didn't I?"

I stared at him, trying to figure out if he was serious this time. He was. Of course, I could have tried to grab a coat from the hall closet before going out, or, as he suggested, I could have taken refuge in the garage.

"If I'd been spotted, arrested by the police and accused of gross indecency, would you have had me released?"

"Hmm! Maybe not that day."

His smile this time was downright sadistic. I imagined myself spending several days half-naked in a cell with the local scum. I didn't know what to say to him.

"Don't worry about it. I'll never leave you in the lurch for long, especially one for which I'm at least partly responsible. And Arthur knows the best lawyers in the country. He'd find one that would make you look crazy, and you'd be out in no time, as long as you went to therapy."

I was speechless for several seconds until he burst out laughing again. He was so amused by his joke and my bewildered expression. I wanted to throw myself at him, to punch him in the face or to make him suffer as cruelly as he tormented Arthur. But I just stuck my tongue out at him.

"Your mouth will soon expiate this mischief," he said.

Then, without telling me what the punishment would be, he took his phone out of one of his pockets.

"Before I forget… I have to call Brazil."

He joined whoever it was to extend his permit to travel in the forest zone to photograph the flora and fauna there. He was asked to email a copy of his current safe conduct. He scanned it and sent it immediately. He was told that he would have an answer to this in a few days.

"This permit doesn't give me the right to travel in the state of Acre, which is particularly well protected, because Natives not contacted by civilization still live there. But it does allow me to go to many places that are off-limits to tourists. And I'm authorized to have an escort. And I told them it'd be you," he said.

We then went to the embassy for the visa, but we would have to go back. They registered my application anyway.

He wanted me to drive. Was he also testing my driving skills or did he want me to be his driver from then on? At least I wasn't too worried about that part. I've been driving since I was sixteen and, without bragging, I'm good at it. It's only in the very heavy, fast-paced traffic of a place I don't know where I feel a little less comfortable.

During all of our shopping trips, he was always keen to get me the best of the best, whether it was for my boots, clothes, all of my trekking gear and even my cameras. I let him have his fun, but I still gave him my impressions, as he asked. He seemed to really care about them. He had checked off the items on his list as he acquired them. There were still a few small purchases to be made, but we were now equipped to leave.

Chapter 25

The next morning, while my master was shaving, I was peeing when a spider hanging from a thread swung out right in front of my eyes. I threw myself back, but not having time to stop urinating, I sprayed all around the toilet. My master stared at me with a questioning and surprised look.

"A spider," I said, pointing in the direction of the ugly bug.

"Where is it? I don't see anything."

"There, above the bowl, at eye level."

He looked. Seeing nothing, he came closer. And, bending his head, he saw it. Then he took the thread and its maker. Holding it out to me, he said,

"This tiny thing? Is that what you're afraid of?"

As he brought it up to my face, I threw myself back, but with my feet caught in my underwear, I fell on the floor.

My master looked at me with a frown, seemingly appalled at my childishly terrified reaction. He still held out his hand to help me up. But fearing that it was the one holding the spider, I did not take it and pushed myself back on my elbows with my feet, now free of my underwear.

"Where is it?" I asked.

"I don't know."

"What do you mean you don't know?" I almost screamed.

I looked on myself and all around, but I couldn't see it anywhere.

"Are you sure it's not on you?"

"Gabriel, that's enough! Get up and clean up the mess you just made."

The very harsh tone pushed me into immediate obedience. But he still looked at me in dismay and even disgust as I scrubbed the bowl and the floor. He, who had traveled the jungle, how was he supposed to perceive my reaction to such a small, totally harmless bug? I was ashamed of myself.

He didn't say anything more, but something in his eyes told me that it was recorded somewhere in his mind, and he wasn't over with it. And that didn't bode well for me.

After our morning ritual, he took several pictures of me and had them printed in the correct format for the visa and my new passport. Then, with me behind the wheel and him in the front passenger seat, we drove off together. We first went to get my police certificate and to the embassy to finalize my visa application. Then we finished shopping for the necessities for the trip.

When we got home, after putting away our last purchases, he ordered me to undress and go lie on my back in the center of the bed in the bedroom. He came and joined me there and tied my wrists and ankles to the bindings on the corners of the frame. My arms and legs were spread wide. I didn't know what his intentions were, and I must admit I didn't feel very safe.

Next, he grazed my nipples, my scrotum and my cock until I was fully erect. He then wrapped a string at the base of my shaft and around my scrotum above my balls, leaving a few inches of string sticking out. I knew that even though he was still fondling me, I wouldn't be able to cum until he released my genitals.

So far, all his cuddling had fueled my pleasure. The only discordant note was that he didn't say anything and looked at me so intently that it made me a little more anxious, which only intensified my excitement.

"You do remember that I owe you a punishment for lying and keeping things from me, right?"

I swallowed my saliva before answering him.

"Yes, Master."

I had hoped to hang from the branch of the big oak tree in the backyard, but apparently, he had other plans.

He then pulled out from under the bed a mysterious purchase he had made while I was waiting alone at the consulate. It was pyramid-shaped with a handle at the top and a similarly shaped cover covering it. Turning his back to me, he uncovered and opened the object, which I could no longer see. He took out something that he tied with the end of the string tied to my dick.

Then he turned around and placed his work on my belly. It was a tarantula! I started screaming and struggling.

"It doesn't have its venom gland anymore. And if you don't scare it too much, it won't bite you."

"Please, Master! I won't cheat you again, I promise."

"Ahan!"

He was still looking at me with that same damn steady gaze.

"It seems to me that you had already sworn to me not to do it again, right?"

I could feel the beast's paws scratching my belly and my master's firm, warm hands holding my hips, preventing me from moving too much and scaring or making the animal slip.

"Try to calm down. If you stay still, nothing bad will happen to you. In fact, of the two of you, it's probably the most scared."

"I… I don't think so!"

He laughed, then began to stroke my nipples, cock and balls with an expertise I had never experienced before. Despite my fear, my orgasm was building. But I couldn't cum with my penis tied up like it was. I closed my eyes and tried to think only of my pleasure. But as I started to get there, eight legs started to twitch and scratch.

I thought another spider was walking on my face and instinctively shook my head, but it was just a tear sliding down it. My heart was racing, as much out of pleasure as of fear. I had never felt such a mixture of emotions and sensations. I was dizzy and heard a dull humming sound that was probably caused by my high blood pressure.

Then I felt my master's mouth on mine. He was kissing me tenderly. I tried to participate as best as I could in this kiss. Then he sucked my tongue with such force that I thought he was going to swallow it whole, raw. Then he started to chew on it while pinching my nipples. It was a mind-blowing experience mixed with fear, desire and pleasure.

I remembered that I had not chosen a safe word and that as a full-time slave, I would probably not be given one. So I couldn't force him to stop.

He untied the spider. I was relieved, because I thought he would put it back in its cage.

"Open your mouth," he ordered, holding the animal's body between his fingers.

I shook my head vigorously. No! It was impossible, he surely didn't want to put that hairy monster in there!

"Please!" I moaned.

"This morning, your reaction to seeing this so small beast it was almost invisible was totally ridiculous. You know that, don't you?"

I was frankly crying now. How he must have enjoyed my fear, this sadistic bastard!

"Do you remember I told you that I would make that mouth suffer for sticking out your tongue at me?"

Nothing ever escaped his notice or his memory! Anyway, he couldn't forget such a good opportunity to torture me.

"Yes, Sir," I said.

"Come on, obey. Open your mouth."

"I promise you I won't cheat you again. I swear to you! I won't make any more faces at you if you don't like it. But don't ask me to... I can't..."

He leaned over, pinched my nose firmly as I shook my head in hopes of breaking free. When, out of breath, I opened my mouth, he placed a few of the beast's legs in it.

"Don't bite it, or it might do the same to you. Wrap your lips around your teeth, like when you give me a blowjob, and hold its legs."

I didn't react. I think I was no longer fully present in that room. I wouldn't have been surprised to learn that I was levitating, so full was my mind of adrenaline and a powerful mix of endorphins.

"Grip them your teeth, but not too tight," he insisted.

I had closed my eyes so I couldn't see what I was biting on. Knowing it was one thing, seeing it was another matter entirely. I managed to convince myself to hold back the hairy legs, as required.

He untied my sex, then began to masturbate me again with the same disturbing skill as before. I could feel the pleasure growing more and more, despite the beast trying to free itself.

"When you've come, I'll put the spider back in its cage. But look at it."

He continued his expert caresses.

"Come on, Gabriel, obey. Do it for me. Show me that I don't have to worry about taking you into the forest where such creatures live."

My eyes opened wide and landed on him first, then on the spider. Where it was, I could only see a clump of chocolate or black coffee-colored hair. I thought it must be very soft. And when I looked at my master, he was smiling at me, so sweetly. Was it pride that I was reading in his eyes? I felt a lot of happiness that I had managed to overcome my fear and please him.

My pleasure had reached its point of no return, when he started to scratch one of my nipples and the head of my cock. The pain mixed with pleasure immediately made me ejaculate with a grunt.

Without waiting, he seized the animal and put it back in its cage. Then he released me and kissed me with a passion he had never shown before. I understood that his dominating nature and his sadistic pleasure were something very special, that what fed them was not only the suffering or the submission of his slave, but above all the demonstration of his determination and his courage.

I unzipped his fly. His stiff cock popped out as if it were ejected. I placed myself between his legs. He had gone out of his way to deliver me from my phobia by associating it with lots of pleasure. I wanted to thank him for it by giving him the best blowjob I could offer. He stroked my hair the whole time I was sucking him off. And when he ejaculated, he grabbed it hard.

We took a shower together. The sight and touch of his body, though beautiful, failed to satisfy all my lust for him. I didn't just want to savor him to my heart's content, I wanted to reach the depths of his being. But the kisses that I put on all that I washed seemed to me insufficient to express to him what I felt. Reaching his ass, I slid a finger down his slit to his anus.

"Kneel down," he ordered.

Then he turned around and pulled out his butt. How desirable he looked in that obscene posture! I spread his buttocks and began to lick him gently. He let me do it until he wanted more.

"Come on, stick your tongue in. Get it in there, as deep as you can."

To satisfy him, I had to stick my nose in his slit. But between his two beautiful firm loaves of white bread, I was running out of air.

"Don't stop. It's so good!"

He had put a hand on my head and was holding my face pressed between his buttocks. With my tongue deep inside him, my nose squashed and water running down my face, I could barely breathe. Although, he must have heard my hard, wheezing breaths, he wouldn't let me stop and told me to continue. I didn't dare to move away, not even an inch, not even a brief moment to breathe a little. I was convinced that this anilingus would not be enough to trigger a new orgasm. So, I reached around him to grab his cock and masturbate it.

"No. Just lick me and push your tongue deeper into my rectum."

I pulled away a little, just long enough to say with a gasp that I was suffocating.

"You'll breathe when I come, not before," he grumbled.

I took a deep breath and went back to work even harder. Did I want to prove my appreciation to him or not? Did my life belong to him or not? Then I imagined myself dying of asphyxiation, with my tongue stuck in his little hole. This vision gave me a hard-on. Suddenly, even my suffocation excited me. His hand holding my head against him, his moans of pleasure, his insistence that I keep shoving my tongue further and deeper again in him, and that I do not stop, not until he ejaculated, all of this became tangled in my mind and turned into a fountain of gushing pleasure, until, sucking hard, I swallowed some of his feces. Shit! Yuck! I gagged!

"Don't you dare stop now or I swear this tongue will know a lot worse than a spider and the few drops you just swallowed!" he growled.

I breathed in, held my breath and went back to work once more, trying to ignore the smell that was coming at me despite my nose being crushed between his buttocks and the sickening taste that coated my tongue.

He's my master. What he's doing to me shouldn't disgust me, it should excite me. What I do to him shouldn't seem repulsive, but make me happy to have the chance to give him such pleasure. I tried my best to convince myself of this, to condition myself to these ideas, but every time his lumpy juices crept into my mouth, they turned my stomach. Then he would press his hand harder to the back of my head in a silent command to continue. And I did. I persevered!

He began to stroke my hair so languidly and gently, to slide his fingers over my cheek so gently that this token of approval and affection brought tears to my eyes. I was happy that I had managed to find favor in his eyes once again. I could hear him moaning louder and louder. His buttocks were twitching and his pelvis was instinctively moving back and forth as he turned around, forced me to do the same and bend over, then lubricated my anus with his organic shower gel and fucked me. Shortly after, he came with a grunt worthy of a madman. Then he waited until he came to his senses, panting under the spray, unconcerned with his coldness. He then cleaned his anus before getting out of the shower. I did the same, then wiped him down.

He looked at me with the same pensive look he had before he started my punishment. Then he tilted his head with a smile and kissed the corners of my mouth, maybe to avoid the taste of his own shit. But it tickled my lips and I shivered with pleasure.

"Thank you, little slave! Your punishment was a real treat," he said with his usual mocking air.

"You're welcome, Master. But don't expect me to give you any more reasons to punish me."

He smiled.

"I hope so! To make mistakes on purpose would be to deceive me. Not only would I discipline you for your false mistake, I'd do it even more cruelly for your true deception."

Chapter 26

The next day, while my master was writing a positive report on Celine's behavior during their last trip to Cambodia and continuing his article on kidnapped children, I went to the passport office by myself to finish my process. I told them not to mail it because I would pick it up. I also went to return the mygale to where my master had gotten it. I told them that the child for whom it was intended was not so happy with his birthday present after all. Fortunately, the pet store allowed a few days of testing and took the spider back without any fuss.

While waiting for my visa and new passport, my master and I looked at my article and report in detail. He would ask me in Brazilian Portuguese why I wrote this and that and if there was anything missing here and there.

"Don't you think that instead of running away from the hospital without your memory card, you'd better meet with the management and ask them about their point of view on the situation?"

Of course, if I had done that, I would have really had the opinion of everyone involved regarding denial of care in general and this one in particular. I acted out of inexperience. Fearing that I would lose what I already had, I avoided doing what would have allowed me to learn more and really understand the situation. Besides, I didn't know how long such a discussion with the director would last, and Mom was waiting for me. That's what I explained to him.

"He had no right to take away your flash cards. All they could've done was refuse to talk to you. But at least you would've tried to get their side of the story. You should always try to get the version of the authorities involved and as many witnesses as possible. You never know which piece of the puzzle will be the most important for your article or story once you've gathered them all and got a complete picture of your subject."

Since he spoke to me almost all the time in Portuguese, I often looked up the dictionary and grammar to understand the meaning of his questions and comments. But he was almost angelically patient, never hesitating to repeat everything to me, even several times if necessary.

He also took on the role of the reader or viewer wondering what I was trying to say with this or that statement. I was sometimes hurt in my pride by his criticism, but I couldn't help but understand that his experience allowed him to see the slightest flaw and what could have produced a misunderstanding or an adverse public impression.

"Do you believe that one should always make the readers or the audience like what one writes or shows?" I asked him in broken Portuguese.

He smiled and asked me the same question, this time perfectly phrased.

"I don't know, Master. If I only present what people hate, I won't have readers or viewers for long. No one will want to publish my articles or broadcast my report. But if I only write what they like, I might not be honest, I might not talk about the... cruel reality."

"The public likes 'cruel realities'. That's not the problem. You have to be as real as possible and at the same time not create too much of a negative reaction to you or your article."

"How can we achieve such a compromise?"

"By remaining neutral."

"Neutral?"

"Yes. You don't have to tell people what they should think. Give them some work to do. But you can give them all the information they need to see things your way. If you do it right, they will. And if they don't come to your conclusion, it won't be your fault. You probably wouldn't have convinced them anyway. And who knows? Maybe they'll give you a new perspective, too."

I looked at him, thinking about his words.

"But..."

"Yes, Gabriel. There is always a 'but'. It's rare that there are no exceptions, cases where you want to be more persuasive, more directive. But remember that you can't convince people by insulting them or by offering them a well crafted, but rational, little article. They will follow you if they like you. To achieve this, you have to speak their language and appeal to their hearts as much as to their minds. Maybe even more to their hearts."

My questions and answers in hesitant and sometimes faulty Portuguese made him smile, but he corrected me gently, without making fun of me, unless the use of bad words or lame turns of sentences had given my speech a so hilarious twist that even I laughed after his explanation. And he was telling me differences between Portuguese and Brazilian. For example, he told me not to call a girl "rapariga", as in Portugal, because that word means "whore" in Brazil, but rather to use "moça". So, I thanked him for saving me from unintentionally insulting people.

In his absence, I had read the article he had written about the abducted children. It contained no negative criticism of anyone, not even the corrupt police officers or the pedophiles who were defiling the souls of these children. But… oh yes, there was a "but"! In a few words and a few pictures, he had expressed all his love for these little victims. But he had only shown the reality. The bloody reality. The shitty reality!

It was Zach Mendel's talent to know how to present, describe, prove, and make people feel in all its intensity the cruelty of mankind. He had experienced it when he was a child. He had felt it and understood it. He could now speak about it with knowledge and wisdom. But he could also show the splendor of our universe. And sometimes he could be truly sublime when he presented our world in its entirety: a mixture of infinite beauty and ugliness.

He made me read and watch some of his old reports, as well as those of other famous or promising journalists. We began to evaluate their achievements, compare them, comment on them and express our preferences and the reasons for them. It was extremely instructive and even fun. My master told me that my observations were very relevant and that he, too, was learning from our discussions; this gave me more confidence.

I was lucky he had become my guide. I was more than happy to follow in his footsteps. So, I signed both contracts, making it clear beforehand on my list of activities that I was not interested in scatology at all and that I was afraid of heights and, yes, spiders again, but not to the point of vertigo or arachnophobia. I said that if I had forgotten any other important limitations and they came to mind, I reserved the right to discuss them with him before any activity involving them or to add them to my list, but I promised him that I would not use this clause to throw tantrums and reject anything that seemed more or less enjoyable.

During those days of waiting, he also forced me to train better.

"You don't know what you're getting into, Gabriel. We'll be riding in the Javari, a place where the terrain is never quite dry and always mountainous. If you're not in excellent physical shape, the combination of heat, humidity, constant obstacles, unstable ground, the weight of your luggage, and concerns for your life or mine will make your trip so difficult that it may seem impossible at times. I need an adventurous assistant, able to follow me where no one else dares to go and just as enthusiastic as I'm about photographing or filming plants and animals that perhaps no one has yet studied or even recorded."

"I want to go there. I'm excited to go!"

"Wanting isn't enough. You have to be able to do it. That's also why I gave you that mygale. I needed to know if you could do it. Morally, you seem to be able to do it, but will you have the physical strength?"

So, he helped me practice Brazilian and we trained as if our lives depended on it. But maybe it would depend on it after all. When you have to live in the jungle, where no one has ever been, it is better to be well prepared.

In addition to exercising on his training equipment, we ran outside, often through the woods, where I had gotten lost. But now I wasn't barefoot; we'd put on Crocs, hiking boots or long rubber boots, because he said we could wear all of that depending on the weather, the time of day, where we'd have to run and what we'd intend to do there.

I was also researching on the web about the flora and fauna of the area we were to visit. I read that the Javari is a territory where the microclimates favor the greatest biodiversity of the entire planet and where three new animal species had been discovered every year for the last ten years. I realized that there were so many different mammals, amphibians, snakes, insects, arthropods, fish, birds and everything else that it was impossible for anyone to know them all. And it was the same for the plants, each one more magnificent than the other. All of this surely contributed to my master's desire to have a home there. It was like settling in the middle of Wonderland or the Garden of Eden. But it was also terrifying because of the wide variety of dangerous and sometimes even deadly plants and animals.

Sometimes he would look over my shoulder at what I was looking on my computer and say with excitement in his voice, "It's beautiful, isn't it?"

Once he dreamed aloud, "Imagine Aliens arriving from their barren and devastated planet and flying over the Earth for the first time and discovering this forest in all its splendor!"

To hear him speak, one would have sworn that he was one of these extragalactic visitors who had just landed on Earth and that he could not believe his eyes, so much so that he had doubted that he would ever find a habitable planet, without ever daring to hope that one day he would discover one as beautiful as Earth.

"Aren't we destroying what we call 'the lungs of the planet'?"

"We did it and, unfortunately, we still do it, but we are trying to protect this forest before it's too late. That's probably what we should be showing: the deleterious nature of our species. We have to find how to highlight this splendor and the horror of its destruction in a way that has never been done before. We must strike the minds and touch the hearts."

If anyone could do it, it was him: this master journalist.

To prepare us for our trip, he showed me what to put in my backpack and in what order to put it, so that I would always have at hand what I would need most and what I might need to access in a hurry.

"There are some things that absolutely must be kept in plastic bags, like all your replacement electronics: memory cards, batteries and so on. If you bring matches, even if they are waterproof, they should be protected. It's also a good idea to put some of your clothes, such as those you plan to wear at night, in bags to prevent them from getting wet. If it rains, you'll be happy to lie in your hammock in dry clothes at night. And the giant orange bags could even be used as an emergency rain raincoat; plus, if needed, they could get the attention of airborne rescue workers."

At the time of purchase, I had wondered about the reason for so many plastic bags; I knew now.

In the evenings, he frequently played guitar or some other instruments. He was fabulously talented. When he played "Just the Way You Are" on the piano, I had tears in my eyes at the end because the music was so beautiful and his playing so perfect.

"What an amazing man," I thought. I once again feared that I was not worthy of him, of someone so talented in everything he did and so eager to do good wherever he can.

"Sublime!" I said, my voice trembling.

"Yes, it's a beautiful piece," he replied, apparently unaware of his talent.

"It's you who are sublime, Master."

He tilted his head like a puppy looking for a better perception of a mysterious sound.

"You play wonderfully," I added.

He smiled and stroked my wet cheek. How many people had told him how remarkable he was? He must not have heard that very often as a child. Even afterwards. If he had been surrounded only by fools like Celine, he must have been seen only as a reckless journalist and a dangerous torturer. Yet he was so much better and more than that!

Moreover, every day he did not hesitate to give me new proofs of his talents as a sadistic master, and all his imaginative tortures ended in bed in an orgy of increasing pleasure.

Chapter 27

The day I got my vaccines, after learning where we were going on the trip, I was prescribed malaria medication. We then went to the pharmacy to buy it. I had several weeks worth of daily doses.

But when I came back, I started to have a little fever. My master took care of me as if I were a very sick person.

While I was sitting on the couch reading Paulo Coelho's "O Alquimista" and looking up words in the dictionary every three sentences that I didn't know what they meant, I watched him smiling as he brought me this and that. I felt like I was the dominant one, so much so that he would go out of his way to serve me well.

"You'd make an exceptional slave, Master," I teased him.

He grunted. I thought I would be entitled to one of his exquisite tortures; but no, he continued to surround me with his constant attention.

"You'll get what's coming to you! When you're fully recovered, you won't laugh so much."

Then, it was I who grunted, of anticipated pleasure.

"Master?"

"Yes."

"Do you remember when I stuck my tongue out at you?

"Of course, I do."

"I didn't do it out of disrespect. I didn't mean to make fun of you or anything you…"

"I know. I thought your reaction was funny."

"But then, why did you punish me for doing it?"

"Did I punish you?"

I looked at him without understanding. He told me he would make me pay for that face and while he was putting that spider in my mouth, he reminded me of it. And I swallowed shit that day!

"You admitted to me that you were once tempted to break a promise you made to me to give me an excuse to punish you, right?"

"Yes, Master. And you didn't like that idea."

"No, because when people lie to me or hide things from me, I start to lose my ability to trust. As the saying goes: 'If you deceive me once, shame on you. If you deceive me twice, shame on me'."

"What does this have to do with me sticking my tongue out at you?"

"If you aren't allowed to willingly push me to punish you, I can take advantage of opportunities from time to time, right?"

Oh, so he hadn't hated my reaction, but had taken advantage of it to justify a punishment and get some sadistic pleasure.

"If we were sitting at a table in a public area of Arthur's club and I said something to you that made you make a face at me or stick your tongue out at me, people around would perceive your reaction as a sign of disrespect to your master. And I couldn't let that go unchallenged. I wanted you to know the risk you were running by doing that. Personally, I like this joking side of your nature. In the future, as long as we're alone, if I punish you for this kind of reaction, it'll be because you have crossed the line. Do you understand?"

"Yes, Master. But I'd never stick my tongue out at you in public. I know it's different, that I must play my part perfectly then; although I don't see what's wrong with joking with your master."

"Imagine I'm the King of England and you were introduced to me, would you immediately hug me or shake my hand?"

"Not until you extend yours to me or allow me to, my king."

He smiled.

"And if the king made a mocking comment to you, would you stick your tongue out at him?"

"Of course not!"

"Yet there's nothing wrong with shaking hands or joking with people, is there?"

Yes, I could see what he was getting at. There are special circumstances where protocol demands that one act with a certain restraint and show the utmost reverence.

"I understand, Master. I'd never shame you. And if I did, it'd be unintentional."

"And I'd still punish you for it."

"Thank you, Sir, for clarifying the meaning of sentences you say to me in Portuguese and for explaining to me how your antique camera works or how to serve you better.

"What? My camera is not antique! But it requires more effort and time to master all its many subtleties."

"Subtleties"? More like complexities.

When he looked at me, eyebrows furrowed, he saw that I was holding back a laugh.

"Oh, you!"

He reached out and touched my forehead and cheeks.

"I think you're much better. Actually, you're doing a little too well," he said, forcing me to put my book away and stand up.

He then set up two chairs facing each other, but about six feet apart, and a third chair in the middle between the first two. I watched him do this, a little worried.

"Get undressed and lie down on your stomach on this chair," he said, pointing to the one in the center.

I obeyed.

"Put your feet on this one and your hands on that one."

I did it. I had my hips on one chair seat, my hands and forearms on another, and my feet and ankles on the last.

"Keep this posture until I allow you to change it," he ordered.

Then he removed the middle chair. I had to remain horizontal between my two support points! I wouldn't last two minutes like this, that was for sure.

"I swear, Gabriel, if you don't hold this posture for at least five minutes, you'll suffer for more than a few minutes and you'll regret it bitterly."

"And if I succeed?" I asked.

I thought I would deserve a reward worthy of the Herculean effort I would have to make. He laughed.

"You little joker! I hope you can keep your sense of humor after we've hiked for hours over difficult terrain in the Amazon."

"I wasn't joking, Sir. I really… hope to be rewarded if… I succeed," I gasped.

"How about I reward you already to show you how much faith I have in your success?" he suggested as he took hold of my dick.

"Nooo!"

"What? What do you mean, no? You dare to say 'no' to your master? Don't you like my caresses?" he asked in a tone that was both cruel and teasing.

"On the contrary… I like them too much!"

He laughed again at my obvious discomfort. But how could I last five minutes under the effect of his too skillful hand job and in this atrocious posture? It was clear that he wanted me to fail.

"Why would I stay… five minutes that way… if you're just waiting for… me to fail so you can… get off?"

"Who says that's what I'm hoping for? I know the difficulty of staying in this posture. Daddy used to make me do it. But he didn't stroke me while I tried to keep it; he whipped me, threatening that if I failed, he'd put my sister there instead of me and that if she screwed up, it would be Mom's."

"Your father was…"

"A monster, yes, I know. But I'm too, in my own way, don't you think?"

"No, Master. You wouldn't do that way to… someone who wouldn't… consent and… certainly not… to children."

I was at the point where I was grumbling my answers more than I was saying them normally. And I had to constantly straighten my ass, which was being pulled down more and more. Damn gravity! If I hadn't trained so well since living with him, I never would have made it. Was this just another exercise to make me stronger or a way to test my will? I still wasn't sure if I would make it, but I was trying hard to keep up with the five minutes required. I was struggling, all right! I imagined my master tortured with unspeakable cruelty if I didn't make it, so I had to succeed. Ah, Lord! When I thought that all this had started with a simple joke. Would I be able to keep that sense of humor that I knew he enjoyed?

He was fondling my nipples as well as my cock and it was really too much for one man to handle.

"Please, Master!"

"My father didn't like complainers and whiners. If I cried under his thrashing, he'd get even more violent. And there was no point in asking for his pity; it was a feeling he was incapable of. So, I learned to bear everything in silence."

I shook my head, for he was the one I pitied now. He continued his stroking while I huffed and puffed under the effort. How could anyone endure that without uttering a sound, especially under repeated beatings? You can't! But he resisted even though he was just a little boy. I'm sure he could do it. For his sister and mother, he suffered in silence.

I focused on what I had to do to hold on. I tried to convince myself that I no longer felt pleasure or pain, that I had become a hard, solid wooden board that nothing could bend. It was really hard, but four minutes later, I was still between my two chairs, not really straight, but still holding on. And I hadn't cummed!

Then, bang! my muscles spasmed and I fell. It was involuntary and impossible to prevent. But I was horribly disappointed. After so much effort, I was on the floor, and he was staring at me with a neutral look.

"How do you think I felt when the same thing happened to me? I'd beg my dad to do whatever he wanted to me, but not to take it out on my sister or my mom. But do you think he listened to me?"

I shrugged my shoulders. But I knew too well.

"He knew that anything he could do to me would seem less unbearable than seeing him torture Karin and Mom because of me. He was a sadist, remember. He always chose what seemed to me the most unjust and atrocious."

"Your marks, Sir, are they…"

"I got one of them during a fight when I was eighteen, and two more on my travels: the first was due to a minor accident, and the second when some small-time gangsters tried to stop me from harming them. But most of them are his work."

"Gangsters!?"

"Ah, they were just young punks who wanted to prove themselves as tough guys. One of them hurt me with his dagger. I'll tell you about it one day."

"But… how could you keep quiet when your father hit you?"

"There were times when I whimpered and screamed and sobbed, even though I knew it'd only make things worse. But sometimes it was… so hard! And the pain he inflicted on me wasn't all physical or leaving marks. It wasn't always visible. One day, shortly before my seventh birthday, Mom asked me what I'd like as a present and, full of hope, I immediately answered a dog. But even though I promised to take good care of it, my father wouldn't hear of it. But when he came home on my birthday with a beautiful turtle that stuck its head out and lifted its nose to sniff the air, I smiled. I ran to it, because I thought it was my present. But Daddy put water to boil in our largest pot and then plunged the live turtle in. I threw myself at him, crying, screaming and calling him names. But he dragged me down to the basement by one ear and laid me down in a long coffin-like box. He closed the lid and screwed it on. He locked me in there almost every time I rebelled against him. And sometimes he left me there for days."

Poor little guy! How I hated his father at that moment! I had tears in my eyes and rage in my heart.

"I wish I could go back in time to hug little Zac and comfort him," I said.

He gently caressed my face with such sadness and tenderness in his eyes that I wanted to cry even more. Then he was the one who hugged me to comfort me.

"Why did he scald that turtle, just to be cruel?" I asked when he released me after kissing me on the forehead and cheeks.

"He wanted Mom to cook him a soup. Fortunately, I didn't have to eat any. I wouldn't have been able to and would've ended up in the basement again for refusing to eat it."

"He must've suspected what you'd imagine. Of all the days to bring that turtle, he chose your birthday, the bastard!"

He nodded and smiled.

"No doubt."

"Were you able to breathe in that box? And you didn't become claustrophobic?"

"There were small cracks between the boards that allowed some air to enter. But while I was locked up and the stench increased with the accumulation of sweat, urine and shit, I imagined all the countries I'd visit later, when I'd be grown up and free to live my life as I saw fit, away from this sicko. I could see myself helping other children like me by freeing them from their torturers and their misery. And luckily, Mom had learned to heal our wounds and comfort us; otherwise, I might've died or lost my mind completely."

I understood now why he was so anxious to free his children, why their fate was so important to him and why he still suffered at the thought of not having them all back.

"Put on some shorts and your new hiking boots, we're going to train outside."

He had said he would give me a hard time for several hours if I failed. I had good reason to think that this workout would be very unusual and difficult.

I was not wrong. We ran outside, but he was chasing me with a riding crop in his hand, and he didn't mind using it if he caught me. He mostly hit my bare flesh areas, like my thighs and arms. But the fabric of the shorts and t-shirt was too thin to protect me effectively. Especially since he was not going easy on me with his crop.

To get away from him, I went into the same wooded area I had walked through when I was naked. Today, I was clothed and shod, but the branches scraped my whip-scarred arms and legs as I was running along them. Every time I thought I had outrun him, I found him right there, in front of me, smiling with all his teeth. I would turn around just as sharply, going the other way, only to find him a little later beside me. My only protection was the trees around me, which prevented or limited his strikes.

After about two hours, I tried to think while running away. I decided to go to the house, to lock myself in before he caught up with me. But while I locked the front door, he came in through the back door, this too-quick and too-smart sadist!

But wasn't two hours of this regime enough? If it wasn't enough for him, it was for me. I was ready to raise the white flag when I saw him approach me brandishing his riding crop. I turned around, unlocked the door and walked out. "Think," I said to myself.

There was no point in running away, because I would have to go back sometime. And then I would be at his mercy. I thought of going in and offering myself to his whip. But I knew that wasn't what he wanted from me. So, what was I supposed to do to satisfy him?

Chapter 28

After running away for several hours and out of ideas, I went to the neighbor's house and called Arthur.

"What?!" he said after my little story.

"I know you'd like nothing better than to make him hate me, but if you did, he'd resent you and make you regret it; so help me find a solution, because I confess my imagination is out of service."

"You could always give him up voluntarily. It'd save me from having to push you to do it," he said.

I was silent for a moment. His answer sounded suspiciously like a threat. Had I just asked the devil for help?

"Arthur, stop it and tell me what you would do if you were me. I can't just go home and say, 'Here I am!' That's not what he wants from me, is it? And there's no way I'm ever going to see him again. So, please, help me catch the damn sadist!"

It was his turn to remain silent. Maybe our master had never pushed him into this kind of dead end and he just didn't know how he would get out of it in such a case. But he probably wouldn't ask for anything better than to replace me.

"I'll think about it. If I want to meet you, where can I find you?"

"I don't have an apartment anymore. My friends are either at work or at college right now. I think I'll go back to my mom's," I said with a note of self-deprecation.

"And where does she live?"

"Ha ha! Don't try to pretend you don't know, Arthur. I'm getting to know you too."

He hung up on me again. This guy really had a bad education and a bad temper. But two days later, I was finishing dinner at my parents' house when Arthur rang their doorbell. Mom opened it for him.

"There's a top model here to see you. I think he's the guy who was on his knees in front of your… boyfriend," she told me, wide-eyed with the confusion of the encounter.

I smiled and went to the door.

"Have you found a solution?" I asked by way of greeting.

After all, he wasn't the only one who could be rude.

"Come on. Follow me."

"Okay, but where are we going?"

"You'll find out."

My parents were now behind me in the hallway.

"Can you introduce us to your friend?" asked Mom.

"This is Arthur Dubois, an old friend of Zac's," I said, addressing my parents. "These are my parents," I finished, turning to our visitor.

Arthur shook their hands without looking at them, as if in regret.

"I'm sorry, but we have to go now," Arthur insisted, taking me by the arm and pulling me towards him.

I followed him, intrigued. He got behind the wheel of his car and I sat down beside him. We drove in silence for almost an hour. We had reached a remote part of town when I started to worry. I thought the drive was unusually long. Where was the bastard taking me?

He stopped, I thought we had finally arrived, but there were only trees around.

"Get out," he ordered as he was getting out himself.

I followed him to the back of the car. He opened his trunk, which was completely empty, like nothing I had ever seen before, except in new cars. The only things in it were a carpet with handcuffs, a gag, and a black cloth bag of some sort on it.

"Turn around," he ordered.

"What?!"

"Do you want me to help you or not? Do everything I tell you or I'll take you back to your parents."

I looked around and wondered if I should run for my life through the woods. Then I turned around. Arthur put the handcuffs on me, the gag, then the bag over my head, which he tied around my neck. Then he picked me up.

"Bend your legs," he ordered.

He then laid me on the carpet. To be kidnapped and transported in a car trunk was one of my secret fantasies. But I didn't have time to enjoy it, because before locking me in, Arthur gave me an injection! Of what? Probably a good sleep medication, because I quickly fell asleep.

When I woke up, I was naked, still handcuffed, in an empty cell, damp and cold, without a window, nor even a bunk. A single light bulb protected by a metal grill lit the room. A ring was fixed to the ceiling. Four others formed a rectangle on one wall large enough to tie a man to it, spread-eagled. A chain riveted to this wall lay on the floor like a sleeping snake. The floor sloped slightly towards its center, where one of the two drains was located. The other was under a faucet.

How long had I been unconscious? If I had slept long enough, I could have been anywhere on the planet. I started to scream.

"You were supposed to help me, Arthur! What are you doing? Where am I? Why am I here?"

I was really scared. But I tried to calm down. I remembered that my master had tried to prepare me for such an eventuality by forcing me to flee, to find shelter somewhere and even to fight my torturers. I wondered if he wasn't behind it all, if he didn't want to check if I had learned what he had taught me. And hadn't he promised to give me a hard time for hours? Was he trying to make sure I really cared about him and that he could trust me?

A man came into my cell. I didn't know him.

"Who are you? Where am I?"

He was a big guy. Unless I was a sumo wrestler, even with all the martial arts classes in the world, I couldn't have competed with him. He took off my handcuffs silently, and then he went out. And since there was no window in my cell, I couldn't unseal the bars even if I had the means to do it. I suddenly felt on the verge of tears. But I had a more pressing urge than to cry; after removing the grating from the central sewer, almost tearing my fingernails off, I was able to relieve myself there.

Two days later, no one had come to feed me, talk to me, torture me, or even look through the skylight in the door. Without a bunk, I had to try to sleep on the rough, lumpy, icy concrete floor. I was afraid I'd catch another microbe and not be able to go to Brazil with my master, if he wasn't already there. At least there was the tap where I could drink by pouring water into my hands. Otherwise, I would have died of thirst before anyone else came.

Every morning during those days of waiting, I tried to work out. I wanted to keep the physical fitness that my master seemed so concerned about me getting.

When walking in the Amazon rainforest, it must be important to have strong legs. But my exercises were mostly to keep my mind occupied and forget for a few minutes what I was going through.

A man in his thirties, of average height and build, entered my cell on the third day.

"Who are you? What do you want from me? Is this Arthur, my master, or did someone else hire you to kidnap and scare me?"

He did not answer any of these questions. He only examined me meticulously from the front before ordering me to turn around.

"Why should I obey you?"

He called out to the muscular giant, who held me back while the other guy inspected me from the other side. I tried not to cry in front of them, but I was shaking, and I didn't know if it was just from cold, terror or both.

Had Arthur lost his mind as a result of being kept out of his friend Zac's life? Had he ever been captured and tortured while serving in the army? Did he want me to experience the horror of it so that I would leave my master, so he could keep him just for himself as he had threatened?

They came out and left me alone, shivering and without a bite to eat, for two more too long days. I thought less and less that this was my master's doing; he had said something about giving me a hard time for a few hours, not days, right? But how could I know for sure how long I had been a prisoner since I could not see the light of day? And maybe hunger and fear were disturbing my memory and distorting my recollection. And the two strangers could be the "brutes" my master had told me about who were in the army with Arthur, the same ones who had helped him find the kidnapped children.

I could hardly sleep and when I did, I had terrible nightmares in which I was kept prisoner for years and my master, having long since given up on finding me, had chosen a new submissive. One night (at least I think it was at night) when I had finally managed to fall asleep, the strong man and two men hooded like the executioners of yesteryear entered my cell and carried me to another room while I uselessly struggled and screamed.

"Where are you taking me? What are you going to do to me?"

They didn't answer or make a sound. After locking the door, they laid me on a kind of seesaw and tied me to it from head to toe. Then they put a basin full of water under the end where my head was. If they let the board fall on that side, my whole upper body would be underwater. I could not have lifted myself even to save my life, because there was a strap around my forehead that held my head on the swing. If they pressed on the other end, my face was out in the open and I could breathe. They amused themselves by plunging me into the water many times until I almost drowned, barely getting me out long enough to swallow a tiny bowl of air. But the most terrible thing was that they didn't even question me, didn't ask me anything, didn't tell me anything.

"What do you want? What do you want from me?" I asked as soon as I had enough air in my lungs to do so.

No answer. Total silence! Then they put my head back in the water. And after an hour or two or more of this horrible process, they took me back to my cell.

Several days later, in the middle of one of the ever-inventive and increasingly atrocious daily torture sessions, I told them I never consented to any of this. As usual, they remained silent. Then I begged them to ask me anything, and I would answer all their questions and do anything they demanded without question if they would put an end to my torture.

And Arthur came in.

"Will you leave him? If you let me have him, I'll let you go right now," he promised.

My eyes almost bulging with terror, I looked at him, trying to catch my breath.

"Have you lost your mind, Arty? You're completely crazy!" I yelled as soon as I could.

"Wait, you haven't seen anything yet."

Desperation overcame me. I was in the hands of a raving lunatic and his criminal friends. And my master must not have even known where I was and he must have been very worried. I ached to think of his pain.

"Why are you crying, wimp?" asked Arthur.

"My master must think I've abandoned him. He must be unhappy and sad. I don't want him to suffer," I replied, stifling a sob.

Arthur looked at me as he had never looked at me before, as if he was discovering me.

"You said before that you'd leave him to me if you could. Now you have the chance. All you have to do swear to me on the life of everyone you care about that you'll never see Zach Mendel again and I'll set you free at once; I swear it."

"When I told you that, I thought you were a good guy, who wanted his friend to be happy. But I was wrong; all you know is how to fuck up his life. And even if I have to go through this hell again to convince you to let me stay with him, I will."

He turned to his acolytes and ordered, "As you can see, he not only consents to being tortured, he wants more. So don't go easy on him."

After almost drowning me again, they beat me savagely. Then they electrocuted me, sending shocks here and there, obviously where it was most painful. I begged, cried, screamed. I insulted them. But it didn't matter. I knew that until I gave Arthur what he wanted, they won't stop torturing me. And what Arty wanted was the most extraordinary man in the world. I didn't really understand it until I was afraid of losing him, but I loved Zach Mendel more than anyone before him and more than anything. If I ever thought I could give him up, I knew now that I couldn't. I would never give him up!

Chapter 29

Days passed again, and I was more and more convinced that my master had left for Brazil with a new assistant. Celine? Flávio? Another handsome young man? Since I couldn't see Arty anymore, it could even be him.

Every day, after being tortured, the strong man would take me back to my cell, carrying me in his arms or on his shoulder. I wanted to ask him why I was there and why I was being mistreated, but sometimes I was unconscious, otherwise I was always so exhausted that I couldn't gather my thoughts or find the strength to question him or plead my case.

The man in his thirties who had examined me on both sides came to talk to me regularly. He had set up a wooden bunk with a thin foam mattress covered with a waterproof canvas. He tended to my wounds of the day, scandalizing at the cruelty of my torturers and raving about my great courage. Then he would sit with me and we would talk about my past, my family, my friends and my hopes for the future.

One day he asked me about my reasons for wanting to be someone's 24/7 slave, and Mendel's in particular.

"I can't tell you about him."

"Who?"

"My master. I promised him I'd keep everything about him a secret."

"Ah. But if you stayed with him full time, it'd be impossible for you to confide in anyone, since in doing so, you'd also be bound to talk about him too."

That seemed like a pretty good point. I thought that I should discuss this with my master when he and I will be back together, to find out what I could tell and what I should absolutely keep quiet about. Then I sadly wondered if I'd see him again.

"It doesn't matter what you can tell about him, since your master has already forgotten you. You should do the same. What's the point of suffering for an unfaithful man like him?"

Was it true? Could I trust this stranger whose name I didn't even know?

"I'll never forget him. NEVER!"

"You're naive if you think that when you get out of here, if you ever get out, you can go back to living with him. Mendel asked Mr. Dubois for help in finding you, but, as you can imagine, Arthur claimed that after investigating, he hadn't been able to locate you. Your master trusted him; he was satisfied with this answer. Then he looked for a replacement for you. He has already found one and he just goes on with his life without you. So why don't you forget him too?"

I heard my master playing "Just the way you are" and other beautiful pieces on the piano again and again in my mind. It seemed to me that my heart would burst with sadness at the thought of losing him. Would I ever get the chance to hear him play something, even if it was just a few notes?

"Because I can't! I love him!"

"You sentimental fool! If you had seen him yesterday. He went to the Deliverance Club with his new submissive. He's so pleased with him that he took the opportunity to brand him. He didn't mark you, did he?"

I didn't even know he was branding his slaves. I touched my fingertip to the spot where he had cut me in the shape of a star. I felt like crying because as it healed, it had almost completely faded away. That must not have been his mark, because it would soon be gone. Why hadn't he marked me? Did he still doubt me? My disappearance must have convinced him that I had run away alone or with someone else and that he was right not to have complete faith in me.

The stranger had left after throwing a picture on my bunk showing my master and a handsome young submissive wearing a star-shaped branding. Was it his brand? Alone in my cell, I sobbed for a long time while looking at this picture. I must admit that I felt abandoned, and despair gradually overtook me.

That night, I woke up and was so sore all over that I felt like my skin had become too tight to hold me in. It was like wearing a wetsuit that was too small and even covered my face; I was suffocating! I called for help, but no one came. Then I managed to calm down and breathe better. I fell back asleep and dreamed that my master was marking me by almost skinning me with his straight razor. Then I looked at myself in the mirror, and it was horrible; I was a real monster! But when I woke up, I was sweaty and erect. It was the very first time I had ever had a hard-on since I had been abducted. I was tempted to masturbate, but I told myself that my sex still belonged to my master and that I had no right to do that without his permission. I couldn't get back to sleep.

When I was let out of my cell the next day, I snatched the big key ring that one of my guards was carrying. It was hanging from a buckle on his belt. I then tried to escape through the big green door at the end of the corridor. But that hallway was long and my legs were wobbly after so many days without food. One of them tasered me. I collapsed. They picked me up and carried me to the torture room, as if nothing unusual had happened. They didn't even comment on my pathetic escape attempt. I heard my master tell me again that if I had to rely on my fighting skills to survive, I would not last long. If a gun had been used instead of a stun gun, I would probably be dead. So, I couldn't quite prove him wrong; but at least I had tried.

Once I was taken back to my cell, the strongman put on my left ankle a metal bracelet fastened to the long chain riveted to a wall. Even if all the doors were open, I couldn't try to escape anymore. He then sprayed me with a garden hose connected to the faucet where I sometimes drank. The cold water soon turned to ice. I crouched down in hopes of retaining some of my warmth and sparing my most sensitive parts. But he ordered me to get up and turn around. I did so because I knew full well that if I didn't, he would force me to obey or he would tie me to the wall or hang me from the ceiling, and my life would be even more miserable than it was with my chained leg.

"Why are you doing this to me? I never wanted to be treated this way," I said through clenched teeth.

As always, he remained silent. He just looked at me shiver with an expression as cold as tap water.

No matter how hard I tried to imagine moments or ways to escape, I couldn't see any. I wondered what I would do to free my master if he were trapped in another cell. I couldn't even offer them my life in exchange for his, because mine was already theirs. If they wanted to, they could take it away from me at any time. My only option to leave this place was to agree to never see him again. And I wasn't ready for that.

"Why am I still alive?" I asked myself. Why a taser instead of a real gun? Who was the man who came to interrogate me every day? He would never tell me, of course. Was he also one of my masked torturers? Was he a friend of Arthur's? If so, why did he refer to him as "Mr. Dubois"?

That night, I dreamed again of the meal my master, Arthur and I had together at the restaurant and what we had said to each other there. Master Lemay wanted to borrow Master Mendel's house in Brazil so that Fausto could temporarily dominate David and try to "break him", as Arthur had said. I woke up with a start.

What if it was Fausto, this man who came every day to talk to me and try to convince me to leave my master for good. He matched the physical description I had been given. And for him, "breaking a man" must have meant pushing him to give up what was dearest to him or betraying those he loved the most.

Had my master consented to all this? I remembered now that he had said that, in order to find out if he could be trusted, Fausto would have to be kept under constant surveillance while he tried to break a "guinea pig". But would he have accepted that I was this guinea pig?

Hadn't he said that any suffering inflicted on people who didn't consent to it was violence, abuse of power and outright mistreatment? Anyway, nothing I had experienced here had felt pleasant or exciting; it had all felt like abuse. No one had asked me if I was willing to be a guinea pig.

Then I remembered! In the restaurant, I had recognized that from the moment I signed my contract of slavery, my master would have the right to do or demand anything from me. He could even offer me to another dominator… "For an indefinite period of time," he had then specified. So would I have consented to this hell without knowing it?

I went back to sleep and dreamed that Master Mendel was sitting at home and watching on his computer screen my torturers who were inflicting various torments on me for hours on end, and me crying and answering Arthur, "My master must think that I've let him down. He must be unhappy. I don't want him to suffer." But he would also see me break my promise of silence when Fausto asked me about him. He would feel my revelations as a betrayal of him.

If at first, I had refused to talk about it, I ended up confiding to my too clever interrogator one small detail, then another, and finally almost everything. Even though I only spoke well of my master and tried to avoid anything too personal, more intimate, I had still failed in my duty, since I had promised not to reveal anything about him and our relationship to anyone. How could any master trust me now?

When I woke up the next morning, I felt like I deserved all the pain I had endured and all the pain that would surely be inflicted on me again.

No one came looking for me or questioning me that day. What was going on?

The next day, Fausto (if it was him) came back. I was lying on my bunk. I sat down immediately.

"You're Fausto, aren't you?" I asked when he came in.

"I don't know anyone by that name," he said with the aplomb of someone telling the truth.

But was "Fausto" just a nickname? If so, he wouldn't have lied: he didn't really know anyone by that name. I still had a doubt, but I pretended I didn't.

"Master Mendel surely did not consent to all this. Did you talk to him personally or did you just rely on what Arthur told you? Arthur wants to get rid of me. Anything is good in his eyes to have my master all to himself."

The man tilted his head and smiled.

"Nice try. You really want to believe that your master had nothing to do with it, don't you? The idea that he might be the one who planned everything that happened to you here disturbs you."

"My master has every right to me. I told him that and I meant it. I also promised him I'd never let him down. So why do you keep lying to me and torturing me? You won't get anything out of me.

With that, Arthur entered my cell."

"All right, then. Since that's the way it is… We'll auction you off on the Deep Web. A beautiful young slave like you, Gaby, should sell for a lot of money, don't you think? That way I'll be rid of you for good. Nobody will ever find you, EVER!" he shouted angrily.

I looked at him, speechless. Then he walked out.

"You said that your master had every right to you, didn't you? What if he was the one who wanted to sell you in this way? Celine left him, but what happened to his previous slaves? Do you know? And who's to say he didn't inherit his fortune and earn it by offering young slaves like you on the world market?" asked the man who looked like Fausto.

"If he sells me, then I'll serve my new master as best I can," I replied with a sob in my voice.

"What if it was an old, fat, ugly, cruel lady who bought you?"

I cried silently.

"All you have to do is give him up, promise that you'll never try to see him again and you'll be free. What do you say to that?"

As I was silent, he stood up.

"When you have chosen, call me or give your answer to Mr. Dubois, so that we know what to do with you."

As he walked away, I thought, "If they sell me, I'll have to be moved somewhere else. Then maybe I'll have a chance to escape on this new trip."

"Sell me," I said quickly as he closed the door.

I saw impatience or anger as a dark cloud settled over his eyes. He must not have liked my decision, because he must have perceived it as his failure to "break" me.

One of my other guards brought me a bowl of rice and a glass of vegetable juice. I took them shaking so hard, I thought I was going to spill it.

"Thank you!"

He grunted before walking out. That was the first sound I heard coming out of either of their mouths. Obviously, he wasn't expecting thanks. But I hadn't eaten anything in days, and I couldn't help but feel grateful for the food.

Since I didn't have a spoon or fork, I started eating with my fingers, thinking that my jailers must have wanted to fatten me up a bit to get a better price for my sale or the food was drugged, and I would fall asleep with my nose in it; this would allow them to transport me without problems.

I didn't fall asleep in the middle of my meal. After washing my fingers with cold tap water, I lay down on my bunk. I felt confident that I had chosen my future in accordance with my values and feelings. I slept in peace for the first time since my abduction.

Chapter 30

Strange noises and screams woke me up. I thought I recognized my master's voice.

"Here, Master! I'm here!" I screamed, my heart beating so fast that the heartbeat in my ears almost drowned out the surrounding noise.

Then there he was, standing in front of my cell, shouting:

"Open the damn door, now!"

When he walked in, I immediately started sobbing. I thought I would never see him again. He came up to me, hugged me, and with his hands on either side of my face, he covered it with kisses.

"Ah, my love! My darling! I found you," he said, his voice vibrating with relief.

His cheeks were wet with tears. I understood that he did not know. He had not instigated all this. It must have been Arthur's evil work.

"He'll pay dearly," he said angrily, as if he had read my mind.

He turned to the one I had come to mentally call Fausto.

"Set him free. And bring me his clothes," he ordered, glaring at the man.

Fausto took off the ankle bracelet that connected me to the long chain.

"His clothes are there, Sir," he replied deferentially, pointing to the cell opposite mine.

My master entered. I followed him, but stayed within the doorway. I was afraid he would be locked up and hurt. I didn't want to take any chances with these crazy people who had been abusing me for days (weeks?).

He handed me my clothes. I almost collapsed trying to put on my pants. My master helped me as he would have helped a sick person. I smiled at him, but I felt new tears welling up in my eyes. He stopped for a moment to kiss me with such tenderness!

"I love you so much!" I said to him with a torn voice.

"Me too, my little angel!"

Daddy used to call me that when I was just a kid.

"My parents must be very worried."

"No, they're not. Don't worry. They think you're already in Brazil. I phoned them when you disappeared and asked if you came by. Your mother told me that you had visited them before you left for Brazil. She wanted to know why I wasn't there with you. I did not deny your story. I pretended that I was going to join you as soon as I had settled some urgent business here. She made me promise to take good care of you."

We then headed for the gate and freedom. My master turned to Fausto.

"You'll be hearing from me!" he said through clenched teeth before walking out.

Beyond the big green door was a huge warehouse that was almost completely empty. During my escape attempt, even if I had managed to cross this threshold, I probably wouldn't have been able to reach the exit and escape my jailers. Not in the state I was in.

Despite all the exercise I had done every day, I was so weak from lack of food that my master had to support me to his car, where he helped me sit in the passenger front seat.

"Where is Arthur?" I asked as we drove along.

"He's at home. He told me that the police had discovered that the woman, the one with the baby, had been put up for sale on the Deep Web. They don't know who the buyer is yet, but they're hopeful they'll find him soon."

That was what must have given Arty the idea to do the same with me.

"He told me they were going to auction me off as a slave."

"What?! Ah, the son of a bitch! He's gonna pay for this, I promise you."

"Did you see the videos of what they did to me?"

I knew that they were recording everything.

"I was given them. But I only took a quick look at them to see if I should kill Arthur before I came to rescue you or later."

I had a little laugh. He smiled sadly at me as he caressed my cheek.

"I love you, my angel!" he said with vibratos in his voice as he turned his gaze to the road.

"I discovered in my cell how much I cared for you. I could hear you playing the piano all the time." I said with damn tears flowing again!

But then he started crying too. His music was so personal, something magical and insubstantial that united us with more depth and strength than any words or even caresses. When he played, it was my very soul that he caressed.

"They're going to pay!" he repeated.

"Who are they?"

"Arthur, Mrs. Bishop, president of the BDSMers Association, Fausto and the doms who tortured you."

"What! I thought they were Arthur's friends."

"No. He told Mrs. Bishop and the others that Master Lemay wanted to lend David to Fausto. And you probably remember when the three of us went to the Deliverance Club together, Arthur was wearing a watch with a camera. He didn't just start recording at the meeting with Mrs. Bishop, the bar owner and Celine, he did it during our entire meal at the restaurant. And he produced an audio-video montage of some of what we said to each other there to prove to the president that we had agreed to have you as Fausto's guinea pig and even to have you on loan to another dom for an indefinite period of time. No one bothered to make sure that this video hadn't been cleverly falsified or to check with you or me if any of this was true before arranging for your abduction and incarceration. The president found doms willing to help her and Arthur."

"But we didn't agree to do it that way! It was only theoretical."

"You and I know that, but not your torturers."

"Did Fausto and the others hear that recording?"

"That's what I have to check. If not, the only two people really guilty are the president and Arthur. But they all should've made sure it was real and got our consent in person, preferably in writing, don't you think, poor darling?"

"While I was waiting in my cell, I had time to think. And I came to believe that I had deserved all this suffering."

I began to sob so hard that I hiccupped. He pulled over to the side of the road to try to console me.

"Come on! Why would a cherub like you deserve all this?"

"I… I betrayed you," I confessed.

"Betrayed me? They told me you refused to give me up."

"Yes, that's true, but…"

"But what?"

"I shouldn't have talked about you at all, about us. I promised you secrecy. But Fausto asked me about my feelings for you and…"

"Don't you think that whatever you revealed, Fausto and the association would be obliged to keep quiet about it? And above all, don't you think you've suffered enough for this alleged betrayal?"

I was still crying. He hugged me.

"I don't deserve you. You are too good for me."

"Stop it! Stop it, Gabriel. You and I will review the videos and you'll tell me where you'd have committed this… unforgivable act in your eyes."

I looked at him. He smiled mockingly.

"You're so…," I began.

"So what?"

He leaned towards me and kissed me passionately.

"Stop or we'll be forced to find a place to… to… I haven't touched myself once since the kidnapping. Yet, when I dreamed of you…"

He chuckled.

"Oh, that was surely the worst torture."

"Yes! Don't laugh. It's true, it's true! It's terrible to be away from the one you love, to fear losing him forever, to dream of him and not be able to do anything about it…"

I hiccupped in surprise when he suddenly put his hand on my dick, which was already too tight in my jeans.

"We'll figure this out at home. That is, if you deserve it."

I felt the tears again…

"But no, my darling. I was just teasing you. You have my respect, and you should be given at least as many hugs and caresses as you experienced sufferings."

Conclusion

Once at home, he ordered me to undress. I did so eagerly. He examined me from all sides before going to get his computer and motioning for me to sit next to him on the couch. He started the first video of my torture sessions.

"You tell me when to stop," he ordered.

"The torture sessions don't matter. Except for the torments and their duration, which varied, it was always pretty much the same. No one spoke to me, neither to explain the reason for their actions nor to question me, let alone to reassure me. But the meetings with Fausto…"

"Good. So, we'll just watch the records with Fausto. I'll take a look at the other videos some other time."

"There's no need to watch them inflict these torments on me, Master."

"Yes, I do need to see what they did to you. If I do the same to you one day without knowing it, you might not react well; you might panic at the memory of your imprisonment. I won't take such a risk."

I nodded, happy to have a master who always wants to be in control of the situation.

"Besides, maybe you should see a doctor and a shrink."

"Nooo! I don't like the idea of telling all this to strangers and having to convince them that you're not responsible. Anyway, my physical injuries are only superficial and will heal quickly. For the rest… As long as I'm near you, I feel safe and secure. If I ever find that I can't forget and that I'm troubled by my bad memories, it won't be too late to go to counseling, don't you think?"

"I won't force you to do it. But don't you dare hide your discomforts from me, if you have any, whether they are physical or psychological. Understood?"

"Yes, Master. Thank you for giving me time to get back to my old self."

"So, if I understand you correctly, you don't want to file a complaint against Arthur and the others with the police either?"

I looked at him, mouth agape, swallowing my saliva and shaking my head. For the tenth time since my return, I felt like crying.

"Do you think this is really necessary?"

"If we ever want our justice system to learn to distinguish between violence and BDSM play, it will have to be involved in bringing charges against people who take advantage of the context to rape and brutalize."

I understood his logic, but I didn't feel ready for that.

"If you don't want to go to the police, I won't force you to. But I think we'll still have to do something to prevent this from happening again."

"I don't know what other solution you can think of, but anything is better than the police in my eyes," I replied.

"Okay. You'll let me handle this then?"

"Yes, I will. I trust you, Sir."

What did he have in mind? I didn't know, but he seemed determined not to leave it at that.

We then looked at samples of the sessions with Fausto. I made a point of making him slow down to watch every part where I had doubts about what I was saying. I also showed him the time when Fausto told me that if I couldn't reveal anything about my master, I couldn't confide in anyone about myself.

"What do you think of that?"

He thought for a moment.

"As long as you remain respectful, you can talk about whatever you want outside of what is our sexuality and our SM sessions. If you were straight and had sex with a pretty girl, would you tell everyone everything about her quirks, her erotic preferences and her little perversions? Would you joke about her squirrel-like cries during orgasm?"

"Of course not."

"It's the same for you and me. I don't care if you tell everyone that I like to eat fast food on occasion, but that most of the time we cook healthy meals together. You can also mention that I had a difficult childhood, but without telling the details. I'd be happy to know that you have a good confidant who can keep a low profile and to whom you'd talk about how you feel about me and even about your difficulties in living this life. As long as you reveal YOUR feelings, YOUR emotions, it isn't about me, but about YOU. Do you understand?"

"I think so, but I'm not sure I always know where the line is between what you think is acceptable and what you wouldn't like me to share."

"Normal. We're starting out together. You'll get to know me better. But in the beginning, you'll just have to ask me whenever you have a doubt. And after telling a good friend about something I'd rather you hadn't, would it be so bad if I punished you for it?"

"No. As long as you still trust me."

The damn tears wanted to come back again. Damn it! I had to have PTSD.

"Is there anything else you'd like me to see on these recordings of Fausto's discussions?"

"Yes."

I couldn't remember when he told me about the mark my master would have given to a hypothetical submissive. It seemed to me that it was the day that Fausto had left me a picture of my master and a young man wearing a scarred star. Had we discussed my little star that day or had I just thought about it? We searched back and forth on the tapes for the spot without finding it. So much so that I wondered if I had dreamed that part of my imprisonment.

"Just tell me what you wanted to show me," my master finally suggested, tired of searching.

I told him, crying.

"It was a photo montage. I don't know anyone with a branding like that and I've never put my seal on anyone. Not even Arthur. At least not in a ritual way. Arthur has marks that are my doing, it's true, but they weren't engraved like my official brand. The closest thing to it is your little star."

"Yes, but it's gone," I said, showing him where it was.

"No, it's not," he said, taking my hand in his.

Looking me straight in the eye, he slid his thumb over the spot where the star had been. But I didn't understand.

"It's engraved here," he said, touching my forehead with his finger, "and here," he added, pointing to my heart.

Yes, I started to cry again.

"Not all marks are visible. The deepest and most beautiful ones are invisible."

His hand was making love to mine, gently caressing that secret mark.

"I didn't see anything you should regret, my darling. On the contrary! You were even more faithful, loyal and courageous than I'd have been in your place. I can't stand being abused anymore. So, in spite of my pacifism, I'd probably have killed half of my torturers and crippled the others."

I let out another sort of bloody laugh.

"It's hard when you're starving, weak, unarmed and…," I started before he interrupted me with a kiss on the corner of my lips.

"Yes, I know, my brave little slave. I couldn't have done better than you."

He then dragged me to his room, probably to prove to me how much he still loved me. He didn't hit me or inflict even the slightest pain. His imagination must have been running wild at the thought of all I had gone through to be able to stay near him. In any case, he was very tender.

After my orgasm, I asked him what he had been thinking when he came so beautifully. I thought he was imagining me being tortured.

"I heard you say over and over again, 'I love him! I'll never forget him' and 'Sell me'."

I snuggled up to him and we fell asleep.

THE END OF THE FIRST BOOK

Other Danny Tyran's Novels

À corps et à cris : cinq fessées érotiques (participation au recueil de nouvelles avec le texte : « *Bonne fille* »)
Éditions Dominique Leroy, 20 août 2013
B00EIKAV0M

À poil ! Recueil de nouvelles de Hugh Masters Questorius
Traduit en français par Danny Tyran
Auto édition, Mars 2022
ISBN 978-2-924400-37-1

Amour en cage
Auto-édition, Juin 2019
ISBN 978-2-924400-28-9

BDSM illimité
Éditions Textes gais, 20 février 2014
B00IJVMC7Q

Cheptel
Éditions Textes gais, 8 juillet 2016
B01I512W38

Conseil de discipline
Éditions Textes gais, 25 sept. 2012
B009GKL6X0

Enlèvement (L')
Éditions Textes gais, 27 février 2015
B00U2FYWEI

Envol : Une découverte du BDSM (L')
Éditions Dominique Leroy, 18 juillet 2013
B00E0LGZL8

Esclave à l'entraînement
Éditions Textes gais, 25 sept. 2012
B009GKLC6Q

Ève et Adam
Édition Le Divin Abricot, 18 juillet 2013
B00E0MCORG

Histoire de Tol (L')
Traduction de Story of Tol par Jack Rowan

Éditons du Tyran, 8 novembre 2017
ISBN 978-292440-02-58

Histoire de Tim (L')

Traduction de Story of Tim par Jack Rowan

Éditons du Tyran, 14 février 2022

ISBN 978-2-924400-3-64

House of Chastisement

Translation of my novel Maison du châtiment

Édition du Tyran, February 2020

ISBN 978-2-92440-29-6

Humiliateur (L')

Traduction du roman The Humiliator par Hugh Questorius

Éditons du Tyran, 26 mars 2017

ISBN 978-2924400-2-03

Livestock

Traduction en anglais de « Cheptel » de Danny Tyran.

Éditions du Tyran, janvier 2021

ISBN 978-2-924400-32-6

M. Benson de John Preston

Traduit en français par Danny Tyran

Éditions du Tyran, 14 juin 2021

ISBN 978-2-924400-3-57

Maison du châtiment (La)

Éditions Textes gais, 5 février 2015

B00T7KTB4A

Missions

Comprend : Tome 1 : Cambodge et tome 2 : Amazonie

Éditions du Tyran, 18 mai 2017

978-2924400234

Obsession

Éditions Le Divin Abricot, 15 mars 2013

B00BURDIEC

Rituels

Traduction du livre *Rituals* par Kyle Stone

Éditions Textes gais

Octobre 2019

Slave in Training

Traduction de « Esclave à l'entrainement » de Danny Tyran

Éditions du Tyran, juillet 2014
978-2924400135

www.ingramcontent.com/pod-product-compliance
Lightning Source LLC
LaVergne TN
LVHW040005200726
843493LV00005B/1123